FANNY AND SUE

Also by Karen Stolz

World of Pies

FANNY AND SUE

A Novel

Karen Stolz

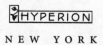

HYPERION

NEW YORK

Library of Congress Cataloging-in-Publication Data

Stolz, Karen.
    Fanny and Sue : a novel / Karen Stolz.—1st ed.
      p. cm.
    ISBN 0-7868-6701-9
    1. Twins—Fiction. 2. Sisters—Fiction. 3. Saint Louis (Mo.)—Fiction. I. Title.
PS3569.T6239 F3 2003
813'.54—dc21

2002032715

Book design by Lisa Stokes

Hyperion books are available for special promotions and premiums. For details contact Hyperion Special Markets, 77 West 66th Street, 11th floor, New York, New York 10023, or call 212-456-0133.

FIRST EDITION

10 9 8 7 6 5 4 3 2 1

This book is for the best readers I know, my parents: Dutch, who generously shared his St. Louis childhood with me, and Jeanne, whose scarlet fever story made me cry. Also, this book is for my supportive and dear sisters, Maggie and Katie, and last and not least, this book is for my son, Danny, a funny and tender character in his own right. I love you all.

ACKNOWLEDGMENTS

I wish to thank my brilliant agents, Gail Hochman, Marianne Merola, and Sally Wilcox, for their good ideas and diligent work. I thank my editor, Leigh Haber, who "gets me" and who gracefully re-choreographs my sentences when need be. I wish to thank the whole marketing/publicity team of Hyperion, who are the hardest working people in the business. I would like to thank Nancy Taylor Day and Sandra Bybee for their support and their editorial good works. Thanks as well to the Texas Commission on the Arts and the Writer's League of Texas, especially Sally Baker. A big thank you to Kathy Patrick, Mary Gay Shipley, and Rona Brinlee.

A few friends I wish to thank for their love and support are Margaret Levering, Collins Selby, Gayle Yelenik, Lynn Anderson, Ricki Ratliff, Sandy and Lottie Shapiro, Herman Wright, Terri Bennett, and Bruce Scoular. And thanks to my Atchison family, especially Margy Stein, Libby Schmanke, Elizabeth Lentz, Dick and Betty Mize, Violet Lehman, and Donna Robertson. And thanks to my aunt, Jean Ahrens, for sharing her St. Louis memories.

Thanks to Lawrence Wright, whose book *Twins and What They Tell Us About Who We Are* was a big help to me and a pleasure to read, and thanks to Mark McCutcheon for his very helpful *Everyday Life from Prohibition through World War II*. Also, thanks to Andrew D. Young for his book *St. Louis and Its Streetcars: The Way It Was*.

FANNY AND SUE

IN 1920, AS THE twins were born, Sue grabbed on to Fanny's foot to come along—Fanny always had to be first in everything! In birth, and in death, as time would prove.

In 2003, when Fanny complained of a clutch in her heart, and fainted, Sue telephoned the ambulance, then tried to pound on her sister's chest. But she could only bear to tap lightly, as if coaxing the end of a flour bag, the soft white flour drifting into a sifter.

Next, Sue looked for a pillow to rest Fanny's head on; Fanny loved creature comforts so on earth, she might as well feel comfortable in leaving it, if that was what was happening. Lifting Fanny's neck, Sue felt of her frizzled hair—a perm she had warned Fanny against, but then felt compelled to copy. For decades and decades, the twins had decried matching clothes and hairstyles, but in their last years they had returned to the ways of their first years.

No pillow was nearby, and so Sue lay Fanny's head on her chest— though they were identical twins, Sue had the larger, pillowy breasts, and good fortune it was now. Sue felt a seizing in her own chest; she thought it was a pang of love for her sister. Something stirred the air deliciously, cooling it and tickling Sue's eyelashes, and then Fanny's eyes closed for the last time ever and, seconds later, so did Sue's.

The ambulance attendants were mystified when they came through the door and saw two women intertwined on the living room floor. Lying on a lilac flower-printed rug, they were each dressed in powder-blue dusters, with rabbit slippers resting at their feet.

"Whoa! Identical twins!" the young attendant with tomato-red hair shouted. A quick exam and the young attendant shook his head. The two ladies had both expired.

"But one of them called!" exclaimed the older attendant, whose arm bore a pink snake tattoo.

"Sure enough," the red-haired attendant said. "They came into this world together, and they left it together."

IT WAS A grand day in August, sunny and iced with cloud wisps. But Sue had a problem. She was sure she'd had a penny in the pocket of her dress. It was one of those teeny-weeny decorative pockets stitched onto the chest of her dress. When Aunt Millie made the girls' clothes, she always sewed on these little extra pockets. So far, in hers, Sue had stored, at different times: five lima beans she was hiding from Mom, a chewed piece of gumball it was awful hard to get off once placed there, a pop pearl from Mom's beads that escaped when baby Bob got hold of them, and a tic-tac-toe game Sue and Fanny had done on a candy wrapper in church with the tiny donation envelope pencil. Sue's worry about the penny was that Fanny had made off with it. She could just picture her now at Beedleman's Grocery buying anything she liked with her penny, but given Fanny's sweet tooth, most likely a whole bunch of candies. I will kill her, Sue vowed.

Just then, Uncle Donald, Aunt Millie, and cousins Myra and Randall arrived at the door with fudge candy. Please, God, let there be no nuts, Sue breathed. She knew Fanny would be praying for the opposite. And just like that, Fanny materialized. She could sense candy from a mile away. She strolled through the door looking exactly like

Sue to most, but worlds opposite to Sue herself. Sue thought this identical twins business was a sad mistake. Mom insisted on dressing them exactly alike each and every minute of their fool lives. And darn it all, Fanny had pulled a switch on the red dresses they wore today, and gotten the loot. Sue marched up to Fanny and then fell upon her, clutching at the little breast pocket to find her penny. Nothing. Pop reached into the flurry of knees and flying hair and righted the two girls lickety-split. "Twins!" he bellowed.

Sue secretly suspected he couldn't tell one from the other. Rarely did he specify names, and he'd had six years to get them straight. "She's got my penny," Sue wept.

Uncle Donald pulled out two pennies and handed them to Sue and Fanny. And then Fanny and Sue's brother, Baby Bob, got one (which Pop pocketed so Bob wouldn't swallow it), and then Uncle Donald and Aunt Millie's own children, Randall and Myra, got a penny each. Now everyone had pennies. The whole world had pennies. But I will still kill Fanny, Sue dreamed.

As punishment for their poor behavior while relatives visited, Fanny and Sue had to help their mother with the afternoon wash. Mom gave Fanny a small scrub brush and made her work at the dirty hem stains of her dress while Sue was set to sorting clothes into piles on a wooden table. The twins stood in the basement in their cotton undershirts and panties, since Mom had made them take off their dresses to wash on the spot. There was a cool feel to the basement, leastways, a relief from the warmth of the day, but the basement was an extremely shadowy place. Fanny was scared of spiders and kept feeling little squishy legs brushing across her feet; however, when she looked down, it was just dust bunnies. She wanted to tell Mom this was really Sue's dress, not her own, so why did she have to work at the stains, but what good would that do? Then Sue would know she had that penny, and Mom would be more emphatic than ever that Fanny clean off the dirt. Fanny hit her own baby finger with the scrub brush. "Owwie," she whimpered.

Sue was preparing the bluing, an ink blue fluid that turned the dull clothes to bright white. This was a job that had only recently been entrusted to her, because it stained like crazy. The first time Sue mixed it, her fingers were blue for days after and she had to wear her white, lacy church gloves around all the time. In truth, however, she loved doing that, though she complained about it for good measure. She liked wearing those little gloves till they got glued together with pancake syrup. Cripes!

"Pour it in, doll-baby," Mom cried out.

It was time! Sue poured in the goo-ishy blue stuff and watched it ribbon into the clothes. Once mixed in, the bluing turned everything stark white. What a mystery.

They were not old enough yet to operate the wringer. They wondered when they ever would be. Mom had caught her apron string in the wringer once, and when she spun around the handle, unaware, the wringer pulled her sideways like she was a ball of cotton fluff and whacked her behind hard. It liked to have dragged in the whole apron and Mom with it, had Pop not been down in the basement at the time tinkering in his wood shop. He dashed over like a hero, and with a pair of rose-pruning shears he cut the apron from Mom, and she fell sideways crying. The twins thought the tears were for her near brush with death, but really she loved that apron; it was pink with small yellow daisies at the borders. Later she cut and sewed the apron scraps into little hankies, edging them in green thread, and the two girls took them to church in their pocketbooks. They were sweet but Sue was nervous that the little yellow daisies looked like tiny bits of snot so she never used hers.

· · ·

Sue was the more nervous twin in general though. In just two weeks Fanny and Sue would be off to start school, and their whole lives would change, Sue believed, not for the better. Their older cousin Randall had warned them about school. All day long you had to sit up, pay attention, learn letters, learn words, he said. It was work, work, work, all the livelong day he said.

Well, that sounded like what Pop did. He had to work all day long every day except Saturday and Sunday. He worked for the Public Service Company, driving streetcars. He wore a crisp, gray uniform that Mom ironed like the dickens every day, freshening it up between washings. Pop had a reputation as the friendliest motorman in north St. Louis and knew all the regular riders by name. The twins rode with him sometimes and saw he was sweet as pie to the old ladies especially. They loved him and sometimes tried to kiss on him or attempted to slip nickels into his pocket. But Pop always told them he did not work for tips! Pop loved the sound the coin collector made when he pushed the wand down, and all the coins went clittery clattery down the chute. Fanny and Sue loved it too; it was a kind of musical sound, and money sounded grand when it joined together.

Pop's working all day wasn't so bad, Sue guessed, but Fanny and Sue couldn't picture themselves working that hard, and as the last days of August ticked by, they were filled with dread for school. Meanwhile, Mom assembled matching outfits for the girls to wear. For the brand-new school clothes, Mom had stitched a little yellow flower on the neck of Sue's outfits, and a little blue flower at Fanny's neck. They wore the same size and didn't know what the reason was for marking the clothes. Would Mom inspect their clothes after school and cast blame if something wasn't right?

September rolled around crisp as a paper kite and full of the good smell of leaves burning. In the air there were speckles of red and yellow from the almost ashes. School had begun. Mom walked the girls there, wearing her good Sunday clothes, as if she might run into the Reverend Bickle all of a sudden, or some such person. She even put on stockings and nice shoes. Sue and Fanny loved the way their Mom looked, like a movie star, similar to Clara Bow, with a laughing look in her dark eyes. And sweet whorls of hair at her cheeks. She even put on lipstick first thing when she got up, just like a movie star would.

Fanny and Sue were united on this school thing. Whatever do we want to learn to count for, what is the earthly purpose, they asked. Okay, it might be good to add nickels and pennies sometimes so that Mom would trust them to go to the bakery and buy a loaf of bread. Though they liked it better when Mom baked the bread herself and they got to help, slicking up their palms in lard to get the pans glistening greasy for Mom. Sometimes they got to whack at the dough, though Mom called it kneading. Anyway, counting out money might be helpful.

The teacher would want to teach the twins how to read, and Mom said, pretend along, even though she'd already taught them. Fanny and Sue could already read real chapter books, and they thought that the books at school were silly. The kids in those stories never tricked their friends with pepper candy, like Fanny and Sue had, they were never nude, and they never used the bathroom, like regular people. Sue and Fanny had seen many things. They saw their pop kiss their mom one time in a way that made Mom squirmy. They had seen Grandpa Logan sneak cigars into the house behind their grandma's back. They had helped him even, creating a distraction with some gum and their own hair. Oh how they'd paid for that, ouch; their hair had stuck out like wild bits of milkweed on a stalk. Mom had had to crop their hair short.

Fanny and Sue sat together in one seat in the classroom. Sue had to fight back the urge to suck on Fanny's collar like she'd done when she was a baby. The teacher, Miss Smoodler, had never had identical twins, so she didn't know what to make of them. "Must you sit in the same chair, girls?" Some of the kids laughed. We'll find ways to get them later, Fanny thought.

"Yes, identical twins sit together," Fanny said, like this was a part of the Bible or something. The teacher didn't know what to do, so she just let the girls sit together. Sue smelled on Fanny's sleeves and felt better. She liked the way Fanny smelled, like her own smell. Like homemade paste, but sweeter.

Miss Smoodler scraped the chalk suddenly across the board, and the sound made Sue jump up into Fanny's lap. How embarrassing. The girls held on to each other all day. When they were supposed to color trees brown and green, Sue colored the trunk and Fanny the leaves. Miss Smoodler frowned. "Girls, you must do your own work!" she screeched.

"We are," Fanny retorted. "I am coloring my very own leaves, and doing it swell, too. Sue is coloring her very own tree trunk."

Miss Smoodler continued to frown as she passed out Animal Crackers. The other kids, they got six Animal Crackers each. Fanny and Sue got six to share. The world looked to be a very hard place, the girls feared.

The twins in their own home were often sworn enemies, but out in the world, they clung together like new kittens to a teat. Teat, a word the girls had learned from Randall the last time he was over. Since he was older, he claimed to remember what the twins had looked like at their mom's teats. He had told the twins they looked like question marks faced backward to each other. They never! Fanny hollered, then punched Randall in the arm. Randall made a face. He had been taught by their uncle, his daddy, that you can never hit a girl, but the twins tested him on this every time. That time he'd pinched Fanny so hard at her wrist that there was a half moon on it for a day.

It was true the girls had seen Mom holding Baby Bob up to her breasts, but they thought she was showing them to him like you might show anything. An ear. Or anything. Milk spurting out of there? Fanny and Sue did not believe that this was a true story.

The Saturday after their first week of school, the whole family went to a church carnival. Pop was setting up picnic tables in the parish hall for everyone to eat pie and cake. Mom had made great-smelling chocolate cake that morning. Fanny had sneaked a swipe of the icing and it was grand. So while the men moved tables, Fanny and Sue waited in their pretty dresses. The other children hadn't arrived yet; there were only people setting things up, and the old folks playing their weekly bingo.

"Pop said, 'Stay right here, twins.' So we better stay here," Sue whispered loudly. She held her box of Animal Crackers close to her chest and listened to herself breathe in and out. She had a cold and her chest sounded like there were little animals in it chattering. Little tiny cookie animals on her chest, little wheezy animals inside.

Fanny looked over to the spot where the old ladies were playing bingo. That looked like fun to her. Why not go join them? Old ladies liked to ride her and Sue on their knees even though they were too old, but sometimes it paid off in pennies.

"B five!" Mr. Gee hollered. He jumped up and tugged on his beard, then sat down again suddenly.

Fanny smoothed her hand down her dress. Today Mom had let them wear different dresses! Fanny's dress was prettier by far, she felt. Her puffed sleeves stood up like clouds at her shoulders, while Sue's lace pinafore sagged a bit. Mom had run out of starch halfway through her ironing. Fanny's hair had curled up a bit too, but poor Sue's had flipped under instead. Fanny was used to being the prettiest, not to mention the best at everything.

"I wish we could eat these." Sue sighed, clutching at her Animal Cracker box.

"Why shouldn't we?" Fanny asked. She knew why. They would be eating pie and cake soon, and these Animal Crackers were to be saved for later. Misses Caroline and Yvette had given them to the girls for being so good while waiting for Pop to finish setting up the tables and Mom to make coffee and heat up food in the church kitchen. The Misses C and Y, as Pop called them, were prone to spoiling the twins a bit.

Baby Bob was too young for the crackers. He would just goo them up and let them run down his little knob of a chin if he got one. For once, they didn't have to worry about it. They didn't have to watch him today; Baby Bob slept in the nursery at the back of the parish hall. A teenage girl named Rosemary watched the babies and got a small bit of change for doing it. Fanny and Sue thought they might like that job when they were older.

"Let's just open one of the boxes and have two or three of them apiece. No one will know." Fanny flipped the flap up—on Sue's box!—with her thumb. She had two in her mouth before Sue could say boo.

At the same time as Mr. Gee hollered out "Bingo!" Pop appeared and saw the open box in Sue's hands, and he swatted her on the behind right there in church in front of God, the old ladies, and of course Fanny, who swallowed down the sweet vanilla-flavored elephant and tiger in her mouth with a delicate, undetected gulp.

CHRISTMAS WAS ONLY weeks away; Fanny and Sue were making presents for Mom and Pop and Baby Bob. Sue had come up with the idea for Mom's present, to Fanny's surprise, since Fanny was usually the idea girl. Sue said that candy wrappers were so pretty, all those colors of the rainbow, so why not save them all till they had a hundred and then make a necklace out of them for Mom for Christmas. Mom loved jewelry and she didn't have very much. She was not the queen of England, Pop sometimes told her when she wished aloud for some necklace or bracelet, though Fanny and Sue thought their mom was kind of a queen. She had creamy skin like a queen. Fanny had spied on Mom once at night in the bathroom and there was Mom with an inch of cold cream on her cheeks, like a creamy ghost.

So the plan was this. Collect wrappers till they had a hundred, then twist them together so they joined real well and became a kind of a bright-colored strand of pearls for Mom. Fanny thought they could add a bunch of water to paste and dip the paper necklace in, and when it dried it would shine! Just like the papier-mâché they'd done at school. It would be a great Christmas present for Mom. The wrappers were in a big pickle jar under their bed. They had washed out the jar and dried it dry as could be, though it still smelled faintly of dill. Everything was coming along fine with the collection till Pop found the pickle jar. "Twins!" he hollered.

The girls were downstairs helping Mom iron. Of course, they couldn't touch the iron yet because it was hot as Hades, but they could help fold things. Sue loved the way hot cotton felt in her fingers and the way it smelled. But when Pop hollered, their blood got a chill to it, despite the cotton.

"Go up and see what Pop wants," Mom whispered.

Sue wanted to ask Mom to go up with them, but she knew better; they were in trouble and had to face it on their own. Fanny and Sue held hands and slowly went up the stairs. Slow till Pop hollered again, then fast. Fanny entered their bedroom first. This was their first real bedroom, and they had gotten a superb pink chenille bedspread for their bed from Kresge's bargain basement, which they adored. In the old flat they had slept on the daybed in the living room. But then they got this house, a tall, funny-shaped house left to them by their tall, funny-shaped Great-Aunt Juliana.

There was Pop, holding the pickle jar up in the air high. From the sunlight shining through the window it glinted its colors like a tree all ablaze in the autumn. For a moment Fanny almost said something smarty about how beautiful it was, then remembered they were in trouble and caught herself just in time.

"What is this?" Pop said loudly. His voice sounded scratchy.

"Well," Fanny began. She felt the tight grip of Sue's fingers on the behind of her dress. She turned around for one second and saw Sue's eyes as big as plums. "Pop, sir, it's an old pickle jar we're keeping our candy wrappers in."

"I know what it is," Pop muttered. He shook his head. "Saving them for what?"

The girls didn't know what a good answer was here. The necklace was a surprise for Mom, after all. They could tell him it was a secret, but Pop had a policy against secrets.

"Well, why not?" Fanny said. She knew that was a mistake right off.

"I'll tell you why not," Pop said.

Fanny felt her hair blown against her neck. A big sigh from Sue.

"Candy wrappers have sugar on them. Sugar brings in ants and other bugs. Bad bugs. Black bugs."

Sue shivered behind Fanny.

"Black bugs?" Fanny asked softly.

"Big black bugs. This long." Pop held up his fingers with more than an inch between them. "Mice too."

"Mice!" Sue spoke up. To her there could be no worse news.

But Fanny puzzled over this. How could a mouse crawl up the side of a slippery jar? Let alone get the lid off! That was like the cartoons at the movies!

"We always keep the lid on, Pop."

"Well, if the mouse smells sugar but he can't get in, he might come up in your bed and try to nibble on you instead."

The twins were speechless. Sue cried in gulps, and even Fanny got wet in her eyes.

"You girls are sweet as sugar so the mouse might be just as satisfied."

Then the girls saw a little glint in Pop's eyes. He was making a joke. Not a funny one however!

Sue choked and gulped on her tears and made the back of Fanny's dress all wet. Fanny still had wet eyes but now she was a little mad too, mad at Pop for scaring them.

"Girls, take this jar out to the ash pit and dump it out. Then come back and wash out the jar. Mom can use it in the kitchen."

"Pop, the wrappers are clean! We licked them off real good!" Fanny could feel the words in the air turning on her. Talking back never served her well, and she had loads of experience to know it.

Pop already had the girls by the shoulders. He had the jar under his arm. He moved the girls down the stairs as fast as if he were a streetcar bent into a curve. They flew out the door and over to the ash pit.

Pop tore the lid of the jar off and shook the jar hard into the pit, and all the wrappers flipped up in a sudden gust of wind for a second then fluttered down like a cyclone of colors into the pit, decorating the orange peels and eggshells and smelly bits of things in the pit that hadn't been burned yet. Pop told the girls to go in and wash up and help their mom with their baby brother. "And no candy for a week," Pop barked.

No necklace for Mom for Christmas.

Christmas morning, Sue and Fanny woke up intertwined; Fanny's red flannel elbow was poking right into Sue's bare tummy. Sue's pajama top had slipped up to her chest and she would have been cold if not blanketed in her sister. When the girls woke, their eyes were looking right into each other's, keen with Christmas glee.

From the top of the stairs Fanny and Sue peered down to see Pop lighting the candles on the tree. It was so pretty, hung with the oranges they'd stuck cloves into the day before. There was a spray of orange mist when they'd thrust the cloves in. A plume of this orange spray had gotten Sue right in her left eye. For a few seconds she'd thought she was blinded and would never get to see her present the next day, but it was fine once Mom patted her eye with a wet tea towel.

Now Mom hollered gaily, "Wait! No opening presents till I have a clean dipe on Baby Bob!"

Mom loved Christmas morning almost as much as the girls did. Pop loved it too, the twins thought, even though he still seemed a bit gruff on the outside. The girls got the shivers waiting for it to be time; they put on wool socks and warm sweaters over their pajamas. Finally Mom, in her thick, white flannel gown, was at the top of the stairs with Baby Bob in her arms. For a second Sue thought Baby Bob looked just like baby Jesus, but then he wailed and she thought, no, baby Jesus would never have hollered and made messes in his dipes like Baby Bob did.

The twins followed Mom and the baby downstairs, then Pop read the story of the Star of Bethlehem from the family Bible. They had heard it last night in church at the Christmas Eve service, but still, Pop always read it Christmas morning too. The girls tried to pay attention but couldn't help casting longing glances at the presents they saw beneath the tree. Please oh please, Sue breathed into Fanny's neck.

Finally it was over, and Pop said okay; they raced to the tree while Pop warned them, "Be careful of the candles, twins!" He handed them their presents just to be sure. Fanny and Sue each got a fine cloth doll, the exact same one. The dolls were dressed in milky pink bonnets and candy pink pantaloons and dresses. The bodies were cloth, but the faces were china. This was the good part: the dolls had cheeks the color of roses and eyes the color of the sky. They had eyelashes that looked real, and the eyes could open and shut. In fact they did whenever Fanny and Sue lifted them about. Sue got a tiny bit frightened that the eyes were watching her, but she didn't tell anyone. Fanny would tease her forever and a year if she knew. Well, so what if the doll was watching her; she was watching the doll, so it was all even.

How would the twins tell the dolls apart? Fanny and Sue giggled; the dolls had the exact same problem they did. No one ever knew who was whom between them, either. Fanny decided to call her doll a very different name from Sue's doll's name, just as their own names were very different. Sue decided to call her doll Jean Louise.

"Two names?" Fanny asked. "Who ever heard of a doll with two names? I'm calling mine Fine."

"Fine?" Sue cried out. "That's not even a name."

"So what?" Fanny retorted. She pinched Sue's arm a bit. "It's like a cat named Fluffy. Fluffy's not a real name either."

Sue blushed. She'd thought it was! Their friend had a white, fluffy kitten with that name, and Sue had even thought that when she grew up she'd name her little girl Fluffy. What a disappointment.

Once they tussled the name question out there was another problem, which was how they would tell whose doll was whose, since they were dressed identically and even had the same curly yellow hair. Mom suggested labeling their dresses with little embroidered flowers just as she did for Fanny and Sue, but Fanny had always hated that practice and could hardly see making their dolls go through it. She came upon a simple solution to the problem: She would cut the hair on her doll into a short, cropped hairdo just like her own.

"Oh no you won't!" Pop ordered. "That's tomfoolery if I ever heard of it." Pop was sitting on the divan wearing a wool flannel robe Mom had sewn him in secret. It was a black-watch plaid, Mom said. And like the plaid, Pop was always watching them.

Fanny crawled onto Pop's lap and kissed him around his mustache. "Please oh Pop o' mine!" she whispered. She'd seen her mom do something similar one time, and Pop had backed right down. Pop hugged her and told her Merry Christmas and thanks for the licorice she and Sue had given him and even whispered to her he loved her, and then he said, "You will not cut that doll's hair, Muffin."

Fanny wondered if Muffin was what Mom called a term of endearment, or if Pop just didn't know which one she was. All right then, Fanny thought, she'd have to come up with another plan. Just for now, she whispered into Fine's ear, "Okay, pigtails for you." She took some ribbon from the package wrappings and tied Fine's hair on each side of her face. It didn't look beautiful, but it looked different.

The baby had gone down for a nap and now Mom was cooking breakfast. Around her neck on a ribbon she was wearing what the girls had given her for Christmas. To their great delight, the girls had found a painted charm in their Cracker Jack box, a little red heart with purple sparkles on it; it was perfect for their mom, and they'd gotten to give her jewelry after all! Pop had given her a new hairbrush with a mother-of-pearl handle, which surprised the twins, who'd noticed that he usually gave her things for the house, such as crocheted headrests for the divan. On the other hand, in one way this gift didn't surprise Sue at all.

One night Sue had gotten up to get a drink of water in the bathroom because she had eaten salt peanuts earlier that night and had a thirst that was sawing her in half. When she walked by Mom and Pop's room she saw this: Pop was brushing Mom's hair. Even in the dark, Sue could see her hair glittering as Pop's hand moved down it with the brush in a way that looked warm and sweet. Not like when she and Fanny had to get their hair brushed, and the horrible tangles made them cry and want to curse. Sue had stood watching, and she'd heard a little sigh from her mother. He must have brushed it about a hundred times. Sue loved watching them and could hardly bear to go back to her own bed. She decided to keep what she'd seen a secret. Fanny's and her minds were not identical, and the only way to be sure of this was to keep different memories in there.

Sue smiled at the memory as she fingered the smooth pearlescent brush handle. What a morning this was! Because it was Christmas morning Mom was making bacon, and it smelled like heaven! She also put some cinnamon inside the butter for the biscuits. Heaven! Fanny sighed with happiness at the good smells of Christmas, and she decided to put Fine on the sideboard so Fine's pink dress wouldn't get butter smears on it. Sue did the same with Jean Louise.

DIRECTLY AFTER CHURCH Easter morning, Fanny and Sue got to go on an Easter egg hunt right in their own yard. Pop had placed the eggs while they were at the service; this was one of the few times Mom wouldn't mind his missing church. His Easter Bunny duties were important!

Fanny was about to crawl under the house to look for eggs. It was not the most likely spot for Pop to have put them, but that's what drew her under, because if an egg were here, it would have to be a very good one, painted in gold even. She could hear Sue whistling a tune to herself as she gathered eggs around the maple tree in the back. Fanny lay her head down on a pillow of dirt by the house, realizing too late that when next she stood up her pale yellow Easter dress would be ruined. She'd be dirty on Easter. Cripes. But, as long as she was there . . . she turned her head toward the little hill that led under the house and saw an extra-hairy caterpillar. Or perhaps it was just that dust plumped its feelers. There was a blue and white ball Baby Bob must have lost, not to mention a great deal of dirt. She closed her eyes and smelled of it. When she opened her eyes she still didn't see an Easter egg, but she did see a pair of eyes peering at her. It was a bunny rabbit! On Easter! Before the bunny could shake its tail,

Fanny had it in her mitts. It was silvery gray with a white tummy, and its eyes were a very deep gray. Fanny filled her lungs with breath in order to holler to Sue, and then she thought, Maybe, just maybe this bunny should be all mine.

Fanny heard Mom call them in to wash up for Easter dinner. Washing up would take a long time in her case. Quick, she must name the bunny, then find a place for him to stay. Since the bunny's eyes reminded her of marbles, she named him after her favorite type of marble, a steelie. Fanny took Steelie to the back shed, and there she found a birdcage that their Great-Aunt Juliana had left them when she passed on. It had curlicues of painted blue wire all around, and Fanny thought it was grand. She had always wanted something to put in it. Would the cage confuse the bunny, make it think it should fly around singing? Fanny had a good laugh at this. But meanwhile Mom had hollered again, and next it would be Pop, and Easter or no, he'd spank her. Fanny kissed Steelie tenderly on his ears, which were soft as pillows, then she pounded on her dress and let the dust mist and crumble off of her. Phew! Not as bad as she'd thought.

Fanny flew to the bathroom and scrubbed her arms and hands with a cake of Ivory. When she got to the table she was the last, but they didn't seem too peeved. Sue gave her a little smarty-pants I beat you to the table look, but that was the least of Fanny's concerns. Mom had been feeding them stews made of cheap cuts of meat for weeks so she could afford a ham for today. It was all dripping brown sugar and smelled divine, with canned pineapple rings too.

After Easter dinner Fanny slipped out to the shed with some carrots in her pocket. Unfortunately, they were cooked ones; she could only hope Steelie would like them better than she did. Well, who should show up like a bad penny behind her, but Sue the Boo-Hoo. That was her nickname for her now. Sue was the crying twin, while

Fanny only cried if their cousin Randall pinched her too hard. Well, now it was all over. Sue would tattle on her about the bunny.

But to her surprise, Sue fell in love too. Though Fanny wanted the bunny all to herself, she let Sue pet him, to keep Sue on her side.

"Whooee," Sue sighed, as she petted him. "He's soft as Baby Bob's hair after it's washed."

Luckily, the bunny ate the cooked carrots. The girls laughed to see the rabbit's tiny mouth working so fast, and they spent the rest of the afternoon finding ways to make Steelie's cage homier. Fanny stole one of Baby Bob's old diapers. It was so worn it was like Swiss cheese. But Steelie would like sleeping warmly on it. Sue drew a little picture of herself and Fanny to put in the cage with Steelie, so he wouldn't miss them when they weren't in the shed with him. Fanny knew Sue couldn't help doing foolish things like this. When God had let them grow together there inside Mom, he had just poured in the smarts a little unevenly.

The twins slept soundly that night, dreaming of sweet Steelie in his cage.

Next morning the girls ran out to feed Steelie some crusts from their breakfast toast before school.

They found Steelie had eaten the picture Sue had drawn him. Sue got teary but Fanny told her that it was because Steelie loved the drawing so much that he wanted it to warm his insides. But he had enough room for their toast crusts.

Normally Mom would have come out to the shed to check on them, but she had a new baby growing in her tummy and it made her tired, and she cried a little sometimes. Also sometimes it made her urp up her breakfast. Fanny heard the noise she made in the bathroom and felt a little sick herself. But Mom was happy about the baby, she said, it just was a lot of work to grow one.

At school, recess was great fun because all the kids told their stories about Easter egg hunts. And candy. One little boy, Timothy, who was usually shy and quiet in the corner of the playground became very popular because he had filled his pockets with jelly beans and let all the children have one. Fanny got orange: the best. Sue got red: the best. Fanny ate half hers but saved the other half for Steelie.

Miss Smoodler was home sick, and they had a Miss Hatcheck (or, that's what it sounded like), who was very nice. She read them stories all day and let them draw pictures. In Fanny's opinion, school should be this way every day.

Fanny and Sue skipped all the way home from school, holding hands, and then running together through the front door. There was Mrs. Shiner from down the block, along with her four-year-old son, Michael. Michael had so much snot and tears all over his face that he was glistening.

"Oh girls!" Mom cried. She jumped up to kiss Fanny and Sue hello like she did every day when they got home from school. "Michael here has lost the bunny rabbit his pop and mom gave him on Easter day. Have you girls seen it?"

"A bunny, no!" Fanny shouted. The words were out of her mouth before she could plan them. Her cheeks burned red.

She turned to Sue. *No,* she breathed very softly. She made her eyes hard against Sue. She could do this as often as needed.

But Sue began to cry. Not gulpy, but tears sprinkled her dress, making it look spotted. Well, that was that, Fanny knew. She reached her fingers around Sue and pinched her hard on the small of her back.

"Yowp!" Sue cried.

Fanny could hear Mom telling Mrs. Shiner that she thought the girls had been acting funny about something out in the shed. "Let's all go out there," she said. She said it all cheerful, like there might be cake and ice cream out there.

Fanny went out to the shed; she felt like her chest was all stove in. That weenie Sue stayed inside boo-hooing on the hall floor. When they were in the shed, Fanny reached into the cage and took out Steelie. His eyes were pleading with her, I like my birdcage and you two girls who look alike. But Fanny knew she didn't have a chance in begging Mom. She kissed Steelie's ears and fed him the half jelly bean before handing him over to Michael.

Michael seemed to love the bunny too, at least. "Hold him like this," Fanny told the boy, and she showed him. Michael was smiling now, and he'd wiped his face off on the behind of his mom's dress.

After all this, the girls were worn out and wanted a nap. They went inside to the hall, and Fanny took Sue's hand and led her upstairs. Fanny even took off both their dresses and shoes and socks for their nap. She felt sorry for pinching Sue, but she didn't want to say so out loud. Sue knew. They went down for a nap in their underclothes in the afternoon sun. Fanny let Sue twine arms with her, and at the end of their arms both their thumbs went into their own mouths.

The Sunday after Easter, Sue woke to a sound of yowling. It wasn't Baby Bob's hollering though. She crept out to the hallway and saw Pop standing in the hallway with Mom in his arms. He was holding her like she was a small child. Mom's face was as white as her nightgown and there was a big red spot on her bottom. Fanny was at Sue's elbow by then.

"Mom, what . . . ?" Fanny cried out.

Sue just began to sniffle.

"Twins, I have to take your mother to the doctor right away," Pop said in a big voice. "Can you watch Baby Bob for me, like big girls?"

"Yes," Fanny said, strongly.

Sue hid behind Fanny and buried her face in Fanny's warm back.

Pop went down the stairs cradling Mom in his arms. But then he hollered upstairs for Fanny to find Mom's coat. He couldn't take her outside in her gown like that. Fanny ran downstairs to the coat closet and got Mom's maroon wool coat. It wouldn't show the blood; Mom would be glad later.

Sue stood in the hallway shivering and gulping, but then Baby Bob began to holler, and she had to make herself go in to him. There he was with his sleep gown twisted all around himself, smelling like pee. Sue would have to change him. She had done it before, but never without Mom there beside her to make sure it went right. He wouldn't stop crying. He wanted Mom, but Mom was sick. Bad sick. Bleeding. Sue got his old wet diaper off finally, though he squirmed and seemed stronger than her. Then a pale gold arc of pee shot right up at Sue's nightgown. Fanny walked into the room laughing, then remembered how things were and stopped. Together, Fanny and Sue pinned a fresh dipe onto their brother, and didn't poke anything or anyone with the pins. Fanny took Bob downstairs to find some breakfast, while Sue changed out of her yellowed nightgown.

Later a neighbor friend, Mrs. Meeter, came over to help them out. She was two feet wide and smelled like camphor. Her hair curls stuck up like question marks. Their pop had gotten word to her from the hospital to come help. Mrs. Meeter didn't say anything about how their mom was, but Sue and Fanny feared the worst. Sue thought, how could your bottom bleed? Mrs. Meeter fixed them some soup for lunch, and she told the girls to lie down for a nap after, like Baby Bob. They didn't even argue, they were so tired from taking care of their brother. They even let Mrs. Meeter tuck them in under Mom's soft wedding ring quilt. As she fell asleep, Sue realized they had missed church that morning. She couldn't remember the last time that had happened.

To their surprise, the girls slept all afternoon. When they woke up, Pop was there. He kissed the girls on their foreheads and petted back their hair, which was sticking up all over from their nap. He had Baby Bob on his lap, and they felt Bob's drool looping over them as Pop leaned to them.

"Twins, I have some sad news. Mom lost the baby," Pop told them.

"He's right there!" Sue corrected him.

"No," Pop said. "Not Baby Bob. You know the new baby Mom had growing in her tummy? That baby won't be coming. It's gone."

The girls held on to each other for a bit, trying to make sense of this news. Sue began to suck on Fanny's collar, like she used to when they were little.

"Gone in the blood?" Fanny asked, her voice ruffled with crying.

Pop said yes.

The next day when Mom came home from the hospital, the twins clung to her coat and told her they loved her. Fanny peeked under Mom's coat. She had on a dress. Pop must have taken one to her at the hospital.

Sue loved Mom's smell and breathed it in hard. Thank heavens. No more camphory Mrs. Meeter. Their own real mom was back home.

Pop cooked dinner that night so Mom could rest. There were scrambled eggs with bits of black in them, and toast with no butter (they were out) and canned pears, and Mom had hot coffee, and the girls had milk. It all tasted good anyway because Mom was there.

When it was time to go to bed, Pop carried Mom up the stairs. He said it was like their honeymoon. When Mom tucked them in, they drank in her good Mom smells, but there was a little bit of a funny hospital smell to her too. Sue filled her hands with her mother's hair. Oh, she was back, her hair soft and slippery in Sue's palms. Fanny put her head against Mom's arm and let the chenille tuft of her robe press against her flesh. Mom sang a short song to them about three little kittens who lost their mittens. When it was over, Sue asked, "Will the new baby that's coming miss her sister?" She patted her mother's tummy, where she felt sure there must be still one baby swimming in there like a lonesome minnow.

Mom had a hard time talking. Salty tears fell off her cheeks. "Oh no, sweethearts. This one was just one baby, like when Baby Bob came. There was only the one."

4

ALREADY IT WAS the end of October; the days had gone from cool to cold, and Fanny and Sue were settled into their new classroom with Miss Binkbaum. They liked her better than Miss Smoodler from last year. She had even taught them how to make popcorn balls, and now Fanny and Sue were making them at home for Halloween. First, they would need to pop about three or four pans of popcorn. Mom had told them, "Wait till I put Baby Bob down for his nap, and I will help you girls pop the corn. Wait for me." She said this last with an eye to Fanny, since Sue wouldn't imagine disobeying Mom. On her own, anyway.

Mom tromped up the stairs with Baby Bob, who at two was not so very much a baby anymore. Mom said he weighed a ton but a ton was a whole bunch of pounds, Sue was pretty sure. She doubted her mom meant it really.

Sometimes Mom had to read to Baby Bob and sing him "Oh do you know the muffin man?" or another song or two before he'd go down for his nap. That really bothered Fanny. Why should a little kid who couldn't blow his own snot out onto a hankie be the one to hold up all their lives? Fanny would never tell this to a living soul, but once she had come awfully close to dropping Baby Bob out the upstairs window. The screen was off the window for Pop to wash down with a garden hose, leaving the window wide open onto the sunny summer day. Baby Bob had just eaten a little Cracker Jack locket Fanny had gotten; on top of that, Mom and Pop didn't seem at all worried that the thing would get stuck in his throat or bother his tummy. After they were sure that that's where the locket had gone, Pop said, "Well, you can look for it in his diaper by end of day." Really! What a mean joke on Fanny! While she was holding Baby Bob that afternoon for Mom to go down to get some dipes off the line, Fanny just for a second began to hold her arms out toward the window. But Baby Bob gave her a sloppy grin, and of course she stopped herself, though there were still times she wished she hadn't.

But now, here were Fanny and Sue waiting, like they waited each and every day of their lives, for Mom to be done with the baby. Fanny got out the corn-popping pan. Easy to tell that this was its job; there were big marble-sized ruts in the pan that made it no good for mashed potatoes or oatmeal.

Fanny put the pan on the stove, and then she found the can of oil behind a tin of sugar.

"Whuh-oh," Sue said.

"What?" Fanny shouted. "I'm just getting it all ready," she argued.

Sue looked out the back door like the popcorn police were going to be standing there with cop sticks. Sue was such a lily-livered fraidy cat, Fanny felt.

Fanny unscrewed the cap off the oil can and hoisted it above the pan in readiness. A few seconds ticked by while she waited for Mom to come help with their popcorn balls that were certainly more important than Baby Bob's dratted nap.

"Fanny!" Sue warned.

That was it. Fanny had to pour in some oil. She curlicued the drips of oil all inside the pan for fun, but Sue saw that a little had messed the outside of the pan too.

Fanny put down the can and then she hollered up to Mom, "Are you coming?"

Sue heard Mom hollering back, "He's almost down, don't make me holler and wake him!" though in fact that's what she seemed to be doing.

"Okay then," Fanny said. She began to root around the kitchen drawers, looking for a box of matches. "Help me," she ordered Sue. She gave Sue the look, the one that made Sue's ideas of good melt into a puddle.

Sue sidled over next to Fanny, and she started rooting around in the drawers too. Finally she spied a bright red and green match box. Why didn't the box have a skull and crossbones on it like poison? Sue tried to hide the matches with a potholder and a tea towel, but Fanny had already spotted it.

"Right here," she told Sue. "Nitwit."

"Fanny, don't!" Sue said it loud so Mom would hear.

"Don't what?" Fanny laughed high pitched like a crazy mockingbird Sue had heard once.

Fanny stood by the stove with a match out, right up to the burner almost, although she hadn't lit it yet.

"Stop!" Sue screamed.

But even though Fanny hadn't struck it, the stove pilot licked up at the match and lit it, along with the web of oil down the side of the pan, and before you could say jackrabbit, these things were on fire: the oil, the pan, and Fanny's sleeve.

Then Mom was in the room, and a loop of water splashed across the kitchen. Mom was throwing water from the dishpan that was handy in the sink but unfortunately a spoon was in there too and it hit Fanny along with the sudsy water. Sue ran to the sink and filled the watering can, and because she was jittery she threw the whole can, not just the water. So, Fanny got burned and beaned all at once. But at least the fire was out, on Fanny and the stove both.

"Owie!" Fanny yelled. Then, she just screamed a high scary shriek; Mom came to her side and started to hug her, but this too prompted a scream.

Fanny's arm began to bubble up all red and yellow oozy, and Sue turned to the garbage pail and lost her breakfast.

Mom said, "There's no time for that!" which made Sue feel ashamed as well as sick in her stomach. "Sue, you stay here with Baby Bob, while I take Fanny to the doctor's."

Mom picked Fanny up in her arms just in time because Fanny's body suddenly turned into a noodle. But Mom had her okay. Their mother was a small woman but with the strength of two Irishmen, Pop said. Fanny's eyes were streaming tears like faucets turned on full force.

Sue held the front door open, and Mom went out lickety-split. Sue ran after her with her purse. Mom had never gone out the door without her purse in her life. In fact, she had never left the house without lipstick on as far as Sue knew, and now Mom's lips looked as ghostly white as her apron had till Fanny began to ooze onto it. Sue sat down on the porch steps fast to keep from fainting or urping again. A searing pain began to gallop up her own arm, and she swatted at it as if it were in flames.

Mom raced down the street to her friend Ethel's house, because Ethel had just gotten a car last Christmas, one of the first on the block to get one. A minute later Sue saw Ethel dash out of the house in a chenille bathrobe with lots of curl-rags in her hair and a set of keys. Mom ran after, with Fanny jiggling in her arms. Sue saw Mom lay Fanny out in the back of the car, while Ethel cranked the engine, then the car roared down the street.

Sue was crying so hard that at first she didn't hear Baby Bob crying upstairs. But after awhile his crying doubled hers, and she knew what she had to do. Choking on her tears, she ran upstairs, wiping her face off with her skirt, which made her trip up the stairs. The burning in her arm would not quit. Baby Bob's face was purple with screaming, and Sue had no idea how to calm him down, but she managed to change his diaper and kiss on him a little bit until he finally got drowsy; his weight seemed to triple once he fell asleep against her in the rocking chair. His breath smelled like bananas from lunch, and even his drool was golden.

Sue put him down in the crib again, and just then Pop came home for dinner, but of course there wasn't any dinner. There wasn't even popcorn. She told Pop where everyone was, and first he hugged on her for a minute, then he went to get Mrs. Meeter to help out with the baby. Once she arrived, he took off on foot for the doctor's, too anxious to wait for a streetcar. It was a mile from their house but their pop had tremendously long legs, and he would walk it fast, Sue knew.

Sue was upstairs in her pajamas in bed, holding on to her doll Jean Louise real tight when Mom and Pop and Fanny finally returned. She heard them talking to Mrs. Meeter downstairs, and then she heard Pop's firm footsteps on the stairs. He carried Fanny into their room and lay her on the bed. She was sound asleep, and her face was pale as milk. Her arm was bandaged up real good, with what seemed to be yards and yards of gauze. Mom came up and took off Fanny's clothes and put her pajamas on her without even waking her. She kissed Fanny and Sue tenderly on their foreheads and tucked them beneath the blankets and their chenille spread.

"Fanny might cry out a little in her sleep, Sue, honey," Mom whispered. "Call for me if she seems to be hurting too much, okay?"

Sue nodded and when the lights were out, she found Fanny's doll Fine and nestled her up against Fanny's side.

5

SUE

W E HAD THANKSGIVING over at Uncle Donald and Aunt Millie's
house, but Mom brought so much of the food we might as
well have had it at our house, Pop said. I had helped Mom make apple
pie and pecan pie. I had just gotten old enough, Mom said, to pare
the apples. But of course, after Fanny's accident, she watched me like
a hawk with that paring knife. I liked the sound the apples made when
you sliced them, a crisp wisp of a sound that made me feel happy it
was fall and getting cold outside. When we mixed the cinnamon and
sugar in with the apples they glistened brown and buttery. Then Mom
put me on duty cracking pecans for pecan pie. Fanny wasn't much
use making Thanksgiving foods, because her arm was still healing.
And though no one would mention it, her burn still oozed stuff a
little sometimes, which was about the last thing you'd want to taste
in a pie. Her arm was healing well, the doctor said, but the times I
saw it unbandaged it still had a scary look to it. There was a look as
if someone had pulled on her skin fast like it was a tablecloth to whip
off a table. It was a little jagged and yellowish from ointment and
purple where the fire had burned her.

Fanny had always run around like crazy to stir up trouble before, but nowadays she was a little slower to do things. Writing at school was hard with her arm bandaged up and hurting, and sometimes I heard her whimper a little when she was writing essays for Miss Binkbaum, like "Why the Pilgrims Gathered for a Feast." "They just do," I heard her mutter. And "They were hungry, why not?" I could actually see Miss Binkbaum fighting off the urge to put Fanny back in the cloakroom, which is where she used to put her when she misbehaved, but now she felt sorry for her I guess.

I think Fanny actually missed the time in the cloakroom. One time when I was sent back to get her from there for us to go to lunch she was standing inside Miss Binkbaum's tall wool salt-and-pepper coat, her head lost in the stomach of the coat and her legs skinny, her socks halfway en route to a heap in her shoes. When I said "Fanny?" she didn't say anything, knowing I was prone to getting the creeps and scared as could be of ghosts. "Mmmmm," she finally said, in a ghostly voice. I walked over and unbuttoned the coat, bottom to top, and when I opened it I saw a hank of hair instead of Fanny's face. She had rotated herself around so I would only see the back of her. Her hair was sticking up and down like a crazy puff dandelion about to be blown to bits. I gulped down a little scream, but just then Fanny emerged from the coat, backing out, and finally I giggled, and we hugged each other and ran off to the lunchroom to eat hot macaroni and cheese, steaming rolls slivered with butter, and cold syrupy peaches.

At school there was a lot of speculation about Fanny's wound, and suddenly I was popular because everyone wanted to ask me about it, behind Fanny's back. I didn't know which I wanted more, to be true to my sister or to acquire a few new friends. Usually the second.

Billy Adams, who always went to school with his shirt inside out or backward and so had little room to cast stones, asked me, "Did Fanny go up in flames all over her body? Did her clothes burn off and leave her nekkid?"

I drew the line there. We were on the playground at the time. I spat at him in response, which I believe he took as a no. It was at this moment that I realized that while Fanny had lost a little of her steam, I might have taken it up. I mean, spitting at a boy was just like Fanny, not me. I smothered a smile beneath my red wool muffler, and later found I had specks of wool yarn on my lips like a sort of wool lipstick.

This reminded me of the time that Fanny had taken the candy-apple-color lipstick Mom had bought at Kresge's, and while Baby Bob was napping she used it to write "hello" on his foot. We stood and admired her handiwork till Bob began to move around in the crib, and we soon heard the gurgling from his rear end sound that told us a poop was on its way. We ran out of the room, then remembered Pop would wallop us for messing Mom's lipstick, but worse yet, for staining the sheets if the lipstick smeared all around there. Quick as could be, Fanny took Bob's foot and pressed it all up her arm, little "hello, hello, hello," red kisses going up to her elbow (this was before the accident, but that same arm). Finally, Bob had smelled up the room and Fanny had reddened up her arm, but Bob's foot was only a faint pink like when he had burned his foot once on the hot sidewalk. Mom was making her way up the stairs singing, "Oh do you know the muffin man?" Pop used to say that before him, Mom must have had a sweetheart who was a baker, she was so enamored of this song. While Mom sang in her high, sweet as syrup voice, "who lives in Drury Lane!" almost as if she were a movie star on the big screen at the Fox Theater, I put the lipstick safe in my jumper pocket, and Fanny had her arm safe behind her back. We escaped undetected.

Speaking of the movies, since the accident, Fanny wouldn't touch a kernel of popcorn. At the theater, she rushed past the popcorn stand because the smell made her want to lose her breakfast. I couldn't eat popcorn at the movies either unless I wanted to sit very far away from my sister. Instead we dissolved Necco wafers on our tongues, making them gritty with soft sugar. The pale brown ones were the best.

Another change that occurred after the accident was that a lot of people—our pop included I think—now had a way to always tell us apart. Fanny's scar was the shape of a fan, triangular, and it was a purplish dark pink. After the accident she was in bandages a long time, bandages that oozed a sharp-smelling yellow medicine, so when finally the burn was healed and we saw it, we said, it could be uglier. Now when Fanny wore long sleeves, of course, she and I were the same again. But when she wore short sleeves, everyone could see the mark on her arm's soft underside. Sometimes it looked almost pretty to me in a strange way—or was I just so relieved to see us made different?

For the first time ever, I had a friend other than Fanny. I began to go around with a girl named Renee, who was full of smart talk, like Fanny had been, and confidence too. But when she tried to take me over and make me always do what she wanted, I found that I could say no. I hardly knew the word before this time. Renee would say, "Let's make our dolls have an afternoon tea, with the tea set my Grandma Suree gave me; it's porcelain you know," and I would say, "No." Just "No," or sometimes, "No, let's jump rope outside. It's a fine sunny day." She was no better than me! I had my own mind and a mouth too.

Fanny spent a lot of time by herself that winter. She got a little spiteful sometimes. When Baby Bob toddled around the house, she would tip him over just to feel her arm do it, I guess. Baby Bob was like one of those tippy toys; he could right himself quickly. His howling moan became abbreviated, just a hiccup of protest, then he was up again and circling the room, looking for things to chew and break. When Baby Bob turned three, he ate a whole crocheted sofa doily, even though it gagged him a few times. Mom said soon he will urp up lace! But it never happened.

6

FANNY

ON NEW YEAR'S Eve, Mom and Pop were going to a fancy party at Pop's boss's house, and a neighbor girl named Lorraine was coming over to keep us company and to watch Bob. Sue and I snuggled under Mom and Pop's pink wedding ring quilt—though there was one yellowish ring on it from Baby Bob—and watched Mom dress for the party. Mom carefully pulled up her stockings, and these made her legs look a yellowy beige not as pretty as her own legs, I thought, but nicely shiny. She slipped a dress over her head that she had sewn herself, with Aunt Millie's help. It was a satiny material, what Mom called a chemise, which meant it floated over her head and then hung still and straight, shivering at her ankles a little because it had a flounce in a different color there. The dress was the color of coffee cream and the flounce was the color of gold jewelry. She looked swell. Pop had forbidden Mom to get one of those bobbed hairdos everyone had, so Mom had twisted her hair into a fancy coil and pinned it with a hairpin made of ivory, but not real ivory. Mom wore cherry-pink lipstick, and she put a little bit on her cheeks too and rubbed it in well, but not well enough, because when Pop came in to have Mom help him tie his bow tie, he spit on his fingers and wiped away the color from her cheeks. I talked about it later with Sue; we think he thought it was a mistake, that some lipstick had gotten loose of her lips and meandered. Mom's face got some color all on her own. Was she mad at Pop, or just excited to go out? To get Pop spiffed up, she got out his brilliantine, which he didn't use every day; he usually just combed tap water into his hair, but tonight he let her dab some on, and his hair glistened in the lamplight, dark brown like chocolate cake.

Lorraine arrived; we knew her from church, but she had never taken care of us before. We liked her right away. She had her hair bobbed, and she let Sue and me feel of it. It was slippery soft where it curled under and kissed her cheeks. She wore her lipstick bee-stung style, dotting the center of her mouth like a big O, and I knew that I would want to do this when I got older. She was a year too young to go out on New Year's Eve, her parents said.

Lorraine was nice about my arm. She looked at my scar and told me it was getting so much better, and that the new year would bring a new look for it. She said that suddenly I would be set apart in a way, as if I had a dangerous past, and that when I got older and fellas started taking me out, they would be intrigued.

"You don't think it's ugly?" I asked.

"No," she said. She pointed to a little dark brown dot on her face which was right in that area between the cheek and the chin, but west a little. "I used to think this was ugly, but then I saw an actress with one. Do you know what they call it? A beauty mark!"

Somehow, I wasn't convinced that my scar would ever be known as a beauty mark, but when it finished healing, it might be lacy looking and not the worst thing that ever marked someone.

Lorraine got out a pan I think for popcorn but then she looked at my face and remembered and said, "Hey girls, how about we make some fudge candy?" This was after Bob had gone to bed, and so she had her hands free to work with and make sure nobody got burned. I handed her sugar and Karo syrup and chocolate squares and she worked at the stove, and her hair sprung out in little curls all down her neck. When Lorraine did the little test to see if the fudge had fudged, as she put it, she looked like a scientist, dribbling a bit of fluid into a beaker.

"Soft ball!" Lorraine cried out, and Sue and I burst into applause. We buttered the plates for Lorraine to pour the fudge in. It smelled like heaven, but we had to wait till it cooled. Meantime, Lorraine told us what a school dance was like, to keep our minds off candy.

Lorraine had only been to a few dances, but she told us everything she wore, from the ground up, as Pop would say. Her brassiere was ivory colored and was meant to flatten her a bit so her chemise fell just right, she said. To the Christmas party she had worn a chemise of violet color.

Sue said, "To match your eyes!"

Lorraine had borrowed her mother's long beads. I mean, they hung to about her thighs, she said! Her hem just barely covered her knees, and only did that because her father insisted. There was a little dimple in the fabric where her mom had to take it down. Her stockings were the new gray color, she told us, and we were awed. It matched the silver color of her beads.

"Only problem was," Lorraine said, "our cat Bingbong got attracted to the long beads and when he tried to play with them, he made a little tiny hole in my stockings."

Sue and I gasped.

"Well, what could I do, we didn't have any extras. I just took a little stitch in them from the back and prayed they'd hold." Lorraine licked some fudge from the corner of her mouth and then she smiled radiantly. "They did!"

The song she remembered most from the dance was, "S'Wonderful." The boy she danced with for that song, Mitchell Barrard, was tall and had glittery hair the color of a fresh ear of corn. He smelled spicy and sweet, and he leaned in against her while they danced. "But not too fresh," she added. "He hummed along just a little while we danced, and he was in tune, even, which you have to be to make it work."

Sue asked Lorraine if she could brush her hair. I could see why, I mean, it looked soft as the softest fur. I washed the fudge pan, and we all sang, "S'Wonderful," while we waited for the new year. Mom had said we could stay up, and we had taken long naps that afternoon to make it happen. At midnight Lorraine kissed us both and then we ran up the stairs to kiss Baby Bob in his sleep. I leaned over his bed and grabbed one hand and Sue grabbed the other, and Lorraine got his forehead. Kiss, kiss, kiss, it was a new year, with new hopes and dreams and fudge too.

SUE

V ALENTINE'S DAY IT was cold out but sunny and bright and smelled like spring wasn't so very far away. This Valentine's Day would be the best ever, I thought. We had new cherry-red sweaters that Aunt Millie had knitted for us, and they had little pom poms hanging from the collar. I mean, we looked swell. Even Fanny didn't mind that they were identical, and she didn't often like for us to match. She had started putting her hair in a different style from mine every day, just so we'd be set apart, using hairpins she'd "borrowed" from Mom. She put them on in the restroom at school when we got there, and she slid them out while we walked home, so I guess she knew Mom wouldn't approve. Sometimes she put a little braid in her hair, just a small section of it, and pinned it up on the side where it pointed to the sky like some crazy twig. I liked my smooth curls better. We had made our very own valentines the weekend before. Some kids brought in store-bought valentines, but Pop thought they were a waste of money, so we made our own. Fanny and I had come up with the idea of taking some red flannel scraps that came from a set of long johns Mom had sewn for Baby Bob and pasting them onto little white circles we cut from old price cards Pop had brought home from the streetcar. I loved the smell of paste something awful and couldn't resist eating a little of it sometimes. Salty, gooey, grand stuff. On Valentine's Day we dressed for school in our cherry-colored cardigans, carrying a shoebox full of valentines to give.

When we were little our teachers made us send valentines to everyone in class, but now in third grade we were allowed to make our own choices. This resulted in some tears and mad feelings but some surprises too. Like, suddenly Fanny opened this valentine that had red yarn at the top and in big sloppy print was Chester Bingleton's signature. A boy! I was getting very mad and jealous but about five valentines farther into my own stack I opened up a valentine that had ratchety edges and a much bigger left loop than a right, and there was one for me from Bert Singman. Fanny and me both, our first real valentines from boys. Fanny sort of acted like it was nothing but I turned almost as red as my sweater, and when I touched my hand to my forehead it felt as hot as a firecracker.

Miss Murphy gave us some cherry valentine lollipops and she let us lick them right there and then, while Mrs. Ferber, our room mother, passed out popcorn balls that had candies stuck on them. Since Fanny still wouldn't touch popcorn, I took hers and slipped it into my schoolbag, which believe me, I regretted later when I realized that my arithmetic homework had stuck to my history homework.

When we got home from school that day Mom gave us valentines she'd made for us. They were little doily things that were lacy and soft; she said we could pin them to our sweaters to wear for a while. Pop had left us shiny new nickels for a treat. He had given Mom a strand of red beads for Valentine's Day. They were lightweight and so long they shimmied at her waist almost. She put them on to show us, and then put them away for the next time she and Pop went out at night, which might be awhile.

But anyway, this Valentine's Day, which seemed the best ever because of getting valentines from boys, changed completely around that night because the way my cheeks had felt firecracker hot was not entirely Bert's doing. I felt really hot after dinner too, and I went up to lie down, but I wasn't there long before I had to throw up in the trashcan next to my bed. Mom came to our room, and she put her hand, which felt like ice, on my forehead. Fanny gave me a mirror to look at myself; I was the color of a devil lady I was so red. I put my tongue out for Mom to look at it, and it was red and at first we thought it was the red lollipop, but then Fanny stuck her tongue out too for Mom to see and no, mine was bright red and Fanny's lollipop stain was gone. I had the look of a strawberry on my tongue, Mom said. And then Pop came into the room and he said, "Oh, my lord heavens," and Mom unbuttoned my cardigan and then she pulled up my undershirt with her icicle fingers, and there was a rash. Unfortunately, we all knew what that meant. I had scarlet fever. Mom turned around to Fanny and Bob, who were standing in the doorway, and she said, "Fanny, go take Bob and keep him in his room, with the door shut. Play puzzles till I come get you. I don't want you to catch this."

Mom went and put a handkerchief on her face, tied in the back, and she looked like a bandit. How funny that my mom was now a robber. I laughed at her and she put a cold washcloth on my forehead, and I could feel all of the little prickly tufts there making my forehead cool off to where there was steam coming off it, I thought. Pop left and soon came back with Doc Reston, who told Mom and Pop to go stand in the corner. It was very strange to hear a man tell grown people to go do that, like they were bad or something. He looked at my chest and he took my temperature, and when he opened my mouth to look at my tongue I tried very hard to not throw up on him. I succeeded, thank the Lord, and then he said, "Yes, it's scarlet fever, she has to go to the isolation hospital right now, tonight."

The next thing I heard was a funny, loud, looping sound, and it was the hospital pulling up to our house. The ambulance I mean, which is the hospital in a car. Two men came in wearing stiff white uniforms and they had on bandit masks; I mean the whole world had turned to robbers. And then one of the men carried me down to the whooping car; there were lights on it, and I was scared. They said that my mom and pop couldn't come with me because I had an infectious disease, and I looked up out of the back of the ambulance, and with my mind I tried to make my hand wave at them, but I felt too sick. Mom tried to hand the ambulance man my doll, telling them, "She can't go without Jean Louise."

But the ambulance man was in a very big hurry as he put me in the little bed in the back of the ambulance and wrapped me up in something cool, and he told my mom, "We could bring the doll, but she won't be able to bring it home because it will be infected and everyone must leave what they come with."

I had a hard time making sense of anything except already my heart was broken that I would have to leave my red sweater with the pom poms too? And then Mom said, "Jean Louise will wait here for you, Sue." And then, "We love you, honey."

And then the men drove me in the dark for a long way and I woke up and fell asleep and woke up and fell asleep again, and the next time I woke up I threw up into a towel, and the man said, "That's okay, honey," like he was a mother almost. I felt a little better hearing that.

When we got to the hospital they carried me up the stairs and put me in a bed. Then a nurse came in and gave me something to drink that made me sleepy, but how would I sleep with no Fanny and no Jean Louise? I had never gone to sleep all by myself in my whole life. I didn't have much time to think about it before I was asleep anyway.

The next morning I felt a little bit better. The nurse carried me to a closet and she said, "Let's find something for you to wear, cupcake."

I had to wear someone else's clothes left behind there because in this hospital you couldn't bring your real clothes here unless you wanted to leave them behind. Just the same as with toys. I wondered if I had turned into a cupcake, from what she had said, and you know, she was talking through a bandit mask too. I heard the nurse say to another nurse who was in the hall, "Her fever's still pretty high and she's a little loopy."

The nurse helped me strip off my old clothes, which was embarrassing because I had been getting dressed on my own for years by then. And she pulled over my head a kind of fuzzy shirt that was pale green like a certain kind of mint, and red flannel pajama pants. It bothered me a little to wear red and green together because after all it was not Christmas, but I had to do what she said. Then she made me get back into bed, and she gave me a book to read that was too young for me, *Three Little Kittens*. In any case it didn't matter because I fell back asleep. When I woke up I saw I had drooled a big quantity of drool onto the book, if I had a measuring spoon I'd say it would be two of them. I smeared the book onto the yellow blanket on my bed till it was dry, I was so embarrassed. I saw that it was getting dark outside and wondered if I'd slept the whole day.

Then the nurse came in and she said, "Guess who is here to see you?" and she carried me to this porch where people could come visit, but they couldn't come in or touch me because I was infectious. I was put into a rocking chair, and I looked through the window and it was Pop! I couldn't stop crying. He held his arms out like he wanted to hug me, but of course he could not. He said my name softly and he said it over and over like it was a song. He told me that they all missed me, and Mom wanted to come see me very bad, but she would probably have to wait to the weekend when Pop could stay home and watch Fanny and Bob. I put my hand on the window, and Pop put his hand on it too, and then he kissed his hand and put it back up on the window, and I kissed my hand and put it up there too.

Pop reached into a brown paper bag and he pulled out a beautiful doll that looked rather a lot like Jean Louise, with the same color hair. He said, "Here, will she do for just a little spell? She will be your hospital doll, and Jean Louise will wait at home till you come back, and she will stay your house doll. Fanny is taking care of her real nice." And a nurse who was outside took the doll from my pop's hands and carried her inside to where I was, and she put her in my arms and right away, I named her Pop Louise, in my mind, but I didn't say it aloud because Pop would think that sounded funny. My, I loved my pop more than I had ever loved him before, and in a way I think it just burst through the window to him because tears rolled down his face too. I had never seen my father cry. The nurse told me that I had to go back to my room, and she picked me up in her arms, and Pop and I said goodbye. Later I found out that Pop had taken the streetcar to the very edge of St. Louis to visit me, and it had taken him an hour and a half there and would take an hour and a half back. Mom would hold his dinner hot, I knew.

The nurse carried me back to my room and put me on the toilet. I had turned into a baby again, it seemed. I peed for her and she helped me back to bed. She gave me some juice and a dry piece of toast, which I couldn't eat, and then left. I have to say, I kissed on Pop Louise like she was a real person, my mom even. There was no other child in the other bed in my room; it was just me, and I was lonely. I missed Fanny something fierce. I wanted to hold on to her and have her tell me everything she thought and wanted, like she always had. I missed her good smell and soft hand to hold, the one that fit mine exactly.

Pop Louise and I looked at the rash on my chest. It was shaped like a branch from a Christmas tree with the needles all poking out. Scarlet was too pretty a word for something that made you feel as bad as this. My cheeks were burning hot still, but my feet were cold as icicles, and I thought about how icicles could snap off branches; I was so afraid my feet might snap off too. I cried for the nurse, but my voice was weak because my throat felt like there was a finger of fire in it. I would try to yell loud, but only this little tiny voice jumped out of me. I wanted the nurse to bring me a pair of socks, but I couldn't get her to come so I got out of bed by myself, but I fell down before I got over to the dressing closet. The nurse later called it fainting. She found me in a heap there with Pop Louise betwixt me and the cold floor. I thought that perhaps this new doll my pop had brought me had saved my life because she made the floor softer and warmer for me till the nurse put me back in bed. When the nurse picked me up she said it was like there was less of me each time she picked me up. I was afraid the heat was making me melt away. But she agreed my feet were ice and she got me a pair of socks that were wool and scratchy but warm, and I fell right to sleep that night with Pop Louise's hands in mine.

In the middle of the night there was a little girl who came into the room with me. I heard the nurse call her Bitsy. She had hair that was very long, like a twiney rope. I saw the nurses putting some cold towels on her and checking her and giving her juice. Bitsy was calling out about her teddy bear, Jimmy Boo, it sounded like. She was loopy too, it seemed. I hoped her pop would bring her a Pop Boo tomorrow but it was hard to know, because I didn't know her pop.

I wanted to introduce myself to Bitsy, but I fell asleep again by accident. In the morning I woke up remembering her, and I went to the side of her bed and touched her arm, and it was like how hot the oven is for Mom to cook biscuits. I felt a lot better this morning; I knew I did because when I had the thought of biscuits it was a good thought and didn't make me feel sick. I was even able to go to the toilet all by myself. It was like yesterday I was a two-year-old baby but today I was a four-year-old. I still couldn't stand up long enough to brush my hair, which I really wanted to do because it had started to look like an overgrown bush that a dog might rub against for scratching. But it was back to bed for me.

I got back in bed and read *Three Little Kittens* to Pop Louise in a small whisper. This time it was on purpose, so we wouldn't wake Bitsy. Bitsy began to make a very bad sound like she was going to throw up so I went to the hall (I could walk that far), and I hollered out with a medium-sized voice, bigger than yesterday's, "We need a nurse right this very now!" I ran back and jumped into bed and pulled my covers over my head so I wouldn't have to see Bitsy throw up. The nurses carried her to the bathroom and shut the door but I heard a sound in there like little birds were being killed. It would probably be a while before Bitsy and I could play together.

When they brought Bitsy back to bed her rope of hair was pinned on top of her head so she wouldn't mess it. Her cheeks were apple red, and her eyes looked almost black because the pupils were big as marbles. The large kind of marble that Fanny always won in a marble game. Did I look that bad too? There was no mirror in the bathroom; maybe we were better off not knowing.

Bitsy fell right back to sleep again after the nurses settled her in her bed. One of the nurses came over to me and said, "Can you eat a little bit today?" and I said yes, thinking of my mom's biscuits with butter and honey, but they took me to a big room where there were a lot of sick children wearing mismatched clothes all with big red polka-dot marks on their cheeks. It was like being in a crazy circus or something. The nurse brought me a bowl of stewed apples. I thought they were too mushed to eat but I spooned up some of the apple soup and ate it.

Later that afternoon when it was just starting to get dark, Pop came again, like I'd prayed he would. He had a letter for me from Fanny and a book to read me, *Winnie-the-Pooh*. The nurse brought the letter inside to me and it said, "Dear Sue, I hate to say this but I miss you. Sometimes you make me mad but now that you are gone there is only Baby Bob to play with, and I don't like his Lincoln Logs and Tinker Toys. I want to play doll dress up with you. I have Jean Louise covered up with Mom's good pink scarf, so she won't get dusty. I talk to her a little so she will remember the sound of your voice, which is I guess a lot like mine. Pop told me you are weak, and so please eat some food and get strong again and come back to us soon. Love, Fanny. P.S., at school the kids miss you too. And Miss Murphy too, who misses the good twin. Ha."

I got teary again and Pop waited for me to feel more cheerful. I told him I had eaten hot apple soup, and he was glad that I had eaten. He opened up *Winnie-the-Pooh* and he read me the first story in it. It was strange to hear my pop read because Mom was usually the one who read to us every night. He read a little too fast, like it was a newspaper story, but when I asked him to slow down he did, and then I could picture Piglet and how he would be pink and small and funny in the story, and how cozy and yellow plump Pooh must be. I loved hearing my pop's voice, which felt like it was touching me softly like a blanket tucked under my chin. When he was finished he got ready to go, putting on his coat and buttoning it high up to his chin. He told me, "Tomorrow is Saturday, so Mom can come to see you." I was very happy. We put our hands up to the window again, and the nurse took me back to bed for a little nap before dinner.

When I got to my room, Bitsy was sitting up in bed and looking at the *Three Little Kittens* book. Her face looked not as apple red, more like raspberry pink red, a good sign. Her eyes looked blurry and a little weird, but she smiled when I introduced myself. I asked about her parents, and she said they lived so far over on the other side of

St. Louis that she didn't know when they could come to see her, plus there were five other children at home. She didn't have her real bear or a substitute bear, but she held a little left behind rabbit whose fur was worn off its behind and who looked too yellow at the ears, but it was something anyway. She was wearing a boy's flannel shirt, it looked like, and a bathrobe that she had come from her home in. I felt tempted to brush her hair and braid it, but I didn't know how set her stomach was, it was probably best not to jostle the bed. So we talked a little and then we fell asleep. Later I went off to eat a little dinner, but she stayed behind and slept because she wasn't to the eating part of her recovery yet. There were strange gloopy noodles for dinner in a chicken broth, and I tried hard not to think about how wormy they looked.

On Saturday Mom was finally able to come and see me. She came right after lunch. I went up to the window and we hand kissed right away but we did it for a long time, like a hug. "Oh baby," Mom said, "my baby girl."

I had dressed up for her as well as I could, the clothes selection being what it was. I wore a yellow dress over some blue pajama pants since it was still pretty cold. Mom had on her good wool coat of dark green, hunter green, she called it, and she had on bright red lipstick that made my heart brim over. On her, Christmas in February looked grand.

I sat in my rocking chair and Mom sat with her chair pulled up as close to the window as it would get, and she leaned her cheek against the window. "I miss you, honey, we all do. How do you feel?"

I showed her how my tongue still had a strawberry on it, but it was a faded strawberry like one that been sitting in cream for a time and the color had dripped out a little. I unbuttoned my dress and showed her my rash, which was still all spindly and spidery looking.

I told her what was true, though, that I had eaten a soft egg for breakfast and though the gloopity part gave me a hard time holding it down, I had done it. They made soft eggs with a cream sauce on it to build up our bones again. I felt better, but not too much better. I still couldn't stay awake for very long. But I could walk around by myself now, I told her.

Mom said the others hadn't caught the scarlet fever, and I was glad of that. "With you two girls as tight as two bugs in a rug, it's surprising Fanny didn't catch it the same place you caught it. We were lucky we didn't have to quarantine the house. The doctor just told Pop not to shake hands with his customers, and Fanny has to sit in the back of her classroom a couple of weeks and stay in from recess. Bob has to stay home with me for a bit and not play with friends," Mom said.

"I bet Bob doesn't like staying inside too much!"

Mom laughed softly. "That's true."

Bob was going to start kindergarten in the fall, and Mom said she was sure ready for that; boys wore you out worse than girls, she said. "Yesterday, Bob found a wooden match that your father had left on the back stoop when he was smoking his pipe with Mr. McGillacutty." Here my mother frowned luxuriantly and then raised her hands in the air. "Bob acted like he didn't know what a match did. He struck the match and he burned up the scraps you girls left behind from when you made those valentines."

Valentine's Day seemed to me like it had been months ago, but Mom told me it was just last week.

"Luckily I caught him in time and I threw my wet dish towel down on the mess and it was over. Your pop lit into him with his belt when he got home, and usually I hate to see this, but yesterday I might have done it myself."

I smiled because I knew she would never have done that.

"When he thinks to pick up a match again, his behind will remind him different," Mom told me. She'd pronounced the word "behind" with great emphasis on the *bee* part.

I told Mom that Bitsy was my roommate and she was a pretty nice girl. She was a little shy but she was a good friend. "At first she just had this old rabbit bunny, but we found a doll that was at the back of the closet for her to play with Pop Louise and me."

"Pop Louise!" my mom exclaimed in wonder.

I turned pinker than usual and had to confess that was what I'd named the doll Pop had brought me. "Don't tell Pop," I whispered.

She said she wouldn't.

"Or Fanny."

"Heavens no! Guess what? I entrusted Fanny with making Pop and Bob a lunch. It's true I made the sandwiches and covered them with a cloth. Fanny mostly just has to uncover them and pour some milk. Come to think of it, Pop will probably pour the milk. But Fanny must wash the plates!" Mom said. "She has been helping me out more, folding the laundry and things you always did for me."

I wondered if they would need me back then.

My mom read my mind. "Of course, you fold them in squares pretty, and Fanny, she makes her own odd shapes! One was a hexagon she told me, but it just looked like a mess to me!"

Mom pulled *Winnie-the-Pooh* from her bag. "Honey, shall I pick up on this where your father left off?"

I wasn't sure, but I thought it had become a Pop book for me. "I just want you to tell me about things at home."

Mom told me the little things, like what flavor cookies Aunt Millie had brought over (almond macaroons) and where Pop had hidden a cigar (behind the sugar cannister).

I didn't understand why, and it didn't really matter why; I could just hear my mother read the recipe for stew or the directions on a box, or hear her hum a tune or anything. Her voice was like a stream that ran behind everything, quietly murmuring. I loved it. In church, my mom had a high, clear voice like the angels, and she sang "Amazing Grace" prettier even than the choir director, and Mom wasn't even in the choir! I closed my eyes now while Mom talked and remembered how she would stroke my wrists while she sang in church, sometimes with her soft fingertips, sometimes with her good-smelling church hankie that had blue roses embroidered on it. I guess I fell asleep for a little, then the nurse woke me to say Mom had to go. I had slept through part of her visit! I began to cry and Mom stayed and sang "The Muffin Man" to me in a soft whispery lilt, and then said if she didn't go that Pop and Fanny and Bob would have to eat raw potatoes for dinner.

She saw me turn a bit green at the idea of raw potatoes. But I hand kissed her and she said she would be back next Saturday.

"A whole week? I'll be here another week!"

Mom looked stunned. She buttoned up her coat slowly like her fingers weren't going too well. The buttons were big coffee-saucer-looking buttons with a sprinkle of sugar in the middle. I remembered when my mom had taught me how to button up my clothes. I could remember back when I was that little.

"I guess no one has told you."

"Can't I come home ever?" I began to cry that crazy kind of crying that is hot fast tears that are rushing down your face and hitting your neck before you know you've gotten started.

"Honey, of course you can come home. But the doctor said the isolation period at this hospital is six weeks."

The tears came down so fast that my yellow dress grew darker yellow like the sun losing its sense. I couldn't believe this. What was six weeks? It was like six years, to me, in my mind and heart. And I hadn't even gotten through one whole week yet.

"But Mom, I feel so much better. I am eating a little bit, and I can walk by myself, and my rash is not so rashy."

"I know honey, but the doctors say your sickness will make others sick too if we don't wait the six weeks."

"When will I come home?"

"Beginning of April."

April was a hundred years away because now it was February and cold and ice and coats and gloves and cocoa, but April was sunny and flowers and cotton sweaters and picnics at the park.

"I can't come home for Easter?"

"The doctor doesn't think so, honey. But he said they have an Easter egg hunt here."

I wasn't very cheered up by the idea of this. I wanted Mom to be able to leave without remembering me wet and crying, though, so I smiled and said, "Okay Mom, will you save me a chocolate bunny or something?"

"Oh honey, two or three at least!"

I loved my mom and pop and even my sister Fanny and my brother Bob, but it was like I had to be in jail for a while even though I hadn't done anything wrong.

"Mom, bye."

8

FANNY

I DIDN'T LIKE to admit I missed her, because my whole life she had been a wrongheaded mirror always looking back at me, the same but not at all the same. She hung on me too much and she needed me too much to decide things. Red or pink? Candy or gum? Jump rope or hopscotch? I was tired of having to know everything! But as pesky as she was, I was used to her. I had to walk to school by myself now. I whistled sometimes, "Me and My Shadow," because now my shadow was gone. The snow was starting to melt and sometimes the sun won over the cold and it was downright pretty outside. I spent some time making circles in the snow slush that was brown and liquidy. But it wasn't as fun without Sue there to tell me we had to hurry and get to school. Then seeing could I make her slush around in it too.

The night they took Sue away was the hardest for me to sleep. I missed her warm body in bed, though it would have been too warm that night; she was like a furnace with the fever. I had to wear socks and I wore a sweater under my nightie that night. This embarrasses me a little, but I had to sleep with my doll, Fine, that night. I mean,

I was too old for that, even though Sue wasn't, but I was lonely and needed someone to talk to. Sue and I always whispered at night to each other till one of us fell asleep. We always did that and we always had. I mean, I wonder if we came out of Mom whispering to each other. We didn't talk about anything important, just about how our teacher's cardigan didn't match her skirt, or how big a pest Baby Bob was with his Tinker Toys poking and scratching us all the time and the way he hollered and threw balls. We didn't understand why boys were like this. Sometimes we would whisper our dreams of what breakfast might be the next day. "Crispy toast with honey," would come over to me on Sue's soft voice like a dream. And soon it would be a dream.

I woke up in the middle of the night scared that I would never see Sue again. Our cousins knew some kids from their church who had died of scarlet fever. When Mom put me to bed she had told me, "We got Sue to the hospital fast and she will get the best treatment there is. If you catch scarlet fever early enough, you get all well. I know it for sure," Mom said, though her lip quivered a little when she said it. I tried to imagine if Sue died, what it would be like to be a twin with no twin. When I imagined it in my head, it was as if half my own body had disappeared, like in a mystery story. I would be half-girl Fanny, with one arm, one leg, half a head of hair, and half lips to speak with. I didn't think my brain would be in half, but I thought my heart might be.

Sometimes when Mom made us say our prayers at night, in my head instead of saying things to God, I would just think, "da da da da da da da," you know, just thinking nothing really, or thinking everything but thoughts of God. But the night Sue went to the hospital I prayed in earnest with Mom and then every time I woke up in the night I put another prayer in to God. I promised some things I could probably not really make good on, and some I could.

As the days went by, I discovered the things that Sue was really good at, because with her gone, I had to do them, and I didn't do them all that well. Sue helped Mom out a lot and I did too, but I realized Mom had picked the easier things for me to do. It was easy to cut up bananas for Bob and to pick up his toys, but it was hard to iron Pop's handkerchiefs and shirts and to cook anything at all. Mom didn't like to trust the ironing to me after I burned my arm, but she couldn't keep up with it. She gave me a long lesson, and I learned to iron without burning myself, but when the things were done they didn't look crisp like Sue's did. In fact, I could see the spots I'd missed, once it was too late. Pop told me that it was okay, since he wore a jacket over his shirt anyway. And surely handkerchiefs got wrinkled fast when you blew in them, Pop said over Sunday rolls and coffee. Bob giggled over this till the rolls were cold and our milk glasses just had whispers of white in the bottom.

I was also not very good at making the beds because I could never tell which was the long way and which was the short way of the sheets. I mean, I started to realize that Sue was smarter than me about some things, and it bothered me no end.

The other thing was that she wasn't there to help me with arithmetic, and soon I would have to stay after school and work on it with Miss Murphy. I didn't look forward to that any so much, because when Miss Murphy said numbers and drew them, my mind went very far away and had a hard time on the return trip. But maybe Miss Murphy would let me slip a little, because when Sue came back, she'd catch me up. Or would I have the job of catching Sue up too, for all the school she'd missed? It was too many jobs for one me.

9

SUE

Now that i had been here two weeks, the hospital was starting to seem like my life. I usually didn't like this life as well as my old one, but I was getting used to the routine. Mostly I felt pretty well. I wasn't quite my old self, but close. I got tired faster than before and had to nap a few times a day like a little kid. But I had grown to enjoy naps. Bitsy and I would bid each other a good nap, and then we'd lie in our each and own beds, me with Pop Louise and her with Mr. Bunny, and we'd whisper to each other like Fanny and I used to do. It reminded me of doing that a lot, so much so that sometimes if I were to drift off a bit while whispering then wake up suddenly to look across at Bitsy I was very surprised to find Bitsy's face so very different from mine, all blowsy cheeked and with hair down to her waist that was a cloud of fox-colored fur, and her eyes chocolate brown. I was so used to looking across the bed to see Fanny's face looking so much like mine, it was like looking in the mirror. Though Fanny's hair would stick up where mine would stick down, and the seams of her pajamas were always crooked, while mine were always tidy. The strong blue-gray eyes were hers and mine both, as was the way our lips curled up at the edges like our mom's did.

I never knew how to feel waking up to Bitsy and not Fanny. Happy, sad? Usually a little of both. Bitsy was a really swell girl. Only thing was she wasn't getting better as fast as me. She took naps between our naps. And when we played dolls she leaned back on her pillows a lot and sighed. We compared our rashes, both a little shy to unbutton our shirts. Hers was a pink-red the color of leaking raspberries, but mine was only a whisper of milky pink like babies wear. On our tongues, my strawberry mark was only a ghost of a mark, and hers was still pink and more triangular than mine. But the nurse said we were both getting better.

I mostly didn't like the food here as much as I loved my mother's. But sometimes they made this mashed potatoes with cream gravy that was good. It was soft and made your tongue happy, and the cream put meat back on our bones, they said. I was sort of thin, and my pajama bottoms would usually billow when I moved around, because there was just less of me to anchor them.

My pop still was the one to visit me most days; my mom could only come on weekends. My pop and I had finished reading *Winnie-the-Pooh,* and now he was reading me *Little Women.* I could tell that he had never read a book like that. It had young girls' thoughts in it. He looked like he was driving his streetcar down a street he had never seen before, which can't happen since they are on their tracks of course. Sometimes Pop even turned a little pink at the ideas of the girls, especially Jo because she had a strong mind. He didn't know if this was good or bad, it seemed to me. Still, I just loved to hear his deep and warm voice, which rose and fell like the Missouri River in a noontime sun. I wrapped a knitted afghan all around me so tight it was like the knitter had knitted me right into it, and I just looked up at my pop, who leaned up against the window. He was gruff a lot in our house, but now I knew that he loved me more than I'd ever suspected. This finally was a time in my life when he never got me mixed up with Fanny. It was clear which twin was where, and I loved that he knew me in my heart in a way I don't think he did before. It may seem crazy to say that in some ways I loved being at this hospital so far from home, but this was as true as anything.

There were no teachers at the hospital, but some of the nurses asked us to name the United States and things just to pass the time and to keep our brains in good care, like a teaspoon of medicine gone through our ears to the insides of our heads. Sometimes the new nurses who didn't know so much about the medicines and treatments read to us, and then, sometimes we older kids read to the younger kids. I read a book about fish and one about trees to some little kids who were five and six. They listened really well and it was fun for me, since Bob would be climbing the walls after three words flat. They would sit at my feet like I was a teacher and listen, and one time they made me read *Coldwater Fishes* five times over. I wondered if I would want to teach when I grew up. I know Fanny would think that stupid because she always tried to get at the teachers any way she knew how. But I liked the shape of the day at school. I also loved the smooth feel of chalk in my fingers. A nurse found a small blackboard for me, and she brought it in with a fresh clean white stick of chalk that was so pretty I hardly wanted to use it. But in minutes the dust of it was flying, and I had drawn some fish on the board for the little kids. I drew a long one, the kind that stays at the river bottom, and I drew a fine fluffy one that looked like a marshmallow with a tail and mouth.

The next Saturday Fanny came to visit me, along with Mom. It was a surprise. I came to the visiting room and there they were. Fanny was wearing a good dress, one I'd never seen before, a pale green one Mom must have just made for her. I was surprised to see her, because it was the first time I could remember looking at her and not seeing myself look back. I knew then how thin and pale I was, because she looked full of warmth and roundness compared to me. Her cheeks were pink from the cold outside, and I remembered suddenly about outside and how good and fresh it felt. Mom always said how the fresh air was the best tonic in the world, and now I wanted some. I leaned up against the window and put my cheek to it and Fanny did the same.

Mom looked happy and sad all at once. But she said, "Isn't this wonderful? Usually they only let one person come to visit at a time, but because Fanny is your twin they said okay." Mom sighed a happy sigh and she unbuttoned her coat, but Fanny and I just stood cheek to cheek and said nothing, even though Fanny was rarely at a loss for words. I cried a little bit and Fanny did too, but only the kind that moistens the side of your eyes, not all underneath.

"I didn't know how much I missed you till I saw you," Fanny said.

"Me too," I told her.

"I'll let you girls talk alone for a while," Mom said, and she went off to a corner of the visiting room and took out some knitting. She was knitting me a new red sweater with pom poms, Fanny told me, since I couldn't bring my infected Valentine's Day one home.

Fanny and I sat down and ooched our chairs close together.

"What's going on at school?" I asked. "Will I have to make everything up?"

"Nah. Miss Murphy will be able to catch you up over a couple of recesses. You're the smart one, remember?"

I smiled and said, "I thought I was the well-behaved one."

"That too." Fanny laughed. "But who's the fun one?"

"You are," I told her. "Fun Fanny. Hey, you should be a movie star and they could have that name on the marquee."

"Maybe so. I've got big plans for April Fools' Day, by the way. You know, you'll be coming home right around then! But if you miss the big day, would you like me to do anything for you? Maybe tie Josie Binkleman's skirt bottom to the end of her blouse?"

"And how would you do that?" I asked. I was filled with admiration for my sister already.

"Well, you know how she always falls asleep when Miss Murphy reads from *Our Great States*? Since I sit behind her, all I have to do is lean over and work real fast. You know, Josie's blouse is always untucked out of her skirt anyway. And this will get back at her for beating you out of the spelling bee."

"Fanny, that was two years ago! And she won it fair and square."

"Doesn't matter to me! Remember how she danced all around you with her little bee pin screeching, 'I won! I won!' You ask me, she's gotten off easy these last two years. I've been planning this awhile, but this is the first year I ever sat behind her."

"All the boys will see her panties!"

"Yeah, what did you think the point was? It will be grand!"

I could close my eyes and see Josie's face turning dark red like blood when she stood up and everyone saw her with this bow on her behind like she was a Christmas package.

Next Fanny told me about how Bob had gotten so excited when he won a game of jacks that he hugged and kissed Nate Freedman. He came home with a bloody nose for doing that. Boy oh boy, weren't all Fanny's stories full of color.

That night at dinner one of the new girls who had come in the week before, Rosalyn, fainted onto her bowl of rice pudding. When the nurses carried her off her face was all freckled with bits of white. No one knew why she'd been allowed to come down to dinner; she was very ill and had clearly been too weak. The kids that were too weak usually got dinner on a tray. One time I had seen this girl Rosalyn's rash on her chest when her pajamas weren't done up right and hers was the color of beets from the can. I hadn't seen her strawberry tongue; of course she was too weak to stick her tongue out at anyone. She was just seven years old, and her parents came to see her a couple of times a day. Usually we could only have visitors once a day, and so the story started going around that Rosalyn would not get better, she would die.

Bitsy and I discussed it and didn't agree that this could be true. This was a terrible illness but we hadn't known of anyone dying. Not in our time here, which was a month now. Why did some kids like to scare others so much? Well, I could ask Fanny about that sometime, she enjoyed it pretty well herself.

I had become the afternoon teacher for all the little kids and I asked them to make get well cards for Rosalyn. The nurses got us some paste and Crayolas and paper, and we went to work on the floor. I had to spell Rosalyn for each and every one of them very slowly, till it started to seem like a song in my mind, "R . . . O . . . S . . . A . . ." and so on. Because of her name, most of the kids drew roses on their cards. That and we had a lot of red crayons.

10

FANNY

MARCH WAS ENDING and soon Sue would be coming home. She had been in that hospital for such a long time! It felt more like six months than six weeks. For when she got back, I thought I would make some plans for us, for fun things to do. While I walked home from school, I relished the cool breeze and yellow sunlight, and I thought, what would Sue enjoy? She had been cooped up in that place for so long, surely she'd like to do some outdoor things. Mom had said that she might have to take it easy for a while, take naps, but I thought, what about a great picnic, just for Sue and me and for our dolls, Jean Louise and Fine. What could I pack for us to take? I thought that Mom would let me take some biscuits from breakfast, maybe ham sandwich biscuits and fresh apples, and some fresh-baked brownies. I would pack it all up in a basket and bring along a jump rope and a fan in case there were bugs. If Sue was too tired to jump rope, she could watch me. And if I could save up a couple of nickels by the time she got home, I could take her to Ted Drewes's Frozen Custard stand if we could catch a streetcar out that way. They had a milkshake there that was so thick they called it the Concrete. One time Bob held it upside down for a minute, till Pop whacked his behind, and not a drop rolled out of the cup. Mom told me that Sue would need to eat a lot of good rich foods to build her blood up again, which made me picture Sue's blood as thin and shivery. I vowed that I would find ways to warm it up again, even a freezy cold milkshake, which would fatten her blood; that would warm it up.

I thought about how glad everyone would be at school to see her back in her seat; she completed the equation (Fanny plus Sue equals the twins). Sue would return in a pretty dress with a smile and a ready hand in the air to answer the questions Miss Murphy had been trying to stick me with in her absence. It was harder for me to enjoy the jokes I played on kids at school when Sue wasn't around to warn me and to make me feel better if one of them went wrong. If we were one girl split into two bodies, I knew she was the nicer half, but I also knew I was the one who might get a laugh or two and who would have plenty of stories to tell my grandchildren sometime.

Bob had turned four while Sue was gone; he had missed her so at his birthday dinner. Now that it was just days before we would go pick up Sue, Bob and I made a welcome home sign to hang in the dining room over the window. Bob cut out all the letters. While the scissors squeaked and flashed in his hands, his tongue stuck out the side of his mouth with the effort to get it right. I hadn't thought very much about how Sue's absence had sat with Bob. He was a boy and he seemed in a different world from us, and he was nobody's twin. Still, he was our brother; I would claim him in spite of the dirt in his ears and the times he made bad noises in church and the way he might bring in a frog to our room every once and again, but he was starting to get into my heart, and about time I guess. I knew he must miss Sue because she was sweeter to him. She read to him a lot and taught him his letters and numbers. She was patient and had a calmness about her that probably got into his skin, almost the way it got into mine. I wondered if he was just now thinking about how sometimes when she read to him, she would pet his hair a little while he nestled next to her on the divan, his face warmed in the sunlight. I saw her smooth his cowlick down a hundred times if I saw it once. One time I heard my pop say about my mom, "She is my better half," and in a way I could sure say the same about my sister Sue.

11

SUE

ICOULDN'T STOP crying. Rosalyn died. Yesterday morning she just didn't wake up. The nurse went in to tend to her and she was gone. Why would this happen? I did not want to know something like this could happen. There was a rumor that the nurse had to place Rosalyn's eyes shut with her own fingertips. I thought, why God? It was hard for me to understand why children would ever die. Very old people and bad criminals, you could see why. But a little girl? I cried till there was no water left in me. I felt dry as a husk. Could I have died here? I'd never really gotten to talk to Rosalyn because she was so ill, much more so than the rest of us; she was usually in a room all by herself or just with doctors and nurses. When the nurses had carried Rosalyn around the hospital, I had seen her Raggedy Ann doll's red yarn hair just dragged along the slippery floor of the hallway, which always smelled like strong cleaner and not like home.

When the nurses told us about Rosalyn's passing, they said we could go to a prayer service and most of us who felt well enough did. The minister there talked about lambs and mountains and things. He didn't talk about Rosalyn much. I thought I had cried out all my tears, but more came.

Otherwise, I thought a lot about home and about how happy I was to be going there in just three days. I felt bad that I was thinking about this during Rosalyn's service, but I couldn't help myself. I wondered what Mom would make for my first dinner home. Maybe chicken and biscuits and gravy. I thought of our pretty china plates at home that had little flowers, all pink and purple and yellow, with green leaves that looked like bird prints left by the tiniest birds you could imagine. Here at the hospital we ate off white plates that were sometimes chipped on the bottoms and never gleamed in the light.

You could always tell how some kids were getting better, which was when they got their meanness back. These kids would torment me with stories of my last day at the hospital when I would have to take a bath in a bitter green cleaner before I would be allowed to leave the hospital. It was supposed to kill the last of the scarlet fever germs so no one else could get sick from me, but they said it turned your skin a little green for a while, and people would think you were still ill.

"You better not wear a red dress any time soon," a girl named Rhonda said. "It'll clash with your green skin!" The other mean girls laughed with her.

I would be happy to leave those girls behind, but I sure would miss Bitsy. I found out where she lived because I thought we might like to play together sometimes after we got out of the hospital, but it turned out she lived far across town. I knew it was farther even than my pop's route. We decided to write each other letters, telling about what life was like for us after the hospital. It was getting a little hard for us to remember what it was like out there in the world. One of the nurses said that sometimes kids wanted to come back to the hospital because it had become safe and familiar, but this hardly seemed possible to me.

The night before I was to leave—and two nights before Bitsy

was—I braided Bitsy's long and beautiful red hair into two braids. As she got her health back, her hair got shinier and more supple in my hands. I loved to braid her hair because it was so long that it took half an afternoon to do, and then we had all that time to talk. I had seen Bitsy's mom a few times on the visitor porch—they lived so far from the hospital her mom hadn't gotten to come very often. She had the very same long red hair, and I thought of how they must look together at night brushing their blankets of hair out till they snapped with the crisp air and made sparks of light in the dark. Fanny and I had pecan brown hair, a bit wavy, only to our shoulders, and Fanny wouldn't let me touch hers much, especially now that she was working so hard to style it different from mine. Bitsy told me that in the first few days at the hospital the doctors threatened to cut off her hair because it got in the way of everything, but the nurses had put it up into high buns to protect it.

The nurses here were kind as mothers, and they looked all crisp and clean in their starched long dresses and thick white stockings. They wore caps that looked like big open coffee cups on their heads. Two of the nurses, Ruth and Jenny, were especially nice, and when Bitsy and I were well enough to care how we looked, they helped us find some decent clothes to wear. One time Ruth even wrapped our hair in rags to make curls. Our hair fell into whirlpool shapes and looked grand.

I would miss the little children I read stories to and played teacher with. A girl named Yvette made a beautiful painting for me to tell me goodbye; it was of Fanny and me. A lot of the kids had never even heard of twins, let alone identical ones, and some of them thought I had made up a good story on them. Yvette's picture of Fanny and me looked just like us. I had told her how Fanny wore her hair different, so she had Fanny's standing up in the air like a fork in a tree and mine curling down to tickle my shoulders. I had told them sometimes

Fanny and I even liked to dress the same, not always, so in the picture she had drawn Fanny in a blue dress with pink shoes, and me in a pink dress with blue shoes. Opposite and the same all at once. That was Fanny and me. And she drew Bob in the corner sneaking up on us with something behind his back.

12

FANNY

ON APRIL 2, WE all woke up filled with excitement. It had been six weeks plus a half week that Sue had been in the hospital. Her doctor believed in the extra half week as a caution. We borrowed a car from our neighbor friend Ethel, and we all drove over to pick Sue up! Bob folded himself into the jump seat even going to the hospital, though there was no need for that till Sue was in the car too. He just wanted to see if he could do it. My pop had taken a day off of work, something I couldn't remember him ever doing before on a day that wasn't officially a holiday. Mom packed up a picnic lunch for us to eat at a roadside park with Sue on the way back. I made lemonade and put it in a big jar, and Mom didn't even yell that the kitchen counter was sticky, she was so happy. The day before, we had made Sue her favorite cookies, sugar snaps, and they were wrapped in a pink checkered napkin, along with sandwiches. Mom had wrapped up in tissue paper the new red sweater that she had knitted for Sue, to replace the one she had to leave behind at the hospital. Pop had bought her a little charm bracelet at Kresge's. It tinkled a pretty sound, and I wasn't even jealous, I swear I wasn't. Bob had finished the welcome home sign, and Pop had helped him hang it from the mantel where our Christmas stockings went. The letters were all different sizes, because Bob didn't know when he cut anything with scissors how it would come out.

I had cleaned up our room as neat as two hands could make it, and done something else I knew Sue would be very surprised by. With Aunt Millie's help, I had sewed a new dress for her doll Jean Louise. Mom had washed the doll in boiling water to disinfect her, and her old dress was faded. We had chosen the new fabric together at Kresge's, Aunt Millie and me, a pink cotton flower print that had happy green leaves nipping around the stems. I had cut out the dress following along a pattern Aunt Millie had, and I had done it very well I thought. As crazy with scissors as Bob was, I had a steady hand for them, though I had managed to sew one of the buttons on upside down and one of the sleeves backward, which Aunt Millie helped me fix. Before we left for the hospital I dressed Jean Louise in the dress and let Jean Louise wear my doll Fine's good satin shoes since they were prettier than Jean Louise's.

We hadn't been together in cars too often, because we usually rode Pop's streetcar or walked when we went anywhere. It was fun watching how Pop got red in the face from cranking the engine and then how he hopped into the car and got a good start to it. Mom turned to me and smiled with a tear in her eye at the time as she clapped her hands in joy. Finally we would be twins again, me and Sue, and Mom would have her whole and complete family back.

13

SUE

THEY WERE RIGHT after all! I had to take a green bath the morning I left the hospital. It was the color of a bucket after it's been left out in the rain for a few days, slimy dark green. It smelled like sulphur a little bit and oats too, but also like a Christmas tree. When I was in the bath, the liquid bubbled like it was alive, this green stuff. Luckily, it was Nurse Jenny who bathed me, and she was gentle with the wash-cloth and told me she had some toilet water that smelled of gardenia that she would put on me when it was all done. I said, "Toilet water!" I mean, could things get worse yet? And she told me toilet water was a French idea for perfume and promised me it had a pretty smell. Afterward, when she wrapped me in a soft towel and dabbed the toilet water on, I kissed her on the cheek. I checked to see if the green had stayed on my skin, but I saw I looked perfectly like my own self as I dressed up in a fresh hospital outfit that had no germs on it. It was a dress the color of baby chicks; I felt lucky to have it.

I had had to say goodbye to Bitsy and Yvette and the others before the bath, because the bath was the last thing you did before you left and after that you couldn't get recontaminated. I had kissed Bitsy's hair and hugged her and I left Pop Louise in her care since I couldn't take the doll out of the hospital anyway. I had hugged and kissed Pop Louise as much as if she were a live girl, because she made me remember how much my pop loved me. I knew Bitsy would also be going soon, so I made Nurses Jenny and Ruth promise to make sure that the next girl who got Pop Louise would treat her like a princess.

I waited in the small, germ-free foyer, and when they got word my family was there, the nurses kissed me goodbye and sent me on outside, because even here there was fear of contamination if someone came inside to get me. When I walked into the sunshine I had to squint my eyes a little at first. I had not remembered how brightly colored the world was! The blue sky was painted with slivers of sparkly cloud, and the trees along the sidewalk all looked green in a glowy bright way. I walked to the gate and there on the other side was my very own family. They all hugged me at the same time, with Bob holding on to my leg like he would never let it go. Fanny hugged me straight on, and Mom and Pop surrounded us from over and around. I couldn't help but cry, and in fact it turned out we were all a little damp at our eyes.

Pop swung me up into his arms and carried me to Ethel's car. I wasn't weak but I loved it anyway; his arms were as strong as I'd remembered, with ripply muscles from switching streetcar tracks. It was such a treat to ride in a car! I laughed to see Bob pop himself into the jump seat with a look in his eyes as if he'd gotten away with something big. Fanny and I sat together in the backseat holding hands, and I could see her looking at me with great curiosity. I was thinner I knew, and I had changed in ways I wasn't sure showed on the outside, changed inside my mind and heart. Once we were on the road, Fanny whispered to me about what had happened on April Fools' Day when she had played her trick on Josie. Usually Mom would tell us it was rude to whisper, but since Fanny and I had been apart for so long, she let it go this one time.

I loved our picnic lunch! I could taste that Mom had made the bread herself, because it tasted a little of honey and salt. When we got to the apples, Pop peeled them with a knife till their skins made a long winding circle I wished I could keep in my pocket forever. Then I let the sugar cookies melt in my mouth. It was all delicious food, food from the world outside! I lay out on the blanket for a few moments after our lunch, and I heard Mom ask Pop if it was because I was weak, but the real truth was I just wanted the sun to fall all over my body.

When we got home, I saw Bob's sign over the mantel, all bright red and yellow and with furry edges from his crazy cutting. I kissed him on his forehead, something he wouldn't normally allow but today, for my homecoming, it was all right. Mom gave me a new sweater with pom poms like the one I had had to leave at the hospital. She had knitted in a little pink heart on the collar, which made me love it even more than the first one. I put it right on along with the pretty silvery-colored charm bracelet my pop had gotten me, which had a tiny flower on it, along with a baby bird, a heart, and a star. It fell off my skinny wrist, and Mom said she'd have to make me a lot of biscuits to build up my arm enough to hold it on! In the meantime I hung it on a string to wear around my neck. Fanny handed me Jean Louise, who was dressed in a new pink flower dress that she had actually made herself! Well, with Aunt Millie's help anyway. It was made of a crisp fabric with a beautiful sheen to it, and was shaped like a bell at the skirt. She had let Jean Louise borrow Fine's pretty white, white shoes. I kissed Fanny right on the lips, which embarrassed us both!

That night I woke up crying. I had had a dream about Rosalyn, the dead girl. In the dream I was walking around the hospital, sockless and cold, in a very tired, slow way, like I was swimming through an ocean of mud. When I got to where I was going it turned out to be Rosalyn's room. I walked through the door and there was a sheet over a body. I had never seen Rosalyn dead in real life, but in the dream I

wanted to look, so I pulled the sheet off the face, and it wasn't Rosalyn's face, it was my own.

I clung to Fanny's warm body and nestled myself into her hair
and breathed in her smell, which I missed like I would have missed
my own blood flowing through me. Her flannel pajama collar brushed
against my cheek like a warm whisper.

FANNY

THAT SUMMER OUR cousin Randall turned thirteen. Aunt Millie and Uncle Donald said yes, now he was old enough to work at the Fox Theater, his dream for a year now. He and a bunch of boys his age got to hand out circulars, and this meant he got paid in free tickets to the talkies. Each time he worked he got two tickets, one for himself and one for a friend. Or a cousin, as it turned out. I loved the movies and sitting in the theater with its dark coolness in the middle of a hot summer day. Even with the smell of popcorn, which naturally I didn't like too well, I loved to be at the theater. When the screen filled with movement and sound, I felt like clapping just for that. I didn't care very much what the picture was; I always wanted to go. My pop took us every two weeks but that wasn't enough. I helped Randall hand out the circulars so that he would take me most often. Mom and Pop wouldn't allow me to do this, if they knew; I was too young and a girl besides.

Sue would tell on me if she knew, so I had to sneak away on my own to meet Randall. But that summer she was playing almost every afternoon with a new girl on the block, Rebecca, and Mom thought

I was going over there too. Instead, I slipped down to a streetcar stop where the man didn't know Pop, and I rode up to the Fox Theater and hopped off the car to meet Randall.

Randall was getting a dark tan from being outside all the time. He had just gotten to change over from knickers to long pants, though he wasn't sure that was such a good thing when it was so hot outside. His shirtsleeves were rolled up and his hair slicked back with Brylcreem filched from his dad. Randall had a fierce cowlick if it wasn't creamed. I wore pretty dresses that drew people to me for the circulars. I wore a kerchief on my arm over my scar like it was some sort of decorative fashion right out of *McCalls*, and no one seemed to think different. Once the circulars had been handed out, Randall grabbed my hand and we ran into the theater. Mr. Laramie, the theater owner, made the circular kids sit in the back, though we got one carton of free popcorn, which I didn't touch, and a free soda too. I always picked Hires Root Beer. On the side of the bottle, it said that Hires was "soothing to the nerves, vitalizing to the blood, refreshing to the brain, beneficial in every way." I didn't know about this, but it tasted fresh and spunky.

One week Randall and I watched the Marx Brothers in *Cocoanuts* six shows in a row, and I can say we never got one bit tired of it. Harpo was a scream. It was funny that now movies could talk, but he was quiet anyway. His curly hair reminded me of a dog you'd like to pet a lot, and his eyes were tender, too.

One time when I was passing out circulars on Grand Avenue, I saw Aunt Millie coming out of Kresge's. I didn't want her telling Mom and Pop what I was doing, so I put all the circulars down the front of my blouse, and I stood there casual but with a stiff chest. Aunt Millie saw me and waved and hollered "Yoo-hoo!" but then you could see she was trying to make out if I was Sue or me. She crossed the street over to me, and she handed me a candy sucker and said,

"Fanny . . ." pausing to see if this was true, and then, "what are you doing out here all by yourself?"

Then Randall ran up and said, "Time to go to the movies!" and he grabbed my arm, and we said bye to his mother as we ran down the street. I dropped my sucker and circulars sifted out from beneath my skirt. They had gotten loose of my blouse and gone right on down through me, but I don't think Aunt Millie saw.

One time Sue said she wanted to go with Randall, but the movie that day was *The Virginian*, and why would she want to see horses and men with guns and such? I made up a lie fast and it was this: I told her that yesterday Randall had been coming down with a stomachache and that he was going to take the day off that day. Then, just because Randall was expecting Sue and not me, I decided to go down to the theater and meet Randall—of course he wouldn't expect Sue to pass out the circulars, just to be his guest—and play like I was Sue.

I got down to a block from the theater, and I slipped into a restroom at Kresge's to comb my hair tidier and straighten out my clothes, since Sue was the neater one. The biggest giveaway would be my scar, but I had managed to filch one of Sue's blouses that had sleeves down to the wrist, and even though it was hot, at least it covered my scar and enabled me to walk in cool and as smooth as a librarian, which is how Sue acted, and I sat right down with Randall. I even took a 7-Up, Sue's favorite, instead of a root beer. While we were watching the movie, I made up some dumb questions Sue might ask Randall, like why the sheriff had on a dark kerchief or how could horses sleep standing up? Then Randall passed me the popcorn, and I remembered that Sue loved popcorn and wouldn't turn it down. Me, I hadn't touched a kernel of it since my burn. My mouth got filled with nervous saliva, and it was all I could do to keep from spitting. I told Randall I had had a very big lunch, which was a lie; in fact I was starved. I filled my stomach with lemon-lime-sweet 7-Up, but still it grumbled so loud during one scene I could swear the whole theater heard it, but it didn't seem to bother Randall.

I had pretended to be Sue before at home (like the time when I took all the praise and glory for a few moments for having won a spelling bee that of course Sue had won) and had fooled my pop but never my mom. But I had never done this in public, and I thought it was great fun. I had gotten a free movie without even working for it.

I had to get up and wash out Sue's blouse late at night, and when Pop caught me in the bathroom washing the blouse with a bar of Ivory, he believed me when I told him I owed Sue a favor and that was why I was doing it. I slipped out into the night as it was all dark and hung Sue's blouse on the line to dry in the night's air, and I would have to wake up in the morning and go back to get it before she got up. It turned out to be easy enough to do this, since I accidentally locked myself out of the house. I lay down on the porch on an old rug in my thin nightie praying no burglar would come around, and I stared up at something on the porch ceiling that I hoped was not a wasp's nest. I must have fallen asleep, and then I woke up when a neighbor dog came and sniffed at my feet. I swallowed down a scream, which hurts you around where your liver is. When I finally got back to sleep I dreamed that the police arrested me for impersonation, and I was in jail with my hands around the jail bars, but in fact, when I woke up, I was in my pop's arms, and fortunately he decided not to tell the others, but in exchange he told me I had to clean his work shoes every night for the rest of the summer. Then he carried me up to bed.

15

SUE

I NEVER THOUGHT I would be very good at anything physical, but I learned how to swim that summer, and I turned out to be a natural. My mother taught me; she loved to swim. The public pool was just one streetcar stop away, and we went there whenever we could. She began to teach Bob too, even though he was still young for it. Fanny didn't care to learn; she was always off doing one thing or the other all summer long, it seemed to me. The bathing suit I wore was a heavy wool knit that sagged when I got out of the pool because it held gallons of the pool's water. But I didn't mind very much because once I got out the hot sun dried me through in a few minutes.

Bob took a little doing, in terms of getting comfortable holding his breath under water. He would come up sputtering and bellowing like the sea lions we visited at the zoo. His face was red and shiny wet in the sun and his hair stuck up in a funny roll with the ends pointing to the sun. When Mom taught him the dog paddle, I laughed to see the crazy shapes of his legs pumping wildly beneath the water. Me, I just seemed to know how to hold my breath by instinct. I rose from the water calm and ladylike, according to Mom. I loved floating the best. I rested on the water like there was a massive lily pad beneath me, cushioning me just so. I squinted up at the sun and sighed with the pleasure of the cold water. There were kids at the pool that I knew, but when I was swimming I liked to be alone. I would find a small portion of the pool to call my own, tuning out the shouts and splashes, and simply relish the water's cool embrace.

Though we took the streetcar to the pool, we often walked home. Mom and I slipped cotton dresses over our bathing suit and stockings, and Bob just walked in his suit and tank shirt. If Mom had a few nickels, we stopped to get a 7-Up at the store near our house, and when the bottle touched my lips with the sweet lemon-lime spray, I was in heaven.

SUE

IT WAS THE fall of 1931, a year when a lot of kids showed up to school obviously hungry and wearing patched-together clothes. Things were bad everywhere, Pop said. Lucky for us Pop's job was okay—people would always need to ride the streetcar, but his salary had been reduced some; Mom had to make our dollars stretch even more. Now she would never, ever throw a leftover piece of food out. She couldn't even buy new material to sew us dresses anymore, and instead she often cut up her old ones and made them over for us. She even did this with Pop's old clothes for Baby Bob, who looked silly in the stiff wool serge pants she made for him.

On the first day of sixth grade Fanny wore a long-sleeved sweater even though it wasn't really cold, but she wasn't fooling anyone. People knew why, that she was covering her scar, except for the new kids, who said things to her like, aren't you getting sweaty, girlie, in your pink sweater? Fanny responded with a steely, "No," but some kids still wouldn't leave it alone. On the playground a mean new girl named Gladys grabbed at Fanny, pretending to grab the end of the jump rope, but then her hand jerked Fanny's sweater right up her arm like an accordion. The scar seemed to pulse there, dark and purply, while Gladys and another new girl said, "Ickity-ickity ick! You are one ug-a-ly girl." Fanny put her scarred arm into Gladys's stomach. Gladys bent at the waist and struggled to not fall to her knees. Fanny's face, during these encounters, would not frown or grimace, but a cold wind seemed to come over her, and turned her face a dark plum color that almost matched her scar. I'd heard people talk about white-hot fury, but Fanny's was cold as ice in February.

Other times, to Fanny's surprise at first, I would stand up for her. I would tell some kids that Fanny's scar was a royal insignia. We had some kings and queens from England in our background, I said. The really gullible kids at school believed this. Another handy technique was to belittle the kids who mouthed off. "At least my sister has good hair," I might say. "Yours is like a steel-wool pad left in dishwater all night." Or, "My sister's arm looks prettier than that scar on your dress." This to the really poor kids who had holes in their clothes. Later in church I would apologize to God, but I wasn't going to let people beat up on my twin.

The part I loved about all this, I was kind of ashamed to admit to myself, was that now I was "the pretty one." People trying to differentiate between us would say this, oh not right in front of us, but I overheard it plenty of times. It was kind of funny in a way, I mean we still dressed alike much of the time, although now that Mom was making over her clothes for us we had less matches. And we had gone back to wearing our hair the same, loose and floppy curls going down our backs, but suddenly I was the prettier one, not because my looks were improved but because hers had been altered just a bit. And all because of a match, some popcorn, and a few drips of oil.

Our mom one time bought some Max Factor pancake makeup, the kind all the movie stars used; it had taken her a long time to save up the nickels for that. She patted some onto Fanny's arm to see what it might do. It changed Fanny's scar into an orangey plum color, which made it even more noticeable, so Fanny burst into tears and scrubbed at her arm with a white tea towel till it was back to its old color.

Mom hugged Fanny and kissed her forehead.

"Sorry you wasted the money," Fanny sobbed.

Mom said, "Fanny darling, don't worry, I can use the makeup on me."

But we knew this wasn't going to happen. Mom never wore a stitch of makeup except bright fire-engine-red lipstick, which she bought when it was on special at Kresge's.

As the weather began to turn really cold, men began showing up at our back door begging for food. My softhearted mother always wanted to give them a little bit, but Pop said he could only feed us and not strangers too, no matter how bad times were.

"We could get by eating a few morsels less," Mom said. "They wouldn't come if they weren't wearing holes in their stomachs." Mom stirred a little sugar into her coffee; she couldn't have cream anymore or even milk because what little we had went to Bob and Fanny and me.

"It's hard enough for me to see you without cream for your coffee," Pop said. "I won't have us going hungry. Don't you want Bob to be a strong boy?"

I guess strong twin girls weren't as important.

"Of course I do," Mom said.

In the background through our window, out of the corner of my eye I saw another man coming to our back door. He was clutching a holey jacket up to his neck but he had no gloves or hat, and his nose was as bright red as Rudolph the red-nosed reindeer's and it was also running. He must not have had a handkerchief because he kept wiping it on his sleeve.

Then came the tat-a-tat on the back door. No matter how old I got I knew I'd never forget this sound. It was a measured plea, wanting to not bother, but needing to and coming from deep in the man's gut. Mom put her hand on a biscuit. It was a slightly burned one, with a whisper of black on its edges. "This one's no good anyway," she said, looking at Pop.

"Jeanette, you may not give that biscuit away, we need it," he commanded, giving her a look he usually saved for us that said, no more now, this is settled.

Mom couldn't seem to let the biscuit drop from her hand. We heard again the tat-a-tat, and then a soft, "Hello there . . ." that sounded like a ghost talking. The men always looked like ghosts rising up from wherever they slept, when they walked up to our door.

"Just sit right there," Pop said. He went to the door and opened it.

"Please sir," the man began.

Pop cut him off right away. "I got five mouths to feed here, we got no extra, move along." He was firm but not mean-sounding. He shut the door and returned to the breakfast table.

Mom still held the biscuit in her hand, and she was quiet, but we could see she was angry.

"Put that thing down before you bust it," Pop said. "I'll eat it for lunch." Pop put his hand out like he sometimes used to have to do to have Bob spit out something that had no business being in his mouth, and Mom turned her hand over and let the biscuit drop into his hand.

From the corner of my eye I saw the man who'd been at our door shuffling off, raising his coat collar up to hide his face.

The next day I was helping Mom with breakfast, and we were talking about something like if Bob needed his socks darned or if the floor needed scrubbing, and when I went to grab the pans for our biscuits I noticed Mom was rolling the biscuit dough out way thin.

You could see the grain of the rolling board underneath one stretched part of the dough. "Mom, you rolled them too thin!" I laughed.

My mother smiled a slight smile, and I saw her lips were pale as the dough; she had no lipstick on so far that day, which was different for her. "Oh well, too late now." She quickly plunged the biscuit cutter all around, making deckle-edged rounds that flew onto the baking pan and into the oven.

At breakfast, Pop poured Bob some milk and then a littler bit for Fanny and for me. He smiled at Mom and slipped a little milk in her coffee. I think it was his way of saying sorry to her about the day before. Mom drank her coffee, and she took off the kitchen towel that had been keeping the biscuits warm.

Bob laughed and took one of the biscuits in his hands. It was flat and small. "It looks like spending money!" Bob said. "Maybe I can buy me some candy with it."

"What happened to the biscuits?" Pop asked. His left eyebrow had shot clear up to his hairline. He held a biscuit in two fingers like it was a coin someone had dropped into his streetcar money collector.

I started to answer for Mom, but Mom gave me a steely glare, and for the first time I can remember in my whole life, I heard my mother lie.

"I think the baking powder got old, so they didn't rise?" Her voice rose in a question at the end.

There was no sound but Bob slurping loudly at his milk.

"Since yesterday it got old?" Pop asked. There was a thickness to his voice I didn't like hearing.

"Everything gets old eventually," Mom said.

Later, after Pop left for work, I saw Mom slipping out back to give a couple of biscuits to the man who had come to our house the day before. She must have rolled them thin so Pop wouldn't know she had hidden some for this. I knew these thin, hard biscuits would taste like the fluffiest, lightest cake to the man out back.

17

FANNY

I ALWAYS HAD dreams of more dresses and blouses to wear, but I knew Mom was too busy to sew me all the new things I wanted, and heaven knows we couldn't afford to buy them ready-made, so I learned how to sew that fall at school. My home economics teacher, Miss Linden, could whip out whole dresses overnight, and she came to school in a smart new one every week it seemed. I didn't think I would be good at sewing, but it didn't take me more than a couple of days to get the feel of the sewing machine's foot pedal. I liked the sound it made, the soft thumping, the humming of the motor, and the clip-clip-clip sound of the needle as it stitched baby blue thread onto the first blouse I was making. The material was a crisp cotton that would look fine with a wool skirt.

There were leaves falling outside, and if I closed my eyes I could hear their swishing sound adding to the music of the sewing machine. The maple-colored leaves had heart-shaped orange splashes, and veins squiggling through. The colorations reminded me of my scar. Why did we think these variations in colors were so fetching when worn on leaves, but not so on flesh?

One day after school I went to the butcher to pick up a pound of beef stew meat my mom had been saving up for. Sue had gone to the school library to get some books for a report, so I was by myself. When I put all the coins out on the counter and added them up, I saw the butcher wrapping our meat in paper, and on his right arm he had a tattoo of a heart. It was a dark, luminous red, and there was a winding black arrow pierced through it. The arrow quivered as he rolled the meat tight in the thick white paper. He was a hearty man with a shock of black hair falling down his forehead. He caught me staring at his arm.

"That's for my missus," he told me. "She deserves diamonds, but we're plumb out of those these days, hey missy?"

"Yeah," I whispered back.

He caught sight of my scar. "What happened to you, little girl?"

I usually didn't like to talk about it. But I said, "Hot oil splatter. For some lousy popcorn."

"Aah, bad luck. But you know," he said, thumping the meat down before me, "it's kind of pretty in a funny way, ain't it?"

I smiled back at him. "You think so? The kids at school don't see it that way."

"Kids, what do they know?"

He leaned in close to me, and I could smell a touch of Brylcreem, along with the raw meat juice smell.

"Tell your ma that she might want to simmer this with a smidge of vinegar in with it, to soften it down."

And me, I felt softened down too. Maybe when I was older there would be grown men like this butcher who would see things his way.

After that time, I often dreamed of tattoos. In dreams I saw men with tattoos of bunnies and tulips and one time a tattoo shaped like a saxophone. My friend Linda's brother Joey had a saxophone, and he was learning to play the new swing jazz. He was a dreamboat: hair with chunks of gold in it and big navy blue eyes. I made sure always to keep my scar covered when I was over at Linda's, in case he didn't see things exactly the same way the butcher did.

I was happy it was fall for a lot of reasons, not least so I could wear sweaters all the time. While I was learning to sew, Sue was learning to knit, so I could keep us in blouses and skirts and dresses, while she kept us in sweaters. That is if she could ever learn how to do corners for shoulders and stop dropping stitches. Mom said she was doing fine, but I noticed she only got Sue yarn she could get for almost free down in the bargain basement at Kresge's. For now I wore old sweaters of Aunt Evelyn's and Grandma Fiedelmeyer's. Grandma's sweaters had a smell of sachet, and they were worn a bit fuzzy at the elbows. Funny, that had been Grandma's favorite expression, "put some elbow into it." (She left the "grease" out of the expression; it wasn't ladylike.) The elbows of these cardigans looked like snowballs, glittery with rayon thread.

18

SUE

IT WAS A week before Christmas when we found out that Uncle Donald and Aunt Millie and Randall and Myra would be moving in with us. Uncle Donald had lost his job during the summer, and their landlord wouldn't keep them on credit anymore. I overheard Pop talking to Uncle Donald about this when I was walking down the hallway with a handful of ribbon I had found from last year to wrap Christmas presents. Naturally we couldn't afford any ribbon this year, or any presents for that matter; we just had homemade gifts. I had found a length of blue ribbon as long as my arm and a pink ribbon twice as long. Pink wasn't a Christmas color exactly but it was my favorite color. I heard Pop and Uncle Donald talking, and I knew somehow not to go into the living room where they were sitting. I touched my hand to the wood molding on the doorway and held my breath and listened.

"How can we all live under this one roof?" Uncle Donald asked.

"I won't have you all put out on the street," Pop said sternly.

"I can't have you feeding us. I know you're short on food already."

"We can get a line of credit at the store if we have to. I've held out longer than most on that."

I had a sudden urge to use the bathroom. I wasn't good at spying like Fanny. But I wanted to hear more.

Then I knew Mom and Aunt Millie were in there too, because I heard crying. Mom said, "We can make do. I can stretch a stew farther than anyone you ever saw. Millie will help me, right honey?"

Millie couldn't answer because of her crying I guessed.

Pop said, "Donald, you couldn't help losing your job. Only reason mine is safe is because people have to ride the streetcar no matter what. Maybe I'll hear about something down at Public Service, though nowadays you have to count on some other fella to die to get a job."

"I hate to do this to you," Donald said.

"You'd do the same for me."

I heard what I knew was the clap of Pop's hand against Donald's back, to end the discussion and finalize it. I had to run upstairs to the bathroom, and while I was in the bathroom, I counted us all up. There would be nine people here in this house waiting to use this one bathroom. While I could, I stayed in there a long time, washing my hands with a special violet soap my mom had been given for her wedding that she had saved all these years and only pulled out when we couldn't afford to buy as much soap at the store as we usually did. Already we were short on soap and food, and here came four more under our roof.

I tried to picture this new life. With the extra leaf in the dining room table, we could fit nine around the table. That part would be like when they came for holiday dinners. It meant it would take a long time for the bread to get passed around the table, but that was not so bad.

There were not enough chairs in the living room, but I guessed my aunt and uncle would bring their furniture over. Where would we put it all? The basement would be stacked to the ceiling with things, so there would barely be room for us if we went down there when it was tornado season. There would be plenty of us to play games though; there'd always be someone who might play cards with me, if there were that many people around.

I guessed that Myra would sleep with Fanny and me, but not in our bed; now that we were getting bigger only the two of us could fit in there. I guessed we could squeeze her little bed in there if we re-arranged everything. And Randall would have to sleep in Bob's room. What joy for Randall, stuck with his little cousin! Where would Aunt Millie and Uncle Donald sleep?

It was hard to picture it all, but we would make it work; many families had doubled up this way. I heard a rapping on the bathroom door. It was already starting! But it was just Fanny.

"Guess what's going to happen?" I asked her.

FANNY

Aunt millie and Uncle Donald and Randall and Myra all moved in on New Year's Day. Myra's rollaway bed fitted into our room okay, as well as Randall's bed scooched into Bob's room. Uncle Donald and Aunt Millie slept on pallets in the living room (they had sold their bed), and they always had them put away before we came down in the morning. Mom fretted over whether everyone was warm enough, but there were so many bodies in our house that we guessed we'd get by on our body heat if the furnace went out.

That New Year's Day wasn't a very festive day like it used to be. For dinner we ate a soup that was a usual soup that Mom made from some meat bones she could get cheap at the butcher's, with potatoes, a couple of carrots, and some nice spices that made it taste okay. Aunt Millie cut up an onion she'd brought from her supplies, and we left it in big pieces for flavor in the soup. With the soup we ate some dry bread that Uncle Donald had gotten when the baker on Grand Avenue was throwing out bread too old to sell anymore. He had waited two hours in line to get it. We laughed when Pop tried to cut the bread because the knife would have nothing to do with it. Finally Pop broke into it with his strong-boned hands and tore off hunks of bread for us. We all put our bread into the soup and pressed it down till it was soft enough to chew. There were bread crumbs everywhere like confetti, so that was our festive New Year's.

My cousin Myra was the shyest girl you ever met. She was ten years old and two years younger than we were. She had lived halfway across town in Walnut Park when they had had their own house, so come her first day of school at Benton School, Sue and I had to walk her to school and take her to the principal's office to get her settled. She would have Miss Murphy as her teacher, and we thought she would like her as well as you could like a teacher. On the way to school, Sue asked Myra a lot of questions about her old school, but Myra wouldn't tell us much. It wasn't that she was unfriendly; she was just so very shy and lived inside her own skin more than most people did. I guess for Sue and me, we had always been intertwined, so it was new to be around someone who didn't share the thoughts and ways that Sue and I shared. Sue and I often finished each other's sentences, and guessed (sometimes correctly, occasionally not) what the other might say or do.

At night Sue and I whispered to each other before we went to sleep like we always did, until Sue said it was rude to not include Myra, but when we asked Myra some questions just to be polite, for instance, who was the best-looking boy in her class, she just lay in the dark until we figured she was asleep or too bashful to have a thought of a boy. We went back to whispering, Sue and me. We had enough thoughts about who was the best-looking boy in our class for all three of us! I voted for Mike Richards, who had eyes the color of blueberries and hair that was fuzzy like a dandelion but the red color of maple leaves. His muscles were so big they seemed to be alive beneath his shirtsleeves, and I often stared at them, transfixed, while Miss Genevieve talked about foreign lands that were exotic and far away, that we'd never see as long as we lived.

Sue liked Jimmy Ritz the best because he was smart about a lot of things, like she was, and because he wore clean shoes every day, which mattered a lot to her, though I couldn't understand why, and because his sun-blond hair was combed sideways every day and glimmered with Brylcreem, which many of the boys could not afford to buy anymore. She liked a tidy boy; I liked more a wild one.

20

SUE

WE ALWAYS LAUGHED to hear Mom and Pop talk about missing the old times because it made them sound so elderly, but I missed them now myself. The house was so crowded all the time. These cold mornings, after Uncle Donald or Pop stoked the furnace, with Randall helping, we sat at the dining room table all cramped around it and prayed to God for the end of bad times. For breakfast we ate the stale bread Uncle Donald had gotten us, moistened with some syrup that we had won a huge gallon tin of as a prize at Bingo a few years ago that we'd never paid attention to before. It had gotten thick as paste, and Mom had to simmer a jar of it in a pan of hot water before we could use it for our breakfast. The grown-ups drank black coffee and only one cup each at that, to get down the syrupy bread. Randall, Myra, Bob, Fanny, and I drank hot water with a bit of sugar stirred into it. I missed when we could have glasses of milk or hot cocoa, but it was rare we could get milk now.

Then Pop went off to work and Uncle Donald went out to look for work. He was looking for something that there was none of; we all knew it, but we knew also that he had to look. There was a spot downtown where day laborers lined up, and once in a while he got lucky and worked for a few hours, but there were no steady jobs to be had. Aunt Millie always made sure he went off in clothes that were clean and tidy as she could make them. Most mornings there was the sound of her whisk broom dusting his wool coat down, and every night she checked it for tears and mended it all as finely as the best New York tailor.

Aunt Millie usually spent the day helping Mom with the household chores, and especially cutting down clothes to make over for us to wear to school. She was a better seamstress than Mom, and I think she felt like she was earning their keep some, but of course we didn't think she should worry about this at all. Aunt Millie took one of her prettiest dresses that was of a pink and blue flower bouquet and was full and billowy in the hips, and she cut it down to make a dress for me. I knew Aunt Millie loved that dress and would have liked to wear it herself, but she wanted to give whatever she could to our family. Mom kept it fresh as could be, so that it could be passed down to Myra one day.

Myra had taken to walking to school with Bob. They were closer to the same ages, and seemed to like each other, maybe because neither of them were big talkers. They could walk for blocks without saying a word, I bet. Also, Myra would throw corkballs to Bob for batting practice sometimes after school, and she wasn't half bad at it either. Fanny and I were just happy to be back to walking on our own, even though we were usually just a block ahead of or behind them.

Randall went to the high school, so he walked off in a different direction. He had grown to almost the height of his father, who was very tall, and looked like a man almost, except that his hair stuck up in funny tufts around his ears. He had strong arms and eyes the color of robin's eggs, and so I think he was popular with the girls at school.

He was a nice boy, after all. When we were little he had teased us all the time, but these days he was sweeter, though mainly he stayed to himself at our house. He never said so, but I think that after school he went to look for jobs too, but he had no luck, like his father. I knew sometimes he met up with his father, and they would take turns in line for bread or vegetables that might be thrown out. They were determined to contribute to our household.

At least this Valentine's Day I didn't have scarlet fever, but otherwise it was a hard day in comparison to other Valentine's Days in previous years. Mom and Aunt Millie made a real effort to be festive; they both wore red in the morning, Mom an apron that was washed so many times it was a whispery red more like pink, and Aunt Millie wore a red dress that she usually saved for church, and it too had seen better times; the collar was frayed and even Aunt Millie couldn't fix that. They also made heart-shaped biscuits for us. Mom had found a small jar of raspberry jam that she had put up with our Grandmother Fiedelmeyer just the year before she died, which was when we were five. Mom loved to tell stories of canning with her mother, who put up the best fruits and vegetables, she said, in these United States. We prayed that the jam would not have gone to mold, as some of the jars did, but the jam was in fact sweet and tart and full of good color.

All of us gathered at the table for breakfast and greeted each other with "Happy Valentine's Day!" instead of "Good Morning." Bob squealed with delight over the red jam; we were all so tired of the gluey syrup on our biscuits. When Aunt Millie passed me the biscuits, I noticed her wedding ring was gone.

"Aunt Millie, your ring!" I cried out. I thought she must have slipped it off to roll biscuits, and I wanted to make sure it didn't wind up married to the square of lard in the kitchen.

Aunt Millie began to cry, but it was that crying that adults do sometimes that is sudden and quiet, so you'd hardly know it was going on if you didn't happen to look their way at that moment. I'd noticed that her skin had looked more sallow lately anyway, and so the tears shone like little bits of gold on her cheeks.

"We had to sell our rings," she said softly. She looked down the table to Uncle Donald.

His ring finger was bare too. It was one thing to see a man without a ring, another to see his wife without one. Even in hard times, most women had their rings; I know Mom loved hers so much. Aunt Millie's was a white gold one with chips of diamond winking in it. Now, her finger only had a whiter band of flesh where her ring should have been.

My father groaned. He turned to Uncle Donald. "Ah, nuts," he said. "That money you gave me last night you said came from getting on a day labor crew? It was the rings?"

Uncle Donald chuckled sadly. "I don't know why I thought I could get away with a lie like that. There's no day labor. There's no labor day or night."

"We pawned our rings," Aunt Millie said, still quietly crying.

"Maybe we can get them back then, Mom," Randall said. "Maybe we will win some money sometime at Bank Night at the Fox Theater."

Bank Night, it was the best, better than when they gave away dishes by far. Winning cash at Bank Night was what we all dreamed of. We went to the movies to see beautiful Jean Harlow in an envelope of silk satin, to see her drink cocktails from a glass shaped like open lips. We knew we'd have to go back home to our watery soup and weak coffee, but for those few hours, we could dream.

That morning Myra left the table crying, her face red as a Valentine and hot tears flying off her like there was a small storm inside our dining room.

21

FANNY

MARCH ROARED IN like a lion, it said in our book at school. It was an odd image to me, because I thought of lions with their hot and fiery breath, and I could hardly picture anything very warm where we were, here in the middle of the country in the Show Me State, where all we had to show were empty pockets and unraveling sweaters and winter coats that covered your knees if you were very, very lucky. The snow felt like it was spanking us as we walked to school. I could feel crystals of frozen snot in my nose. Our cloche hats were getting too small for us; I had accidentally washed them in hot water, and of course they had shrunk, and so now our ears were peeking out from under the frizzled green wool, pinkening more and more with each step we walked. I had no patience for the snow this time of year. In November we could enjoy the clean white, sweeping shapes it made on hills, and sometimes we had fun sledding down the really steep hills, but by March, we were more than ready for spring.

Instead, the snow was dirty and sad looking and there were so many layers of it, it would take an archeologist to unearth, for instance, a corkball that Bob had left out in the yard the previous fall.

At the movies we had seen a film called *The Mummy*, in which a man with hauntingly cavernous eyes was wrapped in yards and yards of cheesecloth, and even though we knew he actually lived in a cold coffin, all we could think about was, he must be warm in all that cloth!

Boris Karloff was the actor in the movie, and he had a sonorous voice that hypnotized us. The character also had this thing he could do with his eyes that made people suffer heart pains and death. He did not even have to be in the room with them to kill them, but when he cast his spell the light around his eyes got whiter while everything else got darker. It was like there was a candle inside him. Sue was jumpy as a cat all through the movie; he was a mummy, after all, but I found Karloff enchanting. Everything the mummy did, he did for love. He had been buried alive and deprived of his one true love! The story was this: There was a girl in the present day who was a descendant of his dead love, and he thought if he could kill her he could bring her back again as his real love. The actress's face was wide and her eyes were swimming with emotion. She wore this satin sort of brocade evening gown in the first part of the movie that I would give anything to have myself. I thought there was nothing as glamorous as the life of actors.

Ever since we had first started seeing talkies, I had dreamed of becoming an actress. I read in a movie magazine that the typical day for a movie star involved manicures and memorizing lines, being fitted for beautiful dresses that dipped way down your back and high heeled shoes that tilted you up from the bottom. Evidently, it also meant an endless supply of champagne to drink with hors d'oeuvres served from a silver tray the butler carried. I could easily imagine myself being painted, fitted, and served lavishly. I would get through school as fast as I could and then move to California. They would be waiting for the next "it" girl by then, and she would be me. In California it is sunshine and oranges and swimming pools each and every day without this miserable snow slush. Everything is jake in Hollywood.

22

SUE

IN THE FALL, when the weather turned cold, I woke up one Monday morning, looked over to Myra, and noticed a bluish color to her skin. Her face looked as if she had washed it with juice that had bled off of blueberries. She had had a terrible cough for a week; I had heard sea lions barking when I went to the zoo, and this is what the cough reminded me of. As we all sat down for breakfast, Myra moaned and fainted off the side of her chair. She went down so fast that even though Uncle Donald tried to catch her, she landed in a heap on the floor.

"Good heavens!" Aunt Millie cried, as Uncle Donald lifted her into his arms, where she curled up like a kitten.

Pop said there was a streetcar they could catch to the doctor's in ten minutes. Aunt Millie put Myra into her own warmest wool coat, and Aunt Millie wore our mother's coat. Mom had to stay behind at the house to see to us.

Myra came to, but after looking around her a bit in confusion, she fell asleep in her father's arms. Randall asked if he could go to the doctor's to see what was wrong with Myra, but was told he should go on to school, then my aunt and uncle and sweet cousin were out the door.

Fanny and Bob and I went off to school wondering how we could possibly learn anything when we were so worried about Myra. At lunchtime, Bob even came to the table where Fanny and I were eating and sat down to eat with us, something he never did. Fanny was so nervous she played with her food, pushing her peaches around so much on her tray that I thought one would take flight like a flying saucer. I mentioned this to Bob, whose favorite radio program was "Buck Rogers in the Twentieth Century." He smiled a small smile in response, which is how I knew he was worried about Myra, because normally he would have said, "That's a scream!" laughing to beat the band. But I noticed that even today his appetite was the same. He ate up all his lunch and then Fanny and I heaped a little of ours onto his plate too.

When we got home from school that afternoon, Myra was back home and in bed with a vile-smelling poultice, made from boiled onions, vinegar, and rye meal, on her chest. An exhausted Uncle Donald said that the doctor diagnosed "mild pneumonia," which he said was a contradiction in terms. "That's like if he said it was a 'soft tornado,' outside," something Uncle Donald's family knew a lot about. (In the tornado of '26, the roof of the house where Uncle Donald and Aunt Millie and the children lived had blown clean off and whipped up into the air, where it became kindling.)

We got tired of smelling Myra's poultice all through the house for several days. But every day Myra looked better, and so we knew it was working. Her skin tone, by the next Saturday, was pink again. That morning her mom had let her have her first bath in days, and at least now the tart twinge of vinegar was gone, and her hair was left soft and good-smelling once more. Fanny, Bob, Randall, and I had all gone to the movies that afternoon (Aunt Millie wasn't letting Myra go outside yet) to see *Tarzan, the Ape Man*, and we crowded around Myra to tell her all about it. Randall did a wonderful imitation of Tarzan's loud yell, so good in fact that his dad was up the stairs in no time hollering at him. But then when he explained what the sound was, Uncle Donald had as big a laugh as anyone.

Fanny wanted to be a movie star now, and I could see how she could be as bold as the actresses we saw in the movies. Maureen O'Sullivan had hair the color of smoke, and she was quite believable as the daughter who fought to go into the jungle with her father. I wondered how they filmed those scenes where she clung to Tarzan while he flew through the jungles. How would they stay glued together in the air? Fanny could do that too, though, I thought. I mean, she had always been able to climb a tree as well as a boy. Me, I was very embarrassed by Tarzan's loincloth. Randall said that they had had to tape Johnny Weissmuller's personal part to the cloth to keep it from jumping out! This was just the sort of thing Randall usually had to say.

Anyway, we were all so glad that Myra was better. That night she sat up at the dinner table for the first time in a long time, and we had a good chicken for dinner, the gravy thickened with real cream that Pop had gotten as a present from a customer. Normally Pop wouldn't have accepted a gift, but he'd made an exception and we were all happy for it.

FANNY

CHRISTMAS HAD COME and gone without much fanfare. We had all made gifts for one another but we had so little to even make homemade things. Sue sewed together a book of poems she had written with red yarn, binding it with a darning needle. She had copied it over for each one of us in the family, twelve pages in her pretty handwriting, then all that sewing to do for each gift. She had written a poem for each month of the year and had found positive things to say for each month, despite what a hard year it had been. In spite of the homeless people who slept with Hoover blankets over them in the park, the sun still rose a golden hue, the crocuses bloomed in the spring, the grasshoppers hopped in the summer, the leaves crisped and reddened in the autumn and shimmied down. These were some of the things she wrote about.

I wanted to sew special pieces of clothing for everyone in my family, now that I had gotten good at sewing, but I couldn't buy all that material, so I made handkerchiefs for everyone, cotton pastels edged in silk thread for my aunt, Mom, Myra, and Sue, and crisp white linen for Pop, Uncle Donald, Bob, and Randall.

For Christmas dinner, we had managed to get a small ham. With the nine of us sharing, we only got a taste of it each, but it was divine, crisp with brown sugar on the fat edges.

New Year's Eve was fun enough. We kids all got to drink 7-Up, and we ate homemade cheese crackers Aunt Millie had made, which turned out so pretty, brown and good-smelling. Aunt Millie went around to all of us and dropped a delicate little warm cracker with pretty deckled edges into our mouths, crying out "Happy New Year!" Uncle Donald got a big kiss too, and that made me wonder what went on down here at night in the living room on their pallets. Our own living room! But then I thought that however a person could have some fun must not be too bad.

We kids put on a show for the grown-ups. We had been practicing for weeks. Sue sang "April in Paris" in a high and pretty voice. She stood with her hands folded neatly in front of her and opened her mouth and let the notes fly out in a way that felt like they were pretty songbirds twittering around. Myra was too shy to sing or dance, so we gave her the job of magician's assistant for Bob. Bob had gotten a magic trick booklet as a prize from eating what seemed like as much as a few gallons of Quaker Oats and then sending in the round lids. The booklet came with some thin props that fluttered around in Myra's hands, like a fakey dove made of stinky old chicken feathers. But when it came time to pull a rabbit out of a hat, Bob actually did it! Later we found out he'd captured a bunny in the woods at the end of Pop's streetcar route and smuggled it home right on the streetcar, risking a sure whooping from our father. But since it was New Year's Eve, we were all trying to feel happy, so Pop let it go. In fact, he was as delighted as anybody when Bob reached in and pulled the gray and white bunny up by its ears and plopped it on Myra, who in turn jumped about a foot in the air and squealed. This caused the bunny to run under Magic Bob's curtained table. Now that she knew what it was, Myra was drawn to the bunny; she rescued him from under the curtain and kissed him on his furry forehead, while the rest of us settled down from laughing.

When the commotion over the bunny ended, I sang "I Guess I'll Have to Change My Plan," a song from the Broadway musical *The Little Show*, I'd heard on the radio enough to memorize it. I wore a pretty pink silk slip that Ethel down the street had let me borrow. It was a slip, but it looked more like a dress. I tucked some powder puffs down the front of the dress where my bubs were starting to grow, but chickened out before I came downstairs—Pop would have murdered me if I'd kept them in! I put on some of Mom's red lipstick and then took it off, using the same reasoning. I ended up wearing a cardigan over the slip and no makeup at all, though I did wear the feather boa that I had also borrowed from Ethel, who was obviously a very chic dresser. Because of the feeling the boa gave me, I entered the room twirling and then began doing a tap dance in time to the music, which was Randall playing his clarinet. Since I had no real tap shoes, I had taped a few pennies to my Sunday shoes, and found this worked well enough. I had practiced to make sure that I wouldn't leave bad marks on the wooden floor, and I don't think I did that night. Randall had his hair combed like the swing-style musicians did and looked altogether dashing in his father's dark tie. I received the most thunderous applause of anyone, naturally, because I would be heading out to Hollywood as soon as I could, to be a movie star. My hands flew out like little sparks of gold in the candlelight that lit me for the show, as I spun around and remembered times could be good in spite of everything.

24

SUE

The many months of our two families living together had certainly made us cranky at times but it had brought us closer too. Sometimes, too close. Our bathroom had a hook-and-eye lock and often the hook flipped off it and didn't work. If you were in a hurry you might not even notice. One Saturday morning in February I barreled into the bathroom with a movie magazine in my hand that had a photo of Greta Garbo in *Grand Hotel*, because even though my hair was lighter brown than Garbo's, I didn't see why I couldn't make it feather about my cheeks like hers, and I needed to have the big mirror to look in, not the little one that came in a brush set I had. Walking in so fast, at first I didn't notice Randall standing up with his pants down, peeing in what seemed to me an enormous arc of pee. I mean, I had naturally seen Bob peeing when he was a little one in diapers, but I had never seen a bigger boy, and I just turned red as an apple right off the bat. Poor Randall stood there with his mouth in a big O, the big arc of pee dwindling to a trickle. And then without thinking about it one bit, I did something I had never done before: I pretended to be Fanny. "I have to see a man about a dog," I said, backing out of the room. It was the kind of line only Fanny would use, straight off the movies.

"Yeah, well mind your own potatoes, Fanny," Randall snarled back.

That was my lesson in how a grown boy looked. I had coincidentally discovered that I could be Fanny as well as she could be me. The trick was all in the demeanor. I was dying to tell Fanny what I'd seen, but this seemed risky considering that I had been impersonating her at the time I'd seen it. Randall had told us a little about the birds and the bees one Saturday afternoon when our radio's signal had gone out and we didn't have much else to do. It was raining hard so we couldn't play outside. Our parents had gone to the movies without us because they needed some time as grown-ups, they'd said. Randall decided to explain to us exactly what "time as grown-ups" sometimes led to, and we could hardly believe it! Fanny and I had both started having our monthlies the Thanksgiving weekend before at exactly the same time, and our mom had vaguely suggested those had something to do with when mothers had babies much later in time, but now with the information Randall had provided, I personally felt that I knew more than I wanted to.

Actually, one time Fanny and I had seen some cats who were having a crazy time in the alley a few blocks from school. I mean, we had heard some very loud cat moaning and hollering, and we were afraid what we were hearing was a cat fight. What we saw was one cat moving on top of another. After Randall told us how babies were made, I thought about this, but I decided surely dads didn't get on the backs of mothers to make babies, and I told Randall what I was thinking. Randall said, no it was tummy to tummy for humans. Well, of all the things to imagine.

Myra said, "But why can't people just leave their pajamas on if they don't want any more children to feed?" We knew that times were hard everywhere, but people were still having babies.

Randall turned a bit of dark red at his ears and neck and he said,

"I guess it's more fun to have your pajamas off sometimes when you're a grown-up."

Now, knowing what I did after seeing Randall in the bathroom, the whole story had a new meaning to me that I couldn't explain. Fanny and I had bubs that were growing rounder under our sweaters and hips that were blooming, while the boys at school got taller and their voices deepened into something rich as dark chocolate sauce. In any case, we were growing into men and women, whether we were ready or not.

25

FANNY

N OW THAT I was sure I would be a movie star, I had to get as much practice as I possibly could, so I became the lead actress, director, and costumer for a series of shows we put on in the neighborhood. We asked all the kids we knew in the neighborhood, and a few we didn't yet know, if they'd like to work on the shows. We got about twenty kids interested, from ages five to fifteen. It didn't take long to see who could sing and act or play instruments; the rest we set to work finding props and costumes (those I couldn't sew myself). I asked Sue to learn how to do makeup and hair, and Randall played the clarinet for our background music, while Myra played a xylophone for the very dramatic entrances and exits. Little Tommy Frieder from around the corner, now he was a real find. He was tiny and wiry, had a big mop of yellowy-white hair like Harpo Marx and a voice as big as the tallest building downtown. You could hear him from about four blocks around, no kidding. Another lucky addition to our cast was a girl named Lucy, who was a friend of Myra's. She was no singer, but there were plenty of nonsinging parts, and she could memorize lines like nobody's business. She was pretty and had good feeling to what she was saying in a show, but was no competition to me, of course.

Right before school had let out, I had talked Miss Snow, our chorus teacher, into lending me some play scripts and music scores to use over the summer. She had spent about an hour describing, in very scary terms, what would happen to me if I lost or in any way ruined any of them. To say that I would be clapping chalkboard erasers till I was eighteen years of age was no exaggeration at all. Miss Snow wrote down everything she was giving me in a ledger and then locked it in one of her desk drawers. But at least now I had some good material to work with.

Part of my inspiration for our shows was the operettas in Forest Park at the Municipal Opera. They had free seats in the back, so most Thursdays, we would go down there on the streetcar at five P.M. to be sure to get the best seats we could, and Mom and Aunt Millie would pack us some ham biscuits and apples to eat for dinner there. We all paid close attention to the shows, so we could use what we learned in our own performances. Even Bob would pay attention through the show; I mean, we were all stuck on music and shows. Bob had found an abandoned snare drum in someone's ash pit. This rooting through ash pits was a new habit of Bob's that Mom didn't exactly approve of, but in this case it was worth it, even when he had to pay the ash picker a penny for it. Now he could play in our productions, right along with Randall and Myra.

The Muny stage was outside, and it was really beautiful to be there when the sun went down and the breezes began to be gentle and sweet with cool. Sometimes if all us kids combined our change, we could buy a bottle of Hires Root Beer and share it while we ate our supper and watched the show. The cold brown foam became mixed in my mind with the thrill of what happened onstage, to the point where I could drink root beer anywhere, anytime and have a show tune come into my mind. One night we saw *Show Boat*, and it actually made me cry to hear the deep bass of "Old Man River," contrasting with the high sweet soprano of the beautiful girl who sang "Make Believe."

There was a tree that grew up through the stage at the Muny Opera, and the stage crew always had to work around it during the shows. For *Show Boat*, the tree was gotten up as a big rigging sail on the boat, with huge creamy expanses of canvas billowing off of it. Bob spotted a fan blowing the canvas from the corner of the stage; he loved details like that.

Inspired by our Muny experiences, we worked hard on our own shows over the summer. Sue collected donations from the neighbors for our shows, like satin dresses that were torn that I could fix up for costumes along with Aunt Millie's help, and little ends of lipstick tubes and almost empty powder boxes and brow pencil stubs to use for makeup. Pretty Ethel down the street gave us some glittery rhinestone hair clips and beaded red and blue glass necklaces she didn't like anymore; they were chipped a little but nothing you could see from the audience.

One day at the end of June we were preparing for a big Fourth of July production that would be put on for the whole block in a vacant lot nearby. Tommy Frieder was going to sing "Night and Day," Sue was going to read her poems, a boy named Walt Morrow, who we'd just "discovered," was going to do a bit of tap dancing. And our showcase piece would be a scene from *Romeo and Juliet*, because I knew that future stars needed experience with Shakespeare. I would perform the balcony scene from *Romeo and Juliet* from a branch up in an oak tree. To play Juliet, I wore a makeshift wig I had sewn from some extra hair that I had Miss Rose, of Rose Salon, save for me. Juliet had to have those long tendrils. Randall was going to be Romeo, against his will, really; I had something to use against him (I'd caught him smoking), and for heaven's sake, we wouldn't have to kiss or anything. But the day of our dress rehearsal, we lost all the boys who would be in the show, including Tommy Frieder, Randall, and Bob, who were the staples of the show. There was a big corkball playoff going on on the next block, and nothing would do but for the boys to play rather than work on the show, no matter what I said about the importance of the rehearsal.

"Corkball is important too!" Bob argued. "St. Louis invented it!"

Corkball, baseball, it was all the same to me. At any rate, we girls took the day off too and went down the block to watch the game. The corkballs were chipped away a little because no one could afford to get a new one. They looked like grizzly spheres flying through the hot air, and once I could have sworn one was on fire. The smack of the stick against cork made a cracking thud that made Sue hop every time. Sometimes our mom said that since the isolation hospital, Sue had a little case of the nerves; if you ask me, she'd always been that way. The game was percolating when our moms called us home to lunch. The boys would not go, so we brought back provisions from the house for them, including a big jug of water with a little ice we managed to chip off the ice block in the kitchen. Sue made them sugar and butter sandwiches, and we brought some oranges. The boys stopped for a few minutes to inhale the sandwiches, and suddenly the air was filled with orange spray while they peeled them fast. Then it was back to the game. We girls watched a while longer, as Randall and Bob scored quite a few points; we discovered Tommy's biggest asset was his voice.

I said, "Let's go back home and work on costumes and props and lines," and that's what we did. Sue and I got the giggles something awful when Sue had to be Romeo down on the earth, and I was Juliet up in the tree. I was shaking leaves off the tree I was laughing so hard. The afternoon was cut short by a sudden thundershower that made the earth sigh with relief and the crickets sing to beat the band. We scrambled inside, and once the boys slid back, streaming with rainwater and cursing about the broken-up game, I got them rehearsing for me once more.

SUE

THE FOURTH OF July was sunny and fresh-smelling from the recent rains. I woke up with a start very early in the morning, only to find Fanny was already up and out of our room. Myra, on her rollaway bed, looked cozy with her sheet tucked up around her cheeks, and her thumb perched on her chin and curled like it was remembering the days when she sucked her thumb. I quickly dressed and ran downstairs. Fanny was drinking coffee with Pop and Uncle Donald. It was a holiday, but our parents always got up at the crack of dawn anyway. Aunt Millie and Mom were in the kitchen making yeast rolls for the nice dinner we planned to have. We had been eating beans and rice for days now to save enough money for a holiday chicken dinner.

Randall walked up to the back door just then carrying the chicken, soon to be our holiday dinner, which was squalling and fussing as Randall swung it from his long arms. Randall saw me standing in the kitchen eating a tiny piece of raw dough (I'd loved doing this since I was little, against everyone's advice, and so far the yeast hadn't hurt me one bit; otherwise my stomach would have risen into the biggest dinner roll of the world). Randall whispered to me, "Send Fanny down!" Meantime, he headed down to the basement by the outside door, and I stepped in the dining room and whispered to Fanny, "Basement." Fanny loved to see Randall throttle and hatchet and pluck a chicken, which I thought was awful of her. I could never stomach it. One time I had merely peered into the little rectangle window through which you could see into the basement, and seeing an arc of blood shoot out onto the floor of the basement, I had to go back into the house woozy and put my head between my legs till I could hold it up again. Fanny not only watched the murder of the chicken close-up, she even helped Randall pluck the chicken. Bob was the one who had to clean down the basement floor from all the mess. In my opinion, chicken tastes good, but might be more trouble than it's worth.

I don't know if I would say that Fanny was a big lover of blood and guts, but she did love drama of any kind, and there was little that beat out killing a chicken for sheer drama. I helped Mom and Aunt Millie upstairs, pinching off dough to make rolls. Later I would dip my palms in some melted butter and feel up the rolls, or that's what Randall described it like. You had to handle them with some butter before you placed them in the oven, if you wanted them gold and shiny and the best they could be.

Fanny washed off the chicken blood in the bathroom sink—and bath night had been last night, darn it all, she said—what had she been thinking? Now she'd be a chicken-smelling Juliet! We all went outside and began to set up the show. Sixteen kids had stuck out the show with us. This meant there would be a lot of family coming to watch! We had no way to get chairs down there, so we laid out some newspapers for people to sit on, since it had rained recently, and the ground was a tad bit mushy.

There was a shed standing on this lot waiting for the house to come up beside it. The shed was a lucky thing for all of us, because it was our dressing room and prop closet. I set to work making up everyone and getting their clothes smoothed right. Fanny had the fanciest makeup because no one was more beautiful than Juliet. I made the liner at her eyes go up and out like cat's eyes. It gave her a questioning look, as in "Romeo, wherefore art thou?" She wore a shade of lipstick called Crushed Berry that we chose because it really looked that way, and Juliet might have been eating berries when her true love called to her from down below. I attached her crown of long dangling locks of hair that fell to halfway down the tree with a sky blue ribbon.

There was never any doubt that Fanny would play the part of Juliet, for many reasons, but for me, the main reason was that Fanny could climb a tree and I could not. She had to do the balcony scene from up above, of course. It wasn't easy to climb up with everyone watching, so she went up there early on and shouted orders down to us like she was God! With her long dress, made from a white bed sheet ruched up at the sleeves and anchored at the bodice with a golden-colored rope, she could easily have passed for royalty.

When everyone got there, we had to do *Romeo and Juliet* first, naturally, since our Juliet was already in her perch. I thought Randall looked dashing in the muslin, overbloused shirt we'd made him, though he felt like a sissy, he said. I had styled his hair in a manner that highlighted his curly hair, but he wouldn't let me near him with any makeup, not even a swipe of a powder puff.

The balcony scene went beautifully, with Fanny's words rich and natural sounding, paying tribute to the poetry of Shakespeare. I felt a creeping feeling in my stomach since I would soon have to follow up Mr. Shakespeare's act with my own poems. Needless to say, mine couldn't hold a candle to his. Randall spoke up full and nice, though he always kept his back to the audience, in an odd demonstration of shyness. It would have been easy to believe Fanny and Randall really were lovers, that is if we didn't know full well they were cousins, except that some dogs from down the street came and bounded up onto Randall's chest with a slobbery kiss, and then clambered up the tree to get a little nip of Fanny's dangling feet. Fanny turned a dark pink that threatened to simmer over and ruin the show, till she decided to turn it all into some shtick, like Fanny Brice would have. Fanny had always said that the mark of a good performer was the ability to *use what you have.* "Yon canines, thee nipping at love's foot arch, can thee but mean the morning is non?" She had the crowd screaming with laughter. After the show, I saw that Fanny had a few teeth marks on her heel. She should have been howling with pain, but instead she was taking her eighth bow. That was our Fanny.

27

FANNY

THE STRANGEST FIGHT I ever heard in my life is one I can never tell anyone about. It was close to October, a time of year I wasn't overly fond of since it was the anniversary of my burn, and I also had a wretched cold that made me shake all over with chills. The cough I had would have scared a young child, it was so loud and barking, so I was staying home from school. My mother had gone to the pharmacist for some camphor to make me a moist chest pack, plus to get some 7-Up to settle my stomach. For the moment I was the only one in the house, and I lay on the divan hoping to stay awake to listen to "Life Can Be Beautiful," which aired on the radio during the day; my mom and aunt listened to it whenever they could and told me the stories of heartbreak and renewal, all punctuated by the Spic and Span jingle.

Aunt Millie and Uncle Donald must have come in the back way, and they didn't know I was there in the living room. They sat at the dining room table to talk.

Uncle Donald said to Aunt Millie, "What's wrong?"

Aunt Millie answered, "That's a *dead* man's coat?"

Well, I can tell you, this made me sit up straight. My blanket slid down, and I clutched it back to my chest and smothered a cough beneath it so I could hear more.

"Baby, people do it all the time. People fixing to get buried, sometimes they're wearing coats, see? They're perfectly good coats that the family don't want cause their relative died in them, but the undertaker gives them away for free! Where else am I gonna get a wool coat for free?"

I could hear my aunt sobbing.

"I can wait around at Druck's Funeral Home and get coats for you and the kids, if you like," Uncle Donald added. Sometimes it surprised me how men could be guaranteed not to know when to quit in saying things.

"We will not wear dead coats!" Aunt Millie cried out.

"The coats ain't dead," Uncle Donald said. "Fact is, the wool came offa sheep that were very alive at the time."

In spite of the drama that was going on in the dining room, I dozed off again because when you're ill that just happens. When I woke, I thought it was a dream about the funeral home coats until I saw my aunt above me looking concerned and tucking my blankets in around me tenderly with her soft and small hands. Her eyes were red-rimmed and damp-looking still. She was sweet as a person could be, and now she was ringless, and her husband was wearing the coat of the dead, and they had to sleep on our living room floor night and night again. I hoped that Mr. Roosevelt was right and that things would get better, that they would get better soon and my aunt could have her ring back, not to mention wear a very fresh new coat, not one from a funeral home!

28

FANNY

THIS CHRISTMAS WAS much better than last year's, because now Uncle Donald had a job. Mr. Monroe, a rod man for the surveyors at Public Service, had died, and Pop had persuaded his bosses to give Uncle Donald a try on the job. It was a job Uncle Donald loved, because he was always outside and using his strong arms. Of course, he would have loved any job, including pooper scooper for the elephants down at the zoo, as he often told us.

They were still going to live with us for a few more months till they could have enough to rent their own house, but this Christmas we had a few store-bought presents again. Also, Pop gave us kids a few dimes to buy gifts, and with the money Sue and I got Mom her favorite red lipstick, Candy Apple, which she had often gone without lately. We got Bob a pair of drumsticks to replace the impromptu sharp sticks he had been using to make music, and Pop a bag of this dark licorice he liked that no one else did. When we were littler the sight of his mouth all black could make Sue jump a foot in the air in fright.

It was happier in the house than it had been for a long time, with

Mom having enough butter and sugar to make gingerbread, which smelled like a spicy sphere of heaven, and for breakfast Christmas morning, hot cocoa with rich milk and thick biscuits like the old days! There was even a slice of bacon each for us, which we ate so fast we were like the pigs that had given it to us.

There was a big crowd of us around the tree that Christmas morning. The year before we hadn't the money for a tree, but this year Randall and Uncle Donald had secretly gone off to chop one down, and there it appeared on Christmas morning, done up with candles and some twinkly silver-threaded bits. Sue and I got real women's camisoles that were hand-stitched by Aunt Millie, and Mom made homemade paper dolls for us. At first we thought we were way too old to play paper dolls, till we saw what they were. Sue's was a teacher doll; Mom had made the doll a smart blue skirt and jacket that a teacher would wear and sensible teacher shoes with thick soles, and there was a tiny pair of glasses to attach, along with props like a pointer stick and a map and a chalkboard. Since Sue had grown to love teaching while she was at the isolation hospital, we all knew that this is what she would be when she grew up.

My paper doll was long and lean like Jean Harlow, and she had a halter evening gown to wear, along with a long strand of pearls, a pair of slingback platform shoes, and a big crazy feather stole, like the one Harlow wore in *Dinner at Eight*! When I first saw that movie I couldn't figure out how Harlow had stopped herself from giggling over each line when she was wearing that stole, because it appeared to be tickling her like gangbusters. My doll even had a prop martini glass, and it surprised me that Mom had included this, since, as Pop put it, she hadn't needed Prohibition to make a teetotaler out of her. All the clothes and accessories had been cut from paper and meticulously shaped, complete with those little side tabs. The dolls were cut from a cardboard, so they would be stronger than if they'd been made from thin paper. Mom had painted them with paints in colors of creamy peaches and vibrant reds and minty greens. It must have taken her hours, working on the dolls while we were at school. Sue and I near crushed her with our strong hugs and kisses that Christmas morning. Her thick flannel nightgown warmed our cheeks like the candles on the tree and the cocoa. With this grand Christmas preceding it, 1935, we all thought, would be a very good year.

SUE

UNCLE DONALD, AUNT Millie, Randall, and Myra moved out at the end of April. They moved to an apartment building only a mile away, so we would see them quite often. What I hadn't really expected to feel when they left was a sense of loss. We had been stepping all over each other for so long, and I couldn't count on two hands the number of times I'd nearly wet my pants waiting to get into the bathroom. Our meals had been stretched thin as thin could be, but still, when they left, I missed them. Myra had become friendlier as time wore on, and we had been her big sisters in a certain way. To prepare her for when she got her monthlies, we told her what ours were like and showed her how to fix a hot water bottle to rest on her stomach. We had also helped her learn how to dress better because now she was twelve and starting to care more for boys. I had taught her how to curl her hair so it fell in soft waves to her shoulders, and Fanny had taught her how to stand up for herself in any uncertain situations. "Shoulders up, lip snarled, and a ready repertoire of comeback lines," was Fanny's motto. Her own personal favorite was, "Don't cast a kitten over it!"

Myra was now wearing all our old clothes from a couple years back, and so seeing her walk out the door when they left was sort of like seeing our old selves leave, never to return.

I felt more mixed about Randall leaving. I was fond of him, but he had almost always been out anyway, doing pickup jobs wherever he could find them, staying after school to play various sports, and he was often off courting girls. When Pop walked home at night from his streetcar, he might see Randall on any number of girls' porches on the way home. He wouldn't say what they were doing, but knowing how intense a color of blue Randall's eyes were, I suspected girls might just be locking eyes with him, and perhaps fingers as well. Lips too, Fanny added, but this was really unseemly! But so like Fanny, of course.

Aunt Millie and Uncle Donald had been able to get new wedding rings; tinier slips of gold than the last set, and while Aunt Millie's had no diamond chips this time, it sure gave a spring to her step having a ring back on her finger. We would miss having Aunt Millie to help us with fancy sewing and needlework, and we'd miss her soft voice and her peach kuchen.

But they all came back for Fanny's and my fifteenth birthday in May, Aunt Millie with a kuchen for us to share, along with the banana spice cake with butter frosting our mom had made. Well, we were two girls, why not two cakes? We had chicken and biscuits and gravy for dinner, along with some fresh-shelled peas that glistened with butter. After dinner we sat down and listened to Jack Benny on the radio while we ate our cake, half a slice of each type of cake at first, then half a slice more! Mr. Benny's voice was so distinctive if I closed my eyes I could just see when he'd have an eyebrow lifted or be rolling his eyes or twirling a finger. He was a riot. We laughed ourselves silly.

After cake came presents. Fanny received a lipstick from Mom in a shade called Baby Red-Pink. I could tell some serious arguing had transpired beforehand with Pop, who did not approve of makeup on young girls, but Fanny was so much of a theater girl and frequently in makeup anyway for school and neighborhood shows, that it wasn't too big a shock to see her with lips the color of not quite ripe cherries. My most memorable gift was a book called *Winesburg, Ohio*, by a Mr. Sherwood Anderson. I couldn't wait to read it. Fanny thought I was a goose for wanting to read something that wasn't assigned at school. Me, I enjoyed the smell of the paper and its ivory color with the black ink capturing people's ideas and memories. I was a book fiend, Randall said, and he knew something about fiends, considering his favorite movies were *Dracula, Frankenstein,* and *The Mummy.* Sometimes Randall liked to hold a candle up near his eyes and imitate the way Boris Karloff's eyes looked right before he cast his murderous spell. I always had to choke back tears it frightened me so much when he did this, but he didn't try this on our birthday, anyway.

We were having some very pretty late spring weather that day, so after opening presents we went outside wearing only our thin cotton church coats. The sky looked violet and velvet; the air was fresh and smelling of lilacs. Mom and Aunt Millie were cleaning up the dinner dishes, and Uncle Donald and Pop were smoking cigars on the back stoop, so we kids all went for a walk up the avenue. Randall's present to us was to take us over to Parkmoor for a milkshake. We were full of chicken and cake, but could a small milkshake hurt us? We thought not.

Fanny and Myra and I walked arm in arm. School would be out soon, and we talked about our plans for the summer. Fanny listed a string of shows a mile long, ones she either wanted to put on or go see at the Muny. Myra wanted to learn how to sew, and she sure had the best teacher in her mom. I would do a lot of reading over the summer, I knew, and I would also try to get off to swim as much as I could. All year, my skin craved the cool surprise of pool water. I had been saving money for a new bathing suit, which I needed because my bubs had grown to the size of pippin apples, and I couldn't stretch the old suit out anymore.

Randall walked a block ahead of us shooting his rubber gun at trees. The ammunition was made from old strips of tire tubes, and the smell of rubber was pungent in the early twilight. Bob had the job of running to the trees and collecting the rubber "bullets." Once or twice Randall let Bob shoot off a round, but mostly Bob was the recovery man. Fanny had just told us all that Frank Bifford had asked her to an end-of-school-year dance, and we were speculating on if Pop would let her go, and more important, what she would wear if he did. And then, up ahead of us, just as the light was starting to give way to night, we saw that Bob, strangely, had darted ahead, and instead of waiting for Randall to hit a tree, had run in a fast arc over to the tree. Randall missed the tree, and—we thought this must be part of a nightmare—shot Bob right in the eye. Bob screamed as loud as a girl, in fact as loud as the girl in *The Mummy* screamed when Karloff seized her. And we heard Randall holler out a bad word that I won't repeat. Soon Bob was down, and we were all around him.

We didn't know what the injury was exactly because there was so much blood and Fanny screamed out, "His eye's gone!" and then she looked about the earth for a minute as if she expected to see his eyeball peering up at her from between some blades of grass. Myra began to cry loud and fierce, and meanwhile Randall picked Bob up in his arms, saying "I'm so sorry Bob!" and ran with him back to the house. We ran right along with them. We still didn't have a car, but our neighbor Mr. Nicholas saw everything from his front stoop and quickly tossed his car keys to Pop, and off Mom and Pop went driving Bob to the doctor's. At the last minute, Randall folded himself up like an accordion into the jump seat, and the last thing we saw was the car's rear light glow red and then fade into the distance. It was hard to forget the look on our mother's face, a look I hadn't seen since I'd lain ill with the scarlet fever. Her heart had broken again, along with the lid of Bob's left eye.

Our aunt and uncle and Myra stayed with us till we got word. We had recently gotten a telephone, and it rang extra loudly that night. We had been all sitting in the living room not saying much of anything, listening to some swing music on the radio, though no one felt too swingy. Uncle Donald picked up the receiver and held it to his ear like it was a big sidewinder question mark. He wasn't comfortable with telephones yet. "Hello!" he boomed.

We listened to his responses, his "Mmm-hmmms," and "That right?" and then he hung up the telephone and said that they would be home soon. Bob's eye was bloodshot, he warned us, and swollen up big as a corkball, but his eye was there, not by the tree down the avenue, and he was not going to be blind. The rubber strip had torn his eyelid bad and they had had to put stitches in it. We couldn't imagine how bad he must have felt, but probably they had given him a whiff of ether so he would be out for it. I pictured him looking like Frankenstein with that crazy zigzag of stitches down his eyelid.

"They know for certain he won't lose his sight in that eye?" Aunt Millie asked. Her voice was tremulous and so soft we could hardly hear her.

Uncle Donald said, "The doc is sure he will see fine once the swelling goes down. I'd hate to be inside of a mile of Bob when he gets those stitches yanked out though!"

We knew also that we'd hate to be within a mile of Randall when he got the whooping he would surely get for shooting off rubber strips when it was getting too dark to do so safely.

30

FANNY

FRANK BIFFORD ASKED to walk me home after school a week before we would be going to the school dance together. So far, Sue hadn't been asked to the dance, which I thought was pretty strange considering she was as pretty as me. She wasn't as outgoing and didn't have as lovely a voice naturally, but she was nice and, being my identical, she must be a swell girl.

It's strange to say, but I guess this was the first time I had walked home from school without Sue, except for when she had scarlet fever. Frank and I came out of the front door of the school together, which was where Sue and I always met to walk home. We walked out and I just gave her a look that said, "Me and Frank are walking alone." She could read my looks. I could see she was a bit wounded; her face quivered a little at the nose, reminding me of that bunny, Steelie, I had nabbed one Easter when we were little and then had to give back. That still griped me. I walked on as cool as you please with Frank holding my schoolbooks along with his, his arm looped in mine. One thing that drew me to Frank was how he was smooth without being slick. Some boys would have fumbled the books, but not Frank. I was glad I was wearing my beautiful blue serge skirt that was the color of rain clouds, with a crisp white blouse. My wavy hair billowed on a breeze.

Frank had a crisp and spicy cologne smell, along with a faint odor of hamburgers and French fries. Frank had a weekend job at Parkmoor, and while Frank's food scent wasn't overpowering, it made me a little hungry to inhale him. We walked at a brisk pace; Frank was an athletic boy, a running back on the football team. His hair was curly and looked like it could shoot right off his head like fireworks. Surprisingly, my pop had agreed I could go to the dance with Frank, even though he was a little concerned that Frank was sixteen, a year older than me. I guess Pop was worried Frank might have some fast moves. Me, I was hoping that he would. I was as ready to be kissed as a cat is to have kittens. I put in a weekly prayer at church to God for patience in this matter, but when I saw Jean Harlow and Greta Garbo and Bette Davis fall into the arms of their suitors when kissed, their shoulders sloping back and their throats extended like white creamy flowers, I couldn't help but want that too.

We were about halfway home when I thought to look back behind me to see if Sue was following us. Mercifully, no. She had probably walked over to Kresge's to buy some new knitting yarn or a Coca-Cola at the fountain. Smart girl.

"Frank, can't you find Sue a date for the dance? One of your friends?" I nestled for just a second on his shoulder even while we walked. I figured he could feel how soft my cheeks were even through his cotton sweater.

"What about Morrie Winnaker? He's in my literature class; he's real smart, like Sue."

I gave him an upended brow to ask, aren't I smart too? Also, I pulled away from him just slightly.

"Toots, of course you're smart too. But Morrie, he's bookish, like

Sue. She wants to be a teacher, doesn't she? You, Fanny, you're show smart, tune smart!"

"Well, that's true. Isn't Morrie a bit of a drip?"

"Heck, he plays softball too. He's not always nosed into a book."

"Okay, see what he thinks!" I smiled at Frank in my most co-quettish way. I had learned it from Claudette Colbert in *It Happened One Night*. Her smile had certainly melted Clark Gable's heart, and he was a crusty reporter in that movie. I started thinking about my favorite scene in the film, when Clark showed Claudette the proper way to dunk a doughnut so it wouldn't disintegrate into the coffee. Thinking of this, I asked Frank to walk me over to Parkmoor for a doughnut and coffee. Their doughnuts melted in your mouth, dunked or not.

The next night Sue got a telephone call from Morrie Winnaker, who asked her to the dance. I saw her look of surprised joy and was glad I'd thought to mention the idea to Frank. After Pop said it was okay, she accepted Morrie's invitation.

"I am counting on you girls to look out for each other!" Pop exclaimed. He didn't belabor the issue, because he was heading out to the back porch for a smoke with his neighbor friend, Bill Blanksy. Our mother did not approve of smoking in the house.

Sue never guessed I was the one who'd set up her date for the dance. She was exuberant. We ran up to our bedroom to start planning our outfits for the dance. We chose flowy skirts, a red one for me and a violet one for Sue, and soft cream blouses. Mom checked them over to see that the skirts covered our calves, our tops did not cling to our bubs, and that we looked wholesome and not hotsie-totsie. She would lend us silk stockings to wear instead of cotton ones, though she made some mild threats of what would happen if we ran the stockings while we danced.

For the next few nights, Sue and I practiced dancing in the hallway that led from the kitchen to the living room. We had learned how to dance in etiquette and decorum classes at school, and we were very ready to try out our steps for the first time on boys instead of girls. Sue and I giggled over the times we had had to dance with Miss Frutt, our teacher. She insisted on demonstrating the steps to each girl in close personal contact. Her breath smelled of sour oranges, and her blouse armpits wore heart-shaped dark stains. She was a tall woman though, which made it good practice for moving on to boys.

"Miss Frutt! Miss Frutt! You are my one and only, my angel girl!" I hollered out, pretending I was a fella.

"Oh, Ricardo, what can I do? I feel faint when I'm around you!" Sue slumped in my arms.

We laughed and laughed till Bob appeared in the hallway asking what was going on. Next we spent an hour trying to teach Bob how to dance. At ten years old, he was still shorter than us, but you could see any day now, he would shoot up by half a foot. He was a wiry boy, with hair that jutted up in so many different directions, you needed a road map to follow it. When I danced with him, I could smell a very strong odor of grass and cork, from his corkball playing. Maybe someday he'd manage a few steps with a girl, but for now, he clung to Sue or me for dear life and made us lead him around. He roped his arms around us like we were lifebuoys. By the end of the hour we had to go soak our toes from where he'd crunched them, and we gave up hope of our own baby brother ever being any kind of Fred Astaire. He said, "Aw nuts!" and stomped outside to throw a ball to a neighbor boy.

31

SUE

I WAS EXCITED about the dance. I secretly suspected that Fanny and Frank had set it up for Morrie to ask me out, but as long as I didn't ask her, I didn't have to know it. He was a nice boy, and he was smart as could be. The things he said in history class revealed a deep mind and a sense of how things all pieced together in the puzzle of our times. I also liked his slender build and shiny face. He had a clear complexion and always smelled of Lux soap.

I got my monthly a few days early and was afraid it would still be with me at the dance on Saturday. Naturally, Fanny got hers early too; we always had ours exactly together, starting within the same hour sometimes. The world of twins. We couldn't try on our dance clothes to check them because we certainly didn't want to stain them. We also didn't feel like practicing our dance steps much more; Fanny and I always got cramps that sent us reeling. Occasionally we had to miss a day of school for them, though Pop took a dim view of that. Easy for Pop, a man! We only had one hot water bottle in the house, so Fanny and I would stay in bed taking turns with it. We told each other funny stories to distract each other from the hurting. Sometimes

Fanny would repeat jokes that she'd heard on the radio, like Baby Snooks, the character Fanny Brice did, or she might sing like Baby Rose Marie.

She was busy trying out all the styles of entertainment to see what she'd specialize in when she went to Hollywood. Last year, when she talked about going to Hollywood, I agreed with Pop and Mom that it was a pipe dream. But the more I heard, the more I believed that she would go. She always said *we* would go. It wasn't that she thought I would break into movies too, but she said they need teachers everywhere; even in Hollywood there were "snot-nosed little kids who have to be taught that four plus four equals eight."

I found it very hard to picture California, its warm and sunny days all year long. Would time feel like it was even passing if the weather was always identical to itself? I thought about how I counted on the summer to mean swimming long, brisk ice-cold laps, the fall to bring beautiful gold and orange leaves crackling under our feet and warm cozy sweaters, the winter to mean Christmas trees swooshing in from the snow, and spring to herald new crocus buds and cardinals popping up plump-breasted to sing the sweet notes of spring. If we lived in California, would we love the sun anymore if there were nothing besides it? Would we tire of short sleeves and hot dogs and Coca-Cola and baseball scores? I wondered. But I tried to keep an open mind.

When Saturday afternoon came, Fanny and I took our baths and washed our hair and put clips in it to set it into pretty waves. We sat on the back porch while our hair dried, drinking lemonade our mother had made because she said lemon was a beauty tonic, whether on your skin or inside you. It was a pretty, sunny day. Bob was down the block playing corkball, but we could hear his whoops and hollers, along with the other boys'. Pop was in the alley washing our new car. We had finally gotten one. For years Pop said we didn't need one because the streetcar would get us anywhere our hearts desired, but finally when he got a great deal on last year's Model T, in a color called Niagara Blue, he relented. Pop already loved the car rather a lot, and he was whistling at the top of his lungs "Smoke Gets in Your Eyes." Smoke did—he was smoking a cigar while he washed.

"Lemonade, Pop?" Fanny hollered out.

"Later, kittens!" he yelled back. "And how!"

I told Fanny that I was a little scared about tonight. I thought that Morrie was a swell fella, but I didn't know him very well. What would we talk about?

"Sue! You two are both bookworms. Talk about what you're reading. Maybe he's read that Whinesboot Iowa you're so crazy about."

"*Winesburg, Ohio*, Fanny!"

"Well, I'm not the smart twin. And I'm not your date, so it doesn't matter what I know!"

"Miss Frutt told us that boys don't like it if the girls are too smart," I said. I crunched on a wisp of ice that was floating in my glass.

"How many suitors do you think bony ol' Miss Frutt has?" Fanny inquired.

"True, true. Okay, I'll just be myself." I sighed.

Mom snuck up behind us and put her arms around our shoulders. "Any boy who doesn't like my smart girls is a dumb boy," Mom pronounced. She kissed our cheeks and we could smell a sweet lemony smell coming from her too. She had rubbed her elbows with juiced-out lemon halves! Next, she did ours too, so our elbows would be smooth as silk when our dates pirouetted us around the dance floor.

Pop looked up to see us sporting yellow elbows and was so surprised he dropped his cigar into his wash bucket.

"Whatever you do, don't laugh," Mom said, smothering a chuckle of her own. "I am going inside to make a very light supper fit for princesses who must be light on their feet." Mom went inside after she had collected our lemon rinds, and Fanny and I whispered about the dance till it was almost growing to twilight outside, the sky pinkening a bit at the edges. Pop and Bob had gone inside to listen to "The Shadow Knows" on the radio.

"Who knows what evil lurks in the heart of man? Only the shadow knows!" drifted outside to us, along with the evil but melodic organ music.

"Girls! Come set the table. We're eating early so you twins can make yourselves pretty."

I had to be very careful passing the plates across the table to Fanny. I was already getting nervous about the dance, but I'd be more nervous if I broke one of Mom's dishes; the dishes were a new pink flower set with a cream ground that we had collected from Dish Nights at the picture shows. It had taken us near a year to get a whole set. Bob had already broken the creamer, and he was still doing penance for that a month later.

We had a ham loaf and fresh-shelled peas for dinner. I hardly ate three bites. Mom let us go upstairs and get dressed while they ate a dessert of macaroon cookies.

I put my camisole on backward! Fanny pointed it out to me, and I sat on the bed and took a few encouraging breaths before I fixed myself. After we had on our skirts and blouses and stockings and shoes (we had allowed quite a bit of time for putting on the stockings, since Mom would strangle us if we ran them), we took the hairclips out of our hair, and then we combed each other's out carefully. Our waves were soft as fur, and slippery too. Our hair glistened in the lamplight, all clean and set for a night of dancing. We had combed sugar water through it when we set it, and that holds the waves, though Mom warned us to be careful outside that no bees added themselves to our hairstyles.

We went downstairs, and the sound of our shoes clicking on the stairs made my heart beat fast. Pop would be driving us to the dance hall, where we would meet our dates. He inspected us and pronounced us pretty. He didn't seem to notice that I was wearing lipstick for the first time! Thank heavens Fanny had paved the way for me on that. Mom kissed our foreheads, and off we rode in our chariot with Pop at the wheel.

32

FANNY

I COULD HAVE sworn Pop had a little tear glinting in his eye when he dropped us off. Our gruff pop! But it was our very first dance after all. Right away we saw Frank and Morrie. They looked grand in their crisp white shirts and billowy wool slacks with knife-sharp creases in them. They put their arms out for us to latch on to, and we went into the dance hall. The lights were twinkling bright in the room, and there was a live band playing, all Negro men, whose chocolate skin appeared dark and shiny against their bright white jackets.

The boys took us out on the dance floor right away, and we slipped in comfortably among the other kids. The first number was a fast one that got us all revved up. I looked over and saw Sue smiling in Morrie's arms and felt relieved that they seemed to be hitting it off. After we had danced three numbers in a row, Morrie and Frank steered us over to the punch bowls, and the girl behind the table, a sophomore, served us some cherry punch in crystal glasses. It tasted delicious; we were perspiring a bit already, and Sue's cheeks were pinkish red. I guessed mine probably looked the same. Frank and I moved off a ways, so we could talk alone. I saw that Sue had a slightly panicked look, but I mouthed "Winesburg" to her, and she nodded slightly and smiled her thanks.

Frank and I found some seats, and we began to talk about what our summer plans were. Frank would be working full-time days at Parkmoor, ensuring that I would be drinking discounted milkshakes all summer, but he was also hoping to take me to the Muny many times over the summer to see some shows. I told him I'd love that. I planned to study the plays and movies I saw over the summer very closely to see how much I could learn from the actresses I saw. I had been entranced with the way that Claudette Colbert walked in *It Happened One Night*, I told him.

"You could tell from her slouch that she was a very rich girl," I said.

"You'd think the rich would have all the reason in the world to stand up straight," Frank said earnestly. We both chuckled.

"Maybe they need servants to go around behind them holding up their shoulders!" I quipped.

I suddenly noticed Frank looking at the scar on my arm. I guessed I had worn sweaters covering it before when we'd been together. Tonight it was there for all the world to see. Most people in school had seen it for years, and I very rarely got teased for it any more. But Frank was new to town that spring.

"It's like a big, exotic beauty spot," Frank said.

I thought for a minute, maybe I was in love.

33

SUE

MORRIE HAD READ *Winesburg, Ohio!* We raved about it for so long we had to sit down. Fanny and Frank had gone back to the dance floor and from the corner of my eye I could see Fanny twirling and swaying as if she were Ginger Rogers. She was a good dancer, now that she had someone to dance with besides Miss Frutt. Her creamy skin was punctuated by the long, red beaded necklace she had borrowed from Mom.

Morrie had a mist of perspiration on his brow from dancing and talking. He had a ready smile and plenty to say on everything, so I relaxed and let the evening wash over me. I was not the life of the party, like Fanny, but I held my own with Morrie, which was all I cared about.

"What will you be doing this summer, Sue?" Morrie asked me.

He had gotten us fresh glasses of punch, and his lips glowed like an ember with the color of the punch. He made it hard for me to listen to his words, he looked so fine.

"Besides reading," Morrie added.

"There's something else to do?" I asked him, half serious.

Morrie laughed. "Yeah, for me anyway. I have to help my dad out down at the store."

I knew Morrie's dad had a dry goods store. In fact, Fanny and I often bought fabric and yarn there. The first time I had seen Morrie outside of school had been at the store. I had watched him whip bolt after bolt of crisp cotton off its holder and rip it off down a straight invisible line. I thought of his arm muscles flexing as he did it, and I blushed till my cheeks felt like they could set a brushfire.

"I can tell you and Fanny when the new fabrics come in!" he told me.

"That would be wonderful," I said.

Just then, the band struck up with "S'Wonderful," echoing my words. Morrie and I had a good laugh at that. It was a song I knew well, because my pop liked to sing it sometimes when he was doing jobs around the house. Our pop had a rich bass voice that made you feel glad.

Morrie and I gravitated to the dance floor and began to move about in what felt like a slow swimming circle. That reminded me. I told Morrie that I would be swimming often this summer, that I loved to swim. He asked if we could go swimming sometime together. I was dumbstruck. I wasn't about to have a boy see me in my swimming costume! The way it nestled to my bubs and the way my legs showed! Oh no! I couldn't say a word.

"Maybe you'd rather go roller-skating?" Morrie said.

"And how!" I nearly shouted with relief.

Soon the evening drew to a close; our pop was set to pick us up at ten o'clock. Morrie and Frank walked us to Pop's car. Certainly they wouldn't try to kiss us tonight, not with Pop there braced against the car staring them down. We introduced them, and Pop gave them his firm handshake, making sure that they returned it with vigor. And then we were driving home, the cool night breeze ruffling over us as we sat in the backseat whispering about the evening. As twins, we had the ability to whisper with only the slightest volume and still hear each other perfectly.

At home, we told Mom a little about the dance while we ate fudge candy she had made for us. She told us she remembered always being ravenous after dancing when she was young. After one dance, she said, she had eaten half a cake all on her own! Mom wanted to know the names of all the songs we had danced to. She asked if Frank and Morrie were good dancers, and we said, yes indeed. Pop came into the house from smoking a cigar, and he waved his arms to us, "Girls, time for bed. It was just a dance, and there will be more, I expect."

In our cotton-lawn gowns, in bed, Fanny and I kept on talking about the night.

"I have a secret," Fanny said. "Frank walked me out behind the hall for a few minutes . . . did you notice we were gone? And he kissed me."

I rolled over and looked at Fanny's face in the moonlight. She glowed there in the creamy light and seemed even to pulse a bit with the moon's aura. I couldn't even form a question, but I guessed my eyes were two question marks poised in the dark for her to see.

"Yeah," Fanny said. "It was real nice. His lips were soft and sweet."

Fanny was always first in everything.

34

FANNY

DANCE MARATHONS HAD been the craze for a few years now, but I had the idea to do a roller-skating marathon instead, as a school ice-breaker a week before classes started up in the fall. This marathon would be for fun, unlike the real ones where people danced to keep a roof over their heads. The skating rink in our neighborhood readily agreed to let us use the rink for the day; it was good publicity for them. Sue and I worked with Miss Snow, my chorus teacher, and Mr. Jennings, the vice principal, to get sponsors for the marathon, for prize money and refreshments. The prize would be one hundred dollars, for the winning couple to share. My plan was to win, of course, and to put the fifty into a kitty I was keeping for leaving St. Louis to go to California to be a movie star after high school was over. I had twenty-eight dollars already in a biscuit tin hidden under my camis in the bureau.

I thought maybe Sue and I could do a switch-off on the skating. We could dress identically, have one twin skate and the other hide out and trade off every few hours. Surely we'd win it if we did this! Sue said it wasn't ethical, and she wouldn't do it. I knew she was right, but it sure took the fun out of being identical if we could never use it to our favor.

We were able to get a radio host to be the marathon emcee. He was a handsome fellow named Rich Richmon. My boyfriend (and skating partner) Frank said that had to be a stage name. Rich was in his thirties and naturally way too old for me, but I figured I could wink at him every time I skated by anyway. Till Frank caught me.

Our mom fretted a bit over us girls competing against each other. This was sweet because it meant she thought it would come down to either Sue or me! It was true that Sue and I were both very good roller skaters. I was especially good where a girl needed to pivot her hips, something I learned in tap dance, and Sue could be fluid in her movements, which I think came from her swimming. Frank and I and Sue and Morrie had been skating quite a bit all summer long. Frank was a little overmuscled in one way for the rink; he played football after all, and was a prize player in fact, mushing down fellows whenever required, though he was gentle as a kitten with me. But his strength came in handy when I got a bit weary. Dancing and skating, we looked fine together.

Morrie was not as built up as Frank, but he matched Sue's agility very well. We could see them whispering their way around the rink, talking about silly books and poems no doubt. After our skating sessions, a bunch of us usually went around to Parkmoor. Since Frank worked there, he could get us discounted hamburgers, French fries for free, and sometimes free milkshakes, but only if his boss weren't there at the moment. Sue told me she always felt a little funny eating in front of boys, like she could feel her lips and teeth moving in an exaggerated way as if she were in some sort of crazy cartoon feature they showed down at the Fox. So she ate slowly and sometimes hid herself behind her checked napkin. Me, I could eat anywhere, anytime, with anyone. Surely this would come in handy in the movies, where you had to pretend to eat but look like you really were. The other thing we discovered that summer was that though we were of course identical in most ways, Sue's waist ran just a little tiny bit to fat. Not me. I was the next "it" girl waiting to make it big, and my waist could rival Claudette Colbert's any day!

Sue and I would dress alike for the marathon, even though we weren't going to switch. There might be photographers there, and they loved twins. Aunt Millie helped Sue and me sew our outfits for the marathon. We used a pretty navy dotted Swiss material for the skirts, which were cut full as spread daisies for movement, and sharp-looking cotton blouses to keep us cool. Aunt Millie in secret made us beautiful ribbons for our hair from the same material as our skirts, to keep our stylish wavy locks out of the way of our faces. The worst thing was when your hair slapped you in the lips in a turn, because it stuck to your lipstick something awful. Skaters had to look poised and pulled together at all times.

The big day came. Mom made us a very light breakfast, fruit and unbuttered toast, so we'd not have our stomachs weighing us down, and Pop drove us to the rink early in the morning because we were part of the setup crew in charge of decorating the rink and also putting some sodas on ice for when the skaters got thirsty. The 7-Up bottling company had donated several cases of soda, and the bottles twinkled like emeralds in a big metal tub. Also, the Hostess Company donated a hundred or so Twinkies! They thought it would be good publicity for how light and satisfying the cakes are, and I thought they would help keep our energy up too.

When Rich Richmon arrived, we girls clamored around him a little. We could hardly help it; he looked like a movie star. In fact, Frank, who was just jealous, thought Rich was too perfect looking, so "pretty" he wasn't even like a man.

The roller rink began to fill up with kids right at nine A.M. To start out, there were thirty-two couples. There would be a ten-minute rest break every two hours, just like the real marathons had. We had set up some cots and some benches with pillows tied onto them as places for the skaters to rest. Everyone sprang to life when Rich Richmon's sonorous voice shouted, "On your mark, go!" No one knew what our mark was, but we went. The only real rule was to keep moving and to hold on to your partner. If you scratched your forehead with one hand, the other better be on your partner's waist.

The marathon began. Very soon I realized that skating rink music was way too heavy on the organ, which played in our head like radio shows, only we weren't listening to see what cowpokes Tom Mix might be sneaking up on, we were only waiting to see who would be the first to drop out of the competition. Frank told me about football practice, and that sort of ran over my head just like the music, sort of lolling there but not really penetrating. To keep from getting tired, I kept my mind busy listing dramatic scenes I had memorized in case a talent scout were to happen by and give me a chance to audition. Finally when the first break came, Sue and I sat down together, leaning up against each other, back to back, on one of the pillowed benches. We needed a little break from the boys. We were so thirsty, which made the 7-Up taste amazing, even better than usual. Sue and I split one soda, because it would be two hours before the next restroom break, and we had to be aware. I asked Sue if she and Morrie were running out of things to talk about, and she said not at all. Maybe a bookish boy had some advantages I hadn't considered. How long could I pretend to be interested in football?

Before we knew it, the break was up and we were back on the floor, and this time the two hours flew by. They'd jazzed up the music a bit, which made it more fun, but also harder for some of the kids to keep up. It was clearly time to tickle a few out of the fray, and sure enough, near the end of the second round, Gladys Murphy and Ron Beener were out; Gladys had a cramp in her leg, though some thought she had the other kind of cramps too; her skin was blue like thin milk.

In the third hour, a total of six couples skated off the floor, leaving twenty-six pairs. Some skated off looking limp as noodles; they had clearly not been practicing before the competition. Some said they were just bored. "You'd have to be a skating *nut* to keep skating this long," George Magson declared as he skated Lori Gennaro off the floor. Success in a marathon took dedication, and not everyone had a good supply of that. After the fourth hour, Sue and I lay down together on a cot, mostly because there weren't many cots to go around, but also because we could whisper to each other about the other kids and compare notes. After a couple minutes, we sat up and ate some Twinkies, then lay back down and let the sugar bubble around into our blood. Before we got up to start skating again, we brushed each other's hair and re-ribboned it, and just then, a photographer from the *St. Louis Post-Dispatch* came by, just like I'd dreamed and planned! Luckily we had just reapplied our lipstick, and with our hair all snapping fresh from brushing, we were ready. I had a little index of types of smiles I was organizing for Hollywood screen tests, which I had taught to a very reluctant Sue. "Number three," I whispered into her ear, and instantly we had matching smiles, a coy and wise and friendly smile no one could resist when doubled by Sue and me.

The next round I could hardly concentrate on our skating, for thinking about the photo of Sue and me that might wind up in the newspaper. I told Frank about it, and he smiled but I could see he didn't know how important this chance for publicity could prove to be. We nicked skates several times, sending little sparks of metal. Outside the afternoon light was turning the rink a golden hazy color, and we could make out dust motes dancing crazily in the air. The hall smelled like Odorono, Brylcreem, and salted peanuts. I began to feel more than a little weary of it all.

But then some friskier music came on, and I got my second wind and started doing fancy loops and things, in case the photographer were still around. Then I realized he'd be more interested in shots with me and Sue, not ones of me with Frank, since everyone loved seeing identical twins. What was I wearing myself out for? I leaned my cheek on Frank's shoulder—what luck to have his big football shoulder at this juncture!—and sort of drifted off a bit and let him roll me around the floor. I woke with a start when the next whistle blew, and Rich Richmon began to name off the couples that remained.

It was down to eleven couples! I hadn't realized how many more had departed, though I should have, since now there was so much more space to maneuver around, even if our strength for maneuvering was depleted. This time during break Sue complained of sore calves, and so I massaged them for her. In turn, she worked on my shoulders a little. My shoulders seemed to slope more with each passing round, and I was glad of the crisp shoulder pads Aunt Millie had placed inside our blouses, so I wouldn't lose shape completely!

It was suppertime now, and so during the next round, some of our mothers brought in triangles of sandwiches for us to eat at the break. Our mom brought deviled ham sandwiches, and they looked out of this world, we were so hungry. Bob had come too, and I could only hope he wouldn't hoot at us or distract us in the next round.

During the next break I skated over to where the photographer was and asked him if Sue and I would make it into the paper.

"I just shoots 'em, ma'am, I don't pick 'em."

"People love to see identical twins though," I told him, practicing my perfect Myrna Loy type smile, personable and vivacious.

"Do they?" he asked me. Then he looked me up and down in a

way that made my stomach squinch up; this fella must have been thirty years old and he looked at me like I might go out with him!

"Oh yes," I murmured faintly, while I backed away, wobbling a bit on my skates, and skated over to the rest area, nearly knocking over a couple of fellow contestants on my way to the restroom. I shook my fist just a little over this photographer's attitude; it was okay he thought we were pretty, but we sure weren't the type of girls to flirt our way into the newspaper.

I came out of the restroom and sat down next to Sue, who fed me one of Mom's delicious sandwiches and offered me some more 7-Up. Sue looked a little pale, and even the effervescence of the 7-Up didn't seem to do much for her.

"I don't know if I can go much longer," Sue said.

It was down to five couples now. "I think we'll have a better chance of getting in the newspaper if we're the last two couples, Sue," I entreated.

"I don't care about the paper, Fanny. I mean, I know you do, but—"

"What about Morrie?" I asked her.

"He's just doing this for me," Sue said. "It doesn't matter to him. And he shouldn't get too worn out, he has to help his father at the store tomorrow."

"Okay then. Well, are you going to try this next one?" I asked. I had more respect for Sue now that she stood up for herself, but it was less convenient for my purposes.

"If you don't mind if we quit, I think we will now. I'm going to go sit up in the stands with Mom and Bob. I may fall asleep I'm so tired, but I'll get Bob to wake me if you and Frank win."

"*When* we win!" I told her.

Frank and I had never spent this many hours together in one stretch, and you sure do learn a great deal about a person in circumstances like these. We had gone through so many moods during the day that it practically felt like we were a married couple. We'd been exuberant when we made it to the final five couples, cranky when the music had a static sound, divided over whether we'd spend some of the prize money together, and truly romantic when Frank nestled my head on his shoulder and kissed my forehead secretively (no public displays of affection was another of the contest rules).

Now it was down to us and one other couple: Jean Morrisette and John Trink. Jean was a bit of a show-off in her bright red satin dress, whipping all around the rink; I had the impression she had been skating since she was barely out of diapers. And John was tall, handsome, and a fine athlete; in fact he and Frank played football together. They were some stern competition for us, but still I thought that this would be our winning round. Jean Morrisette certainly did not have five winning smile styles at her disposal, so I was the better prepared one.

During the last break, Sue had powdered my face and touched up my lipstick for me. I was wearing a new bright pink shade called Jazzy. She gave me a pink mint to perk up my breath too, and it went right along with my lipstick. Mom had brought me an extra pair of shiny golden stockings, which I was happy to put on to replace my old, saggy ones, as well as a fresh blouse to change into, crisply ironed like only my mom could do. So the next time Frank and I skated out onto the floor we had a new lease on life. Or I did, and he got to share in it. Ah, I inhaled him and discovered he had a little fresh cologne splashed onto his jaw. Really, we were all set to make it to the end and collect our honors.

It was down to the wire and the crowd was getting noisy! The music we rolled to was more and more fast paced, and I started to feel a little dizzy as we circled and swooped. I was glad to have Frank's strong arms steering me, because suddenly in spite of everything I wanted to crawl into my bed under my pink chenille spread and suck my thumb, almost! I had never been so tired in my life. The bright lights they'd turned on for nighttime glinted off our faces like car headlights.

During one turn around, I felt Jean's skirt twirl and whip out at my legs. She was going so fast, I felt like I'd been slapped. Was that on purpose? I mean I never . . . ! With only the four of us on the floor, there should have been plenty of space, wouldn't you think?

But she got her just deserts. I turned to see Jean bending a little at the waist and crying out something I couldn't quite hear.

"Kitten, get a wiggle on!" I heard John holler.

But I saw that she was clutching at her stomach, and then she said, "That damn Twinkie!" in a loud whisper that everyone heard.

There was a collective gasp in the audience, and then Jean, burying her face in her hands, frantically sped off the floor to the restroom.

We'd won! There was a loud uproar in the hall, applause and friendly hollering, and then Frank swept me up in his arms and skated me up to the front; we had not planned that, but even I thought it was spectacular. When we got there a local florist, Mr. Beenbaum, handed me a massive bouquet of red roses, and Rich Richmon, who was mysteriously fresh-shaven, gave me a kiss on the cheek and handed Frank and me each fifty dollars in cash! My hand shook as I held the money and beamed at the audience. I threw a few kisses and drank in the applause. I heard a long, crazed whistle from the audience I recognized as Bob's. Frank kissed me on the cheek too, and we did a little pirouette then skated off to the sideline.

My family was suddenly at my side. Pop, who I hadn't even seen come in, gave me a big hug and told me he was proud of me. This meant a lot to me, given Pop's discomfort with "public displays." Mom pressed a cool cloth to my head, I don't know where it came from, and kissed my cheek. "Oh honey!" she murmured. And Sue told me she knew the prize was mine the minute we'd walked into the rink that morning. She gave me a long hug, while Bob asked to hold the cash for just a few minutes. I let him keep it in his pocket "till we get home," I told him.

It was over, and I had done it! I told Frank how swell his skating me to the prize in his arms was, then I fainted for just a moment, and Frank scooped me up and carried me to our car. Pop helped Frank arrange me in the car, and then Sue and Mom piled in, Bob popped into the jump seat and we took off. I waved to Frank out of the back window. I nodded off and woke up a few times on the way home. The gorgeous pale yellow moon was winking at me, I thought. What a long day it had been.

The next thing I knew it was Sunday morning, and I was snug in my bed at home. Mom brought me breakfast—biscuits, honey, and a steaming cup of coffee—in bed! This was unheard of in our house unless you were very ill. And Sue brought me the *St. Louis Post-Dispatch*. There were two photos of me, one with Sue, and another of me with Frank. Sue and I looked really cute, with our hair fluffed out perfectly and bright smiles punctuating our faces. Sue, who had not studied movie star smiles the way I had, looked particularly grand, I thought. Frank and I looked good too; I forgot sometimes what a fine-looking boy he was, how well suited we were to each other. The headline was "Twin win!" and there was a short article about the marathon, the first marathon to feature roller skating in the state of Missouri!

SUE

IT HAD BEEN eight years since my scarlet fever episode when Myra contracted polio. She had come down with a bad cold in February that had lingered worse than all the mounds of snow on every curb. When we had gone to their house for Sunday dinner the weekend after Valentine's Day, Myra looked bluish, like she had the time she had been so sick before, and her cough was so harsh and strong it sounded like a colt neighing. First thing Monday morning Aunt Millie called from the hospital. Myra had gotten up from bed that morning and fell right down; her legs wouldn't work. They got her to the doctor immediately and found out she had polio. They were going to put her in the same isolation hospital where I had been for scarlet fever.

I felt like I was ripping in two. And this time, it wasn't for a twin reason. Half of me was crying for Myra and what she was facing, and the other half was crying to God, not me again, please not me too. We had to miss school and go right to our doctor's. Luckily none of us had any symptoms. They didn't do the spinal fluid test unless you had symptoms.

By the time we were done at the doctor's, early afternoon, Mom said we needn't bother to go back to school. Our doctor's office was close to Crown Candy Kitchen, a malt and candy shop we adored. Mom said we could stop in for a banana malt, the specialty at Crown. They were creamy and sported tiny brown dots from the bananas. We were gathered around a small metal table with our knees bumping against the cool metal curlicue legs and against each other's warm calves, and I was thinking about Myra's immobile legs. It was hard to feel much joy about our malt treat when we knew Myra was in the hospital; we were relieved we didn't have polio, but we were so sad and scared for Myra.

Mom said that a banana malt was just what we needed; they made a person strong of body and spirit. Everyone knew the malt powder was a magic tonic, the kind that gave Popeye big muscles to impress Olive Oyl. "Popeye the Sailor" was a new show on the radio.

"Mom, that's spinach he eats for muscles!"

"But you wouldn't want to drink a spinach milkshake, would you?" Mom teased. She reached out for a handful of Bob's sproingy thick hair and felt of it. "You're my big man, now, no Baby Bob," Mom said, her eyes brimming over a little.

Bob was twelve years old now and had no memory of ever being called Baby Bob, he said. He hadn't had much to say since we'd heard about Myra that morning. He had gotten close to her during the time they lived with us, and I knew his worries were simmering, as evidenced by his kicking at the table's legs till the top vibrated.

Fanny looked very serious. "I was going to teach Myra a few dance steps," Fanny said. "Now we don't know if she'll ever dance again."

"She'll dance," I said. I thought about my weeks at the isolation hospital, and how important it was to believe you'd get better. We had to believe it, for Myra.

"Sometimes kids have to wear those big ugly leather braces all down their legs," Fanny said, as she fished a small hunk of banana that hadn't blended into her malt out with a spoon and ate it.

"There's no need to think the worst!" I told Fanny, as I observed Bob's stricken look.

"Most times the legs recover completely," Mom said confidently, but as I looked at her, I saw it was a mother thing to say, not so much something she was completely sure of.

"I wonder how long she'll have to stay at the hospital," I said. Tears welled up in my eyes with no warning. I closed them, remembering the squealing sound of carts rolling up and down the halls of the hospital, as well as the sharp, strong cleaner and bowls of liquidy food and the bright green and red medicines pooled on spoons and coming down at your throat. I pushed my malt glass away. Bob instinctually grabbed for it, since he would normally polish it off, but he wasn't up to it either.

"Can I go visit her?" I asked.

"Usually they will only let the parents visit, you remember," Mom said. She was buttoning her green wool coat up, so we all started buttoning up our coats too. "I should have made you kids get hot chocolate," Mom said. "Did I forget it was winter?"

"That's okay, Mom, we have the magic malt in our blood," Bob said. And he kissed her suddenly on her cheek, something Bob rarely did voluntarily anymore.

As we walked out of the store, I spotted Wally Johansen behind the counter chopping up walnuts for the heavenly hash candy the store sold many pounds of; he was a boy who had gone to grade school with us, until about two years ago, when he'd left school after coming down with polio. He had never come back. Wally wore leather leg braces, and I could hear the leather creaking as he shifted in his seat. He was a little hunched over and more slender than I remembered, but he had strong color in his cheeks. "Wally," I whispered, staying behind while the others walked out the door. "We miss you at school," I said.

"Aw, nuts!" Wally said. He leaned over and handed me a perfect walnut half. "I miss you too," he murmured, a shy smile on his face.

That night when Pop walked through the door we all looked up at him expectantly. He knew why.

"Donald and me checked out okay," he told us. They had been checked for polio symptoms by the Public Service doctor.

I could hear my mother exhaling, even over the sound of Fred Astaire on the radio entreating us to dance "Cheek to Cheek." Astaire's mellow voice was a fitting background to our relief. Pop went over and kissed Mom, as he always did when he arrived home. But then he kissed us all too, not an everyday thing.

At dinner, Pop said the usual grace before we ate and then he said, "Lord, care for our sweet Myra in her hour of need," and then Pop sliced ham loaf and we passed around the mashed potatoes and glazed carrots, and we ate. Fanny talked about a play they would do at school and sized up her chances for getting the lead: excellent, of course. She tried to talk me into doing makeup for the show, but I didn't feel interested in the show one bit, with my mind only on Myra. How could Fanny rattle on, when Myra was so ill?

Bob told us he had invented a new game in the gym at school. All the kids were dying for spring and the chance to play ball outside, but Bob snared their interest with some sort of new ball game for indoors. I didn't mind his chatter so much, somehow. He was a boy after all, and boys occupied themselves with games no matter what.

I ate my food with little thought for the food itself, not to mention sports or shows. I could only think about what Myra's first night at the hospital would be like.

Fanny and I cleared the table, with Fanny chatting away as if nothing were wrong! We brought to the table some cup custards I had made in the afternoon when we got back from the malt shop. Mom said that they had a nice strong vanilla flavor, and I thought how custard was something Myra might be able to eat before long, its being so smooth and creamy.

After dinner I ironed a dozen shirts and handkerchiefs, my chore for the evening, and the warm cotton made me think of the hot cloths they would put on Myra. I had heard that hot packs were one of the main treatments for polio. When I was at the hospital, the children with the polio were in a different wing, but the nurses said that for polio they cut up wool blankets and soaked them in boiling water, using wringers so they wouldn't be sopping wet. Then they wrapped the wool strips tight around the children's limbs, which sounded horrible to me, but it was an important part of the treatment, the nurses had told us.

That night when Fanny and I got in bed, we talked about the same things we always did, and Fanny made a point of saying she didn't want to talk about Myra.

"There's nothing we can do for her, is there?" she asked me softly.

Sometimes I wondered if God had given Fanny a smaller heart than normal.

"We can pray for her," I told Fanny.

"Okay." And Fanny took my hand and we prayed silently, but I could feel she was really praying. I felt bad for questioning her heart.

After Fanny fell asleep, I remembered how in *The Mummy* Boris Karloff had been able to transmit evil fates to his victims through his mind and his bright white-lit eyes. I thought it was possible to transmit good too, and I warmed my hands together under the blankets and lay them on my own legs and tried to will my warmth to Myra's legs to help her get through the night. I remembered from my stay at the isolation hospital that each night was a struggle, especially that first week. With death hovering all around, each morning you opened your eyes was a gift.

Mom answered the phone when Aunt Millie called the next evening to confirm what my mother had said; only Uncle Donald and Aunt Millie were allowed to visit Myra. After the phone call, Mom came into the living room and sat down on the divan and buried her face in her hands for a moment before recounting the call to us. She said Aunt Millie was exhausted by the long trip to the hospital. She had gone by streetcar because Uncle Donald couldn't miss work, and she didn't know how to drive the car they'd recently bought second-hand. Mom and I had taken over a cold supper of ham and cheese sandwiches and homemade applesauce and left it in their icebox that afternoon. Aunt Millie told Mom she was very grateful.

Aunt Millie told Mom that Myra had spent her first night in the hospital in an iron lung. Bob's eyes grew wide with horror at the idea. Mom explained that an iron lung was a big square machine that Myra had to be locked into, with only her head sticking out the top of it. There was a kind of bellows in there, a contraption that pushed air into and out of the lungs, something Myra needed because her lungs were weak from the illness.

Bob said, "Mom, it sounds like a time travel machine like they have on the Buck Rogers show!"

Pop, who had been fiddling with a broken clock, lay down all the little pieces, including a funny little circular part with fins on it that Pop called a flogan, and said, "Son, what a thing to say! This machine is a serious machine, not some made-up story machine."

Bob looked crestfallen. "Sure, I know," he said.

"Does it hurt?" I asked.

"Millie said that of course Myra was scared when they first put her in there, but then she started breathing much better, and so she calmed down. But she did say she felt mashed down like a pancake on the griddle."

"Will she need to stay in the iron lung?" I asked Mom.

"Well, I guess we'll see," Mom said. "Same with the use of her legs, we just won't know for a while." She turned to Pop. "Jack, do you think that I could drive Millie out to the hospital tomorrow?"

"I guess as long as the streets don't freeze up too bad tonight," Pop agreed.

"Yes, dear," Mom murmured. She rose and kissed Pop on the part of his head that was growing just a little bit bald. She called it the tender spot. "Your flogan has fallen!" Mom said musically.

Indeed, the flogan was whirling across the floor like a little dervish escaping the chore of time. Mom plucked the part off the floor and placed it in Pop's hand.

I thought about the inner workings of Myra's lungs as being like a sprung clock piece and hoped she could be put back together at the hospital as well as Pop was reassembling our clock.

36

FANNY

IN THE MIDDLE of March we had one of the worst snowstorms I can ever remember. During the night, branches cracked and fell from the weight of the ice. We could hear the big crashes in our sleep. When we woke up and looked out the window, the snow appeared to be ten feet deep, but it turned out of course to not be quite that much. We weren't too sure we could make it to school; we weren't even sure there would *be* school. Pop was already gone when we awoke though; Mom said he had to go down early to Public Service to see what could be done for the clearing of the streetcar lines.

Mom didn't wait to find out if school was officially closed; she told us we could stay home from school anyway. I couldn't remember her ever doing this. We had tromped through more snow than a bunch of Eskimos in our lives, arriving at school with stockings that had gotten wet even through our galoshes. Now we enjoyed the big hot breakfast Mom made: bacon and eggs and biscuits, usually a treat reserved for Saturday mornings. Sue and I always drank coffee now just like Mom, so we lingered at the table with her while Bob raced up to his room to work on plans for his summer fort. Bob always looked ahead to good things.

Mom rarely got a chance to just sit with us at the table; she had so much to do every day. But this morning, after we cleared off the dishes, Mom said she would play Monopoly with us. This was a brand-new game that we had just gotten. It was actually Mom's— Pop had given it to her for her birthday. I loved the little metal figurines. Mom chose the flat iron; it seemed we could never get her too far away from her work. Sue picked the baby shoe, and I optimistically selected the thimble engraved with "for a good girl," on it, though there was debate sometimes as to whether I was the good twin. I loved the crisp feel of the paper money in my hands; I even liked the smell of it, almost like real money. The dice made a vibrant, clickety sound when they tumbled across our wooden dining room table. We drank a second pot of coffee while we played.

Sue had a secretive quality to her play, which didn't really go with the rest of her personality. Mom and I had our money organized in piles tucked beneath the board's edge, but Sue kept hers all piled up tight together, fanning the bills beneath her hands when she needed to pay a debt or buy property. In my opinion, Sue and I had very pretty hands, so much so that sometimes I thought that if I had trouble getting work in Hollywood, I could perhaps become a hand model, showing off and advertising gloves, hand cream, and nail enamel. If Sue came with me to Hollywood, four identical hands could be a real asset, it seemed to me.

We played Monopoly for three hours, until nearly lunchtime, which was the longest I'd ever seen my mother go without working. Finally, it was pretty obvious that Sue had most of the money stacked up in her pile, so much that we didn't even have to count it to know she'd won.

"Heavens, girls, we've played from breakfast almost to lunch! And it's still snowing out there."

"I wonder what Pop is doing. I doubt many of the lines are running today," Sue said.

"I wonder what Bob is doing!" Mom cried out. He had been way too quiet upstairs. We were sent up to check on him.

We found that Bob had climbed out the window and onto a tree branch outside. The window was still open and the cold wind was blowing right into his room, and so was the snow; Pop would murder him if he found out about the wasted fuel cost. We looked out the window and there was Bob, sitting on a tree limb, dressed in his pajamas, his wool bathrobe, his winter coat, his galoshes, and several wool caps. His mouth was blue with cold, but he looked happy. He was playing jacks on the tree limb, seeing how many he could keep balanced on the limb and how many ended up tumbling to the earth. The ice made some slip off and crash in seconds, but others he had kept up there for all of two hours, he said.

"You have been out in the cold for two hours?" Sue whispered furiously out the bedroom window, as if Mom could hear us from downstairs, where she was fixing soup for our lunch.

"Oh yeah," Bob said, "it's been a razz. I have eight jacks up here, and there are eight down there."

"What's keeping you on that branch?" I asked Bob. "Are you frozen to it?"

"Nah!" Bob replied. He ooched along the branch cautiously until he reached the window.

"Get a wiggle on!" I entreated.

I put out my hand, and he dropped the remaining jacks into them.

We pulled him back through the window, and took him into the bathroom, where we pounded on him until the icicles rained off of him onto the bathroom floor, and maybe beat some sense into him too.

Bob saw his blue lips in the mirror and laughed. "What will I do to make them red again?" Bob said.

"Mom's soup will do it, but if she sees you with blue lips, it's all over anyway."

Sue found a dry towel and she rested it against the radiator for a while. Then she brought the towel to Bob's lips and rubbed them like crazy for a spell, till they shone like raspberries.

Then we went down to lunch, trying to look normal.

"What did you all do?" Bob asked us.

"We bought and sold houses. Sue won ten thousand dollars!" I laughed, with the tomato soup steam heating my cheeks.

Mom passed oyster crackers and said it had been a fun morning. She never had a clue about Bob.

37

SUE

I HAD WRITTEN Myra a half dozen letters while she was at the isolation hospital, since I couldn't go and visit her. Aunt Millie said that she was doing better with each passing day, and that she hadn't needed treatment in the iron lung since her third week there. The nurses were actually pulling on her legs, a new remedy, and wrapping them in steaming blankets, and she was regaining her use of them. Oh, I was grateful. Aunt Millie said that Myra's weight was down so far that when she or Uncle Donald saw her, they had to try hard not to let the worry show in their faces. She doubted Myra would go back to school at all this season. We would have to spend all summer fattening her up and rebuilding her. Milkshakes, cookies, doughnuts. Maybe even some heavenly hash from Crown Candy Kitchen, which Myra adored. I closed my eyes and pictured Myra with golden brown chocolate on her lips and chopped nuts spilled down her dress. But for now she was still eating the runny mashed potatoes and cream gravy at the hospital. Aunt Millie said they could bring her home by the end of the week. She would probably have to wear the leather leg braces for a few months, but they hoped by the time school started in the fall she would be walking without them.

In my letters to Myra, I told her about "Woman in White," a story she liked to listen to on the radio. Karen Adams Harding was the brilliant nurse who nurtured patients and kept the doctors in good spirits, especially the handsome surgeon who was squiring her about town. I hoped that Myra had some good nurses taking care of her at the hospital, like I had.

I told Myra that when she got home I would bring her some books from school so she could keep up with her reading, since she wouldn't be going back to school for quite a while. Myra enjoyed reading as much as I did, and she was maybe the only person I could imagine lending *Winesburg, Ohio* to, it was so precious to me. Except for Morrie, but he already had a copy of course.

Morrie and I were still seeing each other, but Morrie's dad had decided to close up their shop and move it to Chicago. They would move over the summertime. Chicago seemed like the farthest reaches of Africa, as far away as it felt from me. Was I in love with Morrie? I wasn't sure entirely. But I knew I loved talking to him about books and going to the movies with him, leaning my head on his shoulder there; I loved the softness of his cheek that held a whisper of scraped stubble. We necked, of course we did, and it was pleasurable. I don't think it was quite as wild as the necking that Fanny described she'd done with Frank and that she now did with Bert, her new beau. Did I see myself marrying Morrie and spending my life with him? I guessed not, but I would miss him terribly when he left.

For the first time ever, Fanny and I would be going to the Sunrise Dance in May. This was a dance held at the Casa Loma Ballroom, where the big bands played. Everyone got to the dance at midnight, danced all night, drove to Forest Park to watch the sun rise, then went out for breakfast. I could hardly wait. We were already planning our outfits. Fanny was sewing them for us, and I was crocheting whisper-weight cotton sweaters for us to wear in the cold of the morning. Fanny's dress would be green, mine pink, but the same pattern. Morrie had given us a wonderful break on the price of some shimmery silk fabric with little nubs in it. They would be grand.

The day Myra got home from the hospital, we took over a whole meal to share with Uncle Donald and Aunt Millie and Randall. Randall was nineteen years old and had graduated from high school a year ago. He was working at the Anheuser-Busch Brewery, and he always smelled of hops, a wild yeasty smell that was overwhelming. Aunt Millie had made him put on fresh clothes after his shift so he wouldn't knock down frail Myra with his odor.

We brought beef stew and rolls, and for dessert, I had made a pineapple upside-down cake. Randall let us into the house so we could get everything ready for when Uncle Donald and Aunt Millie drove in with Myra. Fanny ironed a tablecloth, Mom put the food on to heat, and I made a little welcome home card for Myra with my new calligraphy pen. Bob and Pop and Randall threw a football around back behind the apartment building.

When my aunt and uncle and cousin drove up, I burst into tears. I guess I was so reminded of my day coming home from the hospital after scarlet fever. I thought about how Myra must be relishing the cool, early spring air and the green leaves that were starting to peek out from the snow. I thought about how good her parents' arms must have felt enveloping her, her first moments outside the hospital.

Uncle Donald carried Myra into the house.

"She can walk, of course she can!" Uncle Donald exclaimed. "But she's our princess coming home, and I didn't want her slipping on ice!"

Myra had an elaborate set of braces on her legs. They looked like a sort of spider web of leather. But Myra, as slender as she was, had some color in her cheeks and a broad smile on her face. "Hey there!" she cried out, louder than her old self. I wondered what had happened to her at the hospital. Had she lost a little of her shyness at last?

We sat down to supper almost right away, after all the hugging had subsided, and after Fanny had had a chance to do up Myra's hair in a pretty way. She even slipped a little lipstick on her. Randall helped Myra to the table. I thought I saw a little mist on Randall's eyes; he must have missed his sister more than we knew.

We prayed and thanked God that Myra's lungs were all healed and that her legs were better and, most especially, that she was back with us. We ate our delicious meal. Everyone loved my upside-down cake. Bob said you had to eat it upside down and he tried to drape himself upside down from his dining table chair until our pop cuffed him lightly on his arm and said, "Son, quit your horsing around and sit up and honor your cousin." Bob did.

38

SUE

Fanny and bob and I were gathered around the radio to listen to the report on the *Hindenburg's* landing. The German flying machine's arrival was the biggest event since the World's Fair, and none of us were going to miss it. Pop and Mom were getting their coffee fixed out in the kitchen, to join us. Mom had even made an ooey-gooey butter coffeecake, a recipe that was born in St. Louis, like we were. Some called it a cake, some a bread, but the reason we loved it was that it was swimming in sugar and butter. You had to take it out of the oven before it looked done, while it still stared up at you damply. Mom rarely let us eat dessert in the living room, but we were planning to that night, so we wouldn't miss a minute of the report.

Bob especially was fascinated by this astonishing ship made out of gas. He wanted to book a ride on one as soon as he was old enough, perhaps get a job as a crewman. Bob had on a sailor cap that we had gotten for one of our plays, and in the dusk light, I spotted a last ray of sun beaming from the white cotton and off into space, as if to unite with the travelers about to land in New Jersey. The radio broadcaster was Herbert Morrison, with WLS Chicago. Once Morrie moved to Chicago, I could at least listen to WLS and feel close to him.

Mom handed round our plates of cake, but Pop had eaten his so fast it was gone before he finished walking from the kitchen to the living room! We heard our mom's delicate sipping of her coffee, and by contrast, Pop's loud gulping, which was background to Mr. Morrison's report, words I would never forget: "The sun is striking the windows of the observation deck on the eastward side and sparkling like glittering jewels on the background of black velvet." Oh my! What a vivid and beautiful image. I saw diamonds and rubies twinkling on velvet, and it took my breath away. Bob had told us that the ship was long and the shape of a hot dog. But it was really this gigantic billowing and bobbing balloon. It held near a hundred people, but if you were to look at it, he said, it would appear as light as a feather.

We finished our cake and laid the plates on the side table in the living room. We all seemed to list toward the radio like we were waiting to disembark ourselves. We heard a crack of thunder, and Mom said, "My, I hope the lightning doesn't get it!"

Bob gave her a brow-cocked smile and shrugged. "That couldn't happen, Mom, it's the *Hindenburg*!"

But then we heard it. "It burst into flames! Get out of the way! Get out of the way!" Mr. Morrison shouted. His previously melodious voice was now gripped in panic. I grabbed Fanny's hand and nearly drove my nails through her soft palm.

"It's crashing terrible! . . . This is the worst of the worst catastrophes in the world! . . . Oh the humanity, and all the passengers screaming around here!"

Fanny and I streamed tears and so did our mother. I held on to Fanny and buried my face in her shoulder. Our sobs combined and made us shake as if the *Hindenburg* were crashing into our own home.

Bob had turned red and looked furious and betrayed. "Aw cripes, aw noooo." Bob hid his face and cried. Even our Pop got teary-eyed. It was such a shock to us all. Mom led us in a prayer for the passengers. We had never heard anything so terrible in all our lives.

39

FANNY

Sue had written some poems about the tragedy, and Bob was still moping a little and didn't want to listen to the radio as much as he did before, as if such a report might come across the airwaves again. But, "Life goes on," Pop always said, and it was true. Our thoughts turned from the *Hindenburg* to the Sunrise Dance.

Sue and I would be the prettiest girls there, I thought, because my seamstress skills had gotten better and better over the last few years, and when I was done sewing Sue's and my dresses for the dance, I knew I'd created masterpieces. Mine was a green the color of whipped cream run through with mint essence. Sue's was a pink the color of sky at dawn in the summer, with a twinge of orange illuminating it. The material was a duppioni silk that had been hard to work with because I knew I couldn't mess up a single stitch of it, if I was going to have enough. Even with the discount Morrie had given us, it had cost Pop a pretty penny. Pop was happy to buy the material though; he knew that compared to what clothes cost in stores, my fashions were very thrifty. I had worked on these dresses every day for a whole month. I had even done a bit of fancy stitch work on the bodice with a glittery gold thread. Mom was afraid with the gold it would be "too much" but even she had to admit when I finished that it was perfection.

I had given Sue a speck more room in the bustline of her dress; it pained me to admit this, but as identical as we generally were, she had a little bit more in that department. And me the one who had plans to star in movies! I wasn't too worried though; I knew that there were tricks that the wardrobe people did in that regard. And really, to wear the beautiful halter gowns that Jean Harlow wore, it could be an advantage to be a bit smaller there.

I was going to the dance with Bert Singman. He was the first boy ever to give Sue a valentine all the way back on the day she got scarlet fever! Well, Bert hadn't given the fever to her, anyway. He'd grown up into a very fine-looking boy, with blond hair the hue of a silver fox and green eyes the color of the Mississippi River. He had a grand sense of humor; he could sometimes make me laugh by just giving me a certain look. After high school, Bert planned to be a radio announcer, and with his rich voice and spontaneous humor, I didn't doubt that he would do it.

Sue was going to the dance with Morrie; they had been going out for two years now. She knew he would be leaving for Chicago in the summertime, but I don't think it had really hit her yet. Since her scarlet fever episode, she had this philosophy of taking one day at a time, something I had a hard time with, because my dreams lay ahead and made me impatient. Sue would say that I had always been impatient though, and I bore a mark on my arm that proved her correct.

Sue had crocheted the loveliest sweaters for us to wear with our new dresses, fashioning the sleeves to just the right length so that my scar would be covered. The sweaters had a lacy quality from the crochet stitch, and they were beautiful; my sweater was a deep mint color, Sue's a rich pink coral.

Finally it was the day of the dance. Right after lunch, Sue and I decided to take a nap, since the party wouldn't start till midnight, and we wanted to be fresh. It was very funny to be taking naps; we had just turned seventeen, and we had given up naps more than a decade earlier, so now we had trouble settling ourselves down for sleeping. We had taken off our clothes except for our underclothes and pulled a light cotton quilt over us. We turned in to each other, lying on our sides, and let the afternoon sunlight wash over us through the curtains. I looked at Sue, my mirror. As often as I tried to tell myself that we were entirely different girls beneath our identical exteriors, I knew that we had a deep bond, though it wasn't quite deep enough to keep me from trickery. When I had first run into Bert Singman a few months ago at the Fox Theater, he had thought I was Sue; in fact, when he asked me out, he thought that he was asking her.

I didn't let it get out of hand; I only let him think I was Sue during the movies, which, granted, with the two motion pictures, a cartoon, a short subject, and a newsreel, took up nearly four hours. I reasoned that by then it was me he really wanted to be with, anyway, so I told him I was Fanny. He was startled at first but then laughed and said, "Well, okay then. Fanny, will *you* go out with me?"

I had to come clean with Sue about this; it had really been bothering me, his being her first valentine and all. So this afternoon, I reached out my right hand and took Sue's hand in mine. I held it with the comfort I always derived from holding her hand. I said to Sue, "I have something to tell you. You might hate me, though, when I do."

Sue's eyelashes fluttered, I thought in fear of my words. Then a big smile split her face. "You mean, about how Bert thought you were me when he asked you out?"

I lay on the bed dumbfounded. I untwined my fingers from hers and put my hand to my cheek in a questioning look, as I'd seen Claudette Colbert do in the movies. "What the . . . ?"

"I've known the whole time," Sue said. "Who says identical twins can't keep secrets?" Sue laughed a luxuriant, long laugh and took my hand again. "It's okay, I won't strangle you, it would be too scary seeing the look on your face when you went, like looking in a mirror at my own ghostly self. You're lucky, huh?"

I laughed a little too; with so many feelings mixing me up, why not?

"I wouldn't have gone out with Bert anyway. I know Morrie's leaving, but he's still mine."

"You're loyal," I told Sue. I petted her hair away from her face and lay it all back on the pillow.

"Lucky for you!" Sue exclaimed.

We played bridge and drank coffee with Mom in the early evening till it was time to get dressed for the party. Luckily Bob was out of the house; he was at the movies with his friends. Our pop was helping a neighbor hang some shelves, so it was just us girls at the house. Perfect. We took our baths and put on our camisoles and tap pants. Mom had gotten a little vial of perfume as a present from our father for Christmas, and she let us have a drop for each of our shoulder blades, and then she ran her fingers lightly over the curly ends of our hair with perfume. We had fluffed out soft curls, and I wore mine parted to the right, but Sue wore sections of hair clipped up on both sides. We both wore silk stockings—our own pairs this time, no more borrowing from Mom—and shiny satin, high-heeled pumps. Mom had gotten us some fine-netted slips that gave a little extra shape to our figures, though they felt just a touch scratchy. I wore a bright red lipstick and Sue wore a darker red; we were not interested in looking identical tonight. We were ready for our beaus, and right on cue, they knocked on our front door. Pop had already met them both of course; that was the only reason he was not at the house at this moment. Morrie and Bert had both passed muster.

. . .

I hadn't danced too many times with Bert before this evening. The coat Bert wore made his shoulders look as wide as the tree in our backyard, but fortunately he felt softer. He whispered while we danced, and I couldn't make out any words specifically but it seemed to me there was a good flavor to his words.

I watched Morrie and Sue dance in the corner of the ballroom; they had been to so many dances together that they were enmeshed. Sue was a pink halo illuminating Morrie's form. My heart ached a little, watching them, knowing that Morrie would be leaving town before long.

It was about three in the morning when I found myself outside in a yard chair on Bert's lap. My pop had warned me about sitting on men's laps in a general sort of way, but now I knew a specific reason. I could feel Bert beneath me, and what I felt surprised me because it felt like I was resting on a knob of marble, and I didn't know whether to take this as an insult or a compliment. Our etiquette and hygiene class suggested the former, but Bert's smile, which was much more persuasive, communicated the latter. Tentatively, I shifted in a certain way that felt good to me, and then we kissed. Sometimes Bert's tongue felt a little rough, but I enjoyed it somehow.

40

SUE

A T A LITTLE after three, Morrie and I were getting a little sleepy, in spite of all the coffee we'd had at the dance, so we went for a walk. We held hands as we walked, and, as always, I loved the way my palm fit into Morrie's. I wondered if, after Morrie left town, I would ever feel this way again. In the dance hall, I had shed my sweater because of the heat of all those bodies swaying together, but now that we were out in the cool of the night, I took it from around my shoulders and slipped it on. Morrie put his arm around me in a way that made me feel almost scooped and lifted off the sidewalk. We didn't talk at all, and when we came along a park bench in the dark of a tree's shadows, we sat down on it and began to neck. I loved the way Morrie smelled of spicy cologne and his lips that were so red sometimes they seemed like ripe berries.

"I love you, Sue," Morrie whispered.

It was such a soft whisper I worried I had imagined his words. But the look in his eyes told me he had said them. "I love you too," I answered, and I knew it was true.

We necked till our lips ached. I felt him against me.

"Sue," Morrie begged me.

"I can't," I said back, but it sounded like a question even to me.

Even so, Morrie spread out his jacket on the grass, and I lay back on it and allowed him to move on top of me. He touched my breasts through the silk of my dress, and suddenly I was grateful that the dress buttoned in the back. Morrie ran his hands up the silk of my stockings until he got to the flesh of my thighs. His hand pressed up farther, and my hands pressed him too. We breathed and sighed and kissed. We discovered some very new things, but with our clothes mostly in place.

41

FANNY

I WAS IN trouble now. It seemed we had gone to the place where, our hygiene teacher warned, there was usually no turning around. And all this on a chair! But there was a high-pitched whistling sound from the dance hall that helped put us to rights. The band leader was signaling for a change in dance beat, and I looked to the heavens that had thrown down a crown of stars above me and winked my thanks. Bert and I straightened and smoothed our clothes down, and we stood. I headed into the dance hall for the restroom, while Bert hung behind to have a sip from a fellow's flask. I could hardly blame him, now.

When I came out of the restroom, I saw Morrie and Sue coming in from a side door. Sue's hair was so messed it made me gasp. I waved her over to me and took her into the restroom where I worked for nearly twenty minutes trying to get her hair back into some order. There were some bits of grass in among the wavy strands, which I picked out and sifted into the waste can without comment. Sue turned a little pink, she was so embarrassed even in front of me.

. . .

Those of us who were still awake drove to Forest Park to watch the sun rise. The sky was the luminescent pink color of the inside of a seashell, with streaks of gold fire. In the chill of the morning, our sweaters weren't enough, so both Sue and I wore our dates' suit jackets at our shoulders. We sat on the grass on newspapers. I enjoyed the nubby feel of the fabric, and the smell of Bert's cologne. His face was nubby by now too, with stubble outlining his face like a picture frame. I saw that Sue had fallen asleep against Morrie's chest. She breathed in and out lightly, and I saw her lipstick was nibbled away again slightly. And after our careful reapplication in the restroom!

"Rise and shine!" Bert sang out. "Breakfast!"

Sue's eyes popped open, then she hid them beneath her hand. "Did I fall asleep?" she inquired.

"Not at all, baby, not at all." Morrie laughed softly.

We all drove over to get breakfast at Parkmoor, where we drank pots and pots of coffee and ate eggs and toast. Jeff Frinkstein built a little house out of his toast, which he sprinkled with sugar, like snow. He was always doing things like this, which made him fun to have around, but perhaps not the best date, I guessed from the look on Janet Marvel's face.

The boys drove us home and kissed us good night, or good morning really. I sensed Bob peeking through the curtains at us. Once we were inside, Mom asked us questions about the evening, but Sue and I had rings under our eyes that practically extended down to our cheeks, so we told everyone we were going right to bed, and that's what we did. I cast off my clothes as fast as I could and got under the covers. Of course, Sue hung her clothes neatly, then did the same for me. Finally she got under the covers too, and we both sighed with pleasure. No bed ever felt better than one that held you after a long night awake. We were asleep before we could exchange a word.

42

SUE

I THINK MR. Sherwood Anderson would say that our romantic feelings had been heightened by Morrie's imminent departure. In one part of my mind, I knew this was why, but on the other hand, I just wanted to spend every minute with Morrie and didn't care why. He was a year older than me, and he graduated a few weeks after our Sunrise Dance. He was even valedictorian. After the ceremony, we went to a jazz club, which was my first time. The music was rousing and sad at once, and I soon decided the saxophone was my favorite instrument, and not just because I knew Morrie could play it himself.

That night Morrie put a nip of gin into my 7-Up. I hadn't had any alcohol before this, and it gave me a warm, fuzzy feeling I admit I liked. But when he offered to "flavor" my next bottle of 7-Up I declined. I was having trouble staying a "good girl," during these months, and I didn't need anything to steer me away.

After the club, we went to a doughnut shop and got doughnuts and coffee to make sure Morrie was sharp when he brought me home, in case Pop was on the porch when we pulled up. We ate them in the car and one moment we were feeding each other doughnuts and next thing you knew, we were necking and pressing into each other. Morrie asked if we could drive to Forest Park and walk around, but I said no, and Morrie drove me right home. No Pop on the porch, so we kissed in the car for a while, but I wasn't comfortable, knowing my family house was staring down at me. I told Morrie I'd see him the next day, and I ran into the house, knowing it was only one month till he and his family left St. Louis for Chicago.

I cried a little into my pillow that night. Fanny was already asleep. Her breathing made the edge of her pillowcase puff up the slightest trace with each release of breath. Her hair was falling over her shoulder and about to drift into her mouth, so I put my finger gently beneath the strand and moved it over behind her cheek and back to her pillow. She opened her eyes for less than a second, giggling a little about something sweet in her dreams. I dried my eyes against my pillowcase and went to sleep, hoping to meet her in her dreams.

Fanny and I had gotten a summer job in the soda shop at Kresge's. We took turns working; at first our boss, Mr. Binder, could never figure out who was whom, so he called us both "Fanny Sue," to cover his bases.

Sometimes we took people's orders at the counter and served them and poured coffee, and other times we helped prep the orders. I loved to make the grilled cheese sandwiches, watching the cheese ooze out the sides, and I enjoyed the burned little remnants of cheese that made comma shapes on the grill. I did not like peeling potatoes to make French fries; they purpled fast if you didn't put them in the oil right off. Fanny refused to do the fries altogether, because she was still afraid of hot oil. She didn't mind making the egg salad or chicken salad, however.

Some of the boys who came to the counter tried to flirt with me, and when I told them I was seeing a boy already, they said, "You were awfully friendly yesterday!" Fanny, of course. I told them I had an identical twin who worked on the days I didn't, and they all shook their heads like I must be some kind of swell storyteller.

Kresge's was just a couple blocks from Morrie's dad's store, so on my breaks I would try to meet him there or he'd come over and join me for lunch. Morrie and his dad were now spending nearly every day packing fabric for the move to Chicago. Fanny spent her first paycheck on fabric there, since prices were reduced for going out of business.

Our boss was quick to point out that our work habits were different, and that's how he finally figured out which twin was which and knew our names. I was good at refilling all the metal prep containers, so there was always clean lettuce ready for sandwiches, ketchup to fill paper cups, cheese presliced, and so on. I kept the counters clean with soapy bleach-water solution, and liked shining up all the equipment too. On the other hand, Fanny had a bad habit of flirting with the boys to the point that the Cola glasses overfilled, and there was a sticky trail following her behind the counter. One time she forgot to clamp the milkshake cannister onto the spoke, and she had a rain shower of milkshake. She joked that all the movie stars took milk baths, why not her? She forgot to wipe down the counter and tables till the customers complained about them. And she wouldn't put her hair back into the required hairnet because it was "unattractive."

When Fanny came home with the news that she'd been fired after only two weeks' work at Kresge's, Pop thought she was a bit too nonchalant about it. He took her out back for a stern lecture about responsibility. He didn't spank us anymore, but his lectures could sting pretty hard too. Meanwhile, I got a phone call from Mr. Binder, offering me the extra hours at the counter. I took them; it would mean less reading time for me, but the money would be good.

Anyway, it was a good thing Fanny had purchased all that discounted fabric from Morrie's shop, because she sewed up a couple of dresses and took them in to show an alterations lady in the bridal department at Famous Barr department store. They hired her on the spot to do hems and to nip in waists that nervous brides required and even to stitch on extra lacework and seed pearls. Now Fanny had a job she was really good at, free of the distractions of boys.

At twelve, Bob was old enough for the job of passing out circulars for the Fox Theater this summer; they still gave the kids free movie passes in exchange for this job, and Bob planned to see as many monster movies as possible over the summer. He often stopped in for a soda or a milkshake before or after the movies. One day he came by on my break, so I made him a chocolate milkshake with extra chocolate syrup. I thought he was a little too thin. Times were so much better, as Roosevelt said, but we were making up for some lean years still. Mr. Binder squirted a big dollop of whipped cream on Bob's milkshake for me; he was as fond of me as he'd been perturbed by Fanny. Bob tapped his foot on the footrest of the counter till it rang with noise; I whapped him lightly on his thigh. "Please cut it out, mister!" I whispered loudly. Boys were awfully strange at that age. He was taller every time I saw him, taller even from breakfast to supper, and full of nervous energy. Pop said they could run a streetcar on the commotion Bob kicked up, without it needing any other energy source. Bob had just seen *A Day at the Races,* with the Marx Brothers, whom he adored. In fact, to effect silence in our house, we only had to say to Bob, "Be Harpo," and Bob would take on the angelic, light-suffused affect of Harpo, quiet except for the beep-horn (Bob got a hold of one like that at a certain point and Pop quickly relieved him of it). Bob even had Harpo's curls, though Bob's were not a platinum blond, but rather a coffee-brown crown.

"Harpo is the one who knows everything," Bob told me. "People think he's simple, but it's just the opposite, don't you see?"

"So why doesn't he talk?"

"Talking's too obvious," Bob said. With his thumbnail he ran a little design down the frosty side of the chilled glass. "If Harpo spoke, he could get them all out of the jams they're in, so there wouldn't be anything to watch."

"I see." I drank my coffee and looked at the big clock on the wall. I had my monthly and that made my legs ache a little, since I was on them most of the day. In five minutes I would be back on duty. I kissed Bob lightly on his curly hair. "You're a little more like Groucho, though, aren't you, crazy boy?"

"Yeah." He raised his eyebrows and held a French fry like it was the trademark cigar. Then he chomped it down in one bite. "Well, I better go. Thanks for the shake, and for sharing your fries, Sis."

The night before Morrie left St. Louis forever, we decided to cancel the plans we'd had with Fanny and Bert, to spend our time alone instead. Fanny and Bert didn't seem too disappointed. We chose to go and sit for a while at the Jewel Box, which was a glass-enclosed, cathedral-shaped greenhouse in Forest Park. The Public Service Company had built it just the year before, and it was only my second time there. We just walked around the grounds staring at the pink and yellow and red blooms aflame in the darkening sun. Morrie softly sang to me from "The Way You Look Tonight."

"You look pretty swell yourself," I whispered. And I memorized his look tonight, his fine corn silk hair combed but still hectic looking, his gray-blue eyes that smoldered now, his square shoulders underneath his shirt that was both crisp with starch and smooth, soft, the way cotton could be both at once.

He kissed me and I tasted tears, though I wasn't sure whose. "Sue, why don't you marry me?" Morrie asked.

I stumbled backward a little. I couldn't speak.

"I don't think I can be without you," Morrie begged.

"Oh honey," I told him. I don't think I had ever called him honey before this. "I haven't finished school yet even! And how could I go to Chicago, I don't know how—"

"Don't you love me, Sue?"

"I love you, but I'm too young to get married, Morrie."

He held me at my waist and shook me very slightly. "I don't want to be without you."

"I don't either, honey, but how could I leave my family, how could I leave Fanny and school and my job?"

"I know, I haven't thought anything through," Morrie said. He sat down suddenly on the grass like a disappointed child and buried his face in his hands.

I draped myself over his back and kissed his neck. Later we got up and walked to the car without talking.

We agreed to write to each other and to see how we felt as the year went by. I told him that Fanny expected me to go to teacher's school and then to Hollywood with her. She would act in the movies, and if it took her a while to break in, I would be able to teach and therefore keep us both fed and clothed. Also, if there were any good parts for twins, we could both act, she said; I didn't argue this, but I had no intention of trying to be in movies. Anyway, this was Fanny's plan, Morrie said, and he tried to convince me that it didn't have to be my plan. But he had never been an identical twin of Fanny, so what did he know?

Morrie and I embraced and kissed in his car till my father flipped the light on and off in the living room. Since Pop was against wasting electricity, I knew he meant business. I couldn't get over that this might be the last time I ever saw Morrie. I simultaneously cried and tried not to cry, which meant that I choked on my tears and ended up with hiccups! I kissed Morrie once more, between hiccups, and then fled to the house.

Mom had already gone up to bed, and Pop didn't know what to make of my blurred face and my hiccupping. He seemed torn between lecturing me and comforting me, but the latter won. He held me in his arms and let me cry my heart out. My hiccups shook us both so hard that he dropped an unlit cigar he had been holding and no doubt hiding from my mother. Finally, when neither the crying nor the hiccups seemed close to abating, Pop gently steered me down the hall and to the kitchen, where he filled a glass of water for me and told me to drink down ten sips fast. I did it, and the hiccups stopped for a minute, and then they got louder. Pop took me out back, and we sat on the back stoop with me shuddering against Pop and him petting my back. Finally, my exhaustion beat back the hiccups, and I kissed Pop and went upstairs to put on my nightgown and crawl into bed. Fanny was still out with Bert, so now Pop had a new vigil to wait out. But, at least he had a cigar to pass the time.

I realized that Pop and I had not even talked about Morrie and me, or about anything, really. In point of fact, I was all talked out anyway. I pulled the quilt up over me even though it was hot outside. It was a comfort quilt, at least that's what my Grandma Logan had always called it. Its furrows of stitches made a small nest for my chin, and I fell asleep, with the sound of Morrie's voice still tickling my ear.

43

FANNY

Lucky for me I was fired from that dreadful counter girl job at Kresge's; I was much more suited to this job at Famous Barr in the bridal department. It was supposed to be only a summer job, but they liked me so well they kept me on, to work after school once a week and also on Saturday mornings. I was very happy working in the lush surroundings of the bridal parlor, amid the fine Italian silks and cottons, Irish lace, tiny buttons made of real bone, buttons so tiny they could fit beneath your fingernail. I loved meeting the brides too, and I often gave them free bonus advice about hair and makeup, seeing as how I had studied up on this for Hollywood.

One of the Famous Barr clients, a bride's mother, planted a seed in my mind. She suggested that when I got to Hollywood, if Louis B. Mayer didn't snatch me up instantly like he certainly should, I might consider trying for a job in the costuming department. Her thinking was that this way I would be able to support myself, and still be around actors and actresses all the time. I pictured myself measuring Clark Gable's arms and nearly gave myself a fit!

While this was going on, Sue and I were also beginning our senior year of high school. Sue was moping around quite a bit about Morrie, from whom she got letters about twice a week. I told her that it wasn't good to be tied to one boy at our age, but she said I didn't understand, and, I guess, in truth, I didn't. Morrie was a very sweet boy, but he was gone, and I believed nothing should spoil our final year of high school, especially a boy who was living all the way up in Chicago!

Sue and I were taking English classes from the same teacher, but at different times. Miss James never mixed us up; from the start of the semester, she seemed to know easily how to tell us apart. I was excited because we were reading Shakespeare aloud in this class. Naturally, I always wanted the lead female part, and further, I always wished I could perform it in front of the class like a real play. Usually we just sat and read from our chairs though, and of course Miss James had to spread the good parts around a little to be fair, though she told me privately after class that I had the makings of an excellent actress.

When we got to the third play, *Romeo and Juliet,* I was reminded of the time years ago when Randall and I had done part of the play for our neighborhood show. Now I shuddered to think of my childish interpretation of Juliet. This time around, I was able to draw on Sue's grief at Morrie's leaving for the role. Juliet had become more than just a character to me. Joel Mironi, who was playing Romeo, was perfect for the part. He was not hard to look at either, with his angular jaw and dark purple eyes. I found him easy to love, during English class hours, anyway.

I stayed after class to ask Miss James's advice about my reading of Juliet.

"Fanny," Miss James said. "Do you really want to know how you can *manifest* Mr. Shakespeare's Juliet?"

Manifest? This was making me a little scared. Did she mean something ghostly here, like transmitting her spirit? "Hear the words," Miss

James said. "Really listen to them, when you say them, when Joel says them."

"I hear the words," I said before I had a chance to think what she might mean. "Of course I do."

"In one way you do," Miss James said. She sat on the edge of her desk and crossed her legs.

Miss James had pretty legs, I saw, and the way she sat on the edge of the desk made her seem like a regular person, not a teacher. Her eyes were almond-shaped and even the irises were almond-colored. She wore her hair back in a tight chignon, which made me wonder what she looked like with her hair down and flowing. It was rare to meet a teacher I could imagine existing outside of school, but I realized I had begun to see Miss James as a real woman.

"You read the words beautifully," she said. "You articulate them well and hit the rhythms in the lines perfectly. This is no small thing!" Miss James looked at me intently. "But still my dear, I don't think you are really listening to the words."

"I know the lines, Miss James." I felt my cheeks color a bit at the suggestion that I might not know my Shakespeare. "I understand what is happening. I'm not as smart as Sue, but I know what the story is."

"Oh yes, I know you understand the story. But you don't savor the words, you don't taste them."

Now I thought she was getting a little strange, not to mention a little pushy. I gathered my books up and told her that I had to get to my next class. She had some nerve, I thought.

Later, Sue told me that Miss James was the best teacher she'd ever had. She'd stayed after class to talk to Miss James too.

"What did you talk about?"

We were taking shirts and chemises off the clothesline, one of our after-school chores. There was a loud plunking as we threw the clothespins into an empty pickle jar. Sue folded the clothes carefully even though I pointed out to her that we would still have to iron them later; I simply tossed the clothes into the basket.

"So, did you talk about me?" I asked, as I batted a wispy-winged bug away from my face.

Sue disappeared behind a shirt of Bob's, and when her face emerged her countenance was quarrelling between a grimace and laughter. "We didn't talk about you! Not everything is about you!" Sue said. Her laughter won out even though she tried to smother it beneath Bob's shirt.

"Well, hey, I know that," I answered. I whipped clothes into the basket so fast that I had to kick the basket along the earth to keep up with me. "It's just that she told me that I wasn't hearing the words when I read Shakespeare."

"The words when Joel says them or when you do?"

I stopped and blew a butterfly off the elbow of one of Pop's Public Service Company emblems on his uniform shirt. "Oh cripes, I don't know for sure," I admitted.

"Talk to her again," Sue said. "She knows a lot about things." We lifted the basket up and swung it between us as we walked to the house. "It's getting chilly out," Sue observed.

It was true each year that St. Louis turned from summer to fall like a faucet suddenly snatched on to full stream. The leaves that had softly given under our feet the day before, it seemed, now crunched a fall sound. I could listen, see, I really could.

On the next class day, I decided I would get to school early so I could speak with Miss James right away. I would be reading the balcony scene in class with Joel, and even though we weren't performing on stage, I wanted to improve my technique.

Sue and I ate our breakfast of cinnamon toast while we walked to school. As was always the case, our strides fell right in with each other. Other kids had always teased us about it, "Here come the Same Step Twins, right left, right left." We were good-natured about it, since it was as natural as breathing for us.

When we got to school, Sue told me she was glad that I was keeping an open mind with Miss James, but the truth was it was not about Miss James, it was just that I would do anything in my power to become a better actress. I told Sue this, and she said, "I know it. It makes me proud to be your twin, Fanny-o-mine."

I smiled. That was something she hadn't said to me since we were smaller. I waved goodbye to her as she headed to the library down the hall.

Miss James came into the room wearing a crisp, chocolate-brown balmacaan coat that smelled like smoke and leaves. "Fanny, wonderful to see you," she said. She set down the cup and saucer she'd been carrying from the faculty lounge. "You don't mind if I drink my coffee while we talk, do you?"

"Not at all." I sat down in the desk I sat in for class, by habit. I turned my palms up and asked her, "How? How do I hear the words?"

Miss James sat in her chair and took a small sip of her coffee. I saw a scarlet, heart-shaped imprint of her lipstick on the edge of her cup. "The words mean things, but they also have their own shape and height and depth and taste. Some words have *heft* like an apple or a slab of wood, and others have an eerie lightness and seem to practically float away as you utter them. Words bounce, throb, even echo."

I sat down, stunned. "They do, don't they?" I said softly. I realized this was one reason I loved to perform. I loved how the words themselves had different rhythms, how some were icy smooth in my mouth like a milkshake, others were crisp like the hot cinnamon toast Sue and I had crunched on that morning.

"Do you ever notice the way an actor says a word that seems like a word they particularly savor? It doesn't even have to be a pretty word. My boyfriend loves the word 'cantaloupe.' Who knows why? But when he says the word, you just can't wait to eat some!"

It was strangely personal to think of her boyfriend relishing cantaloupe. I smiled at Miss James and watched her sip her coffee.

"I like the phrase, 'hot cup of coffee.' " I said. "Not just for what it is, though I do like coffee, but you can hear the sound of the cup clanking against the saucer, and you can feel the sharp feeling coffee gives you in the crisp sound of the word cup."

"Yes, that's just it," Miss James said. "So it's about bringing the words alive, infusing them with what they do in the world."

"And that's what makes an actor great?" I asked. I was on the edge of my seat, literally, since I wanted this knowledge, I realized, as much as I wanted pretty clothes and jewels and the chance to kiss Clark Gable.

"And then there's something else," Miss James continued. "You also have to listen as closely to the words that Romeo, in this case, Joel, says. You can tell in an actor's eyes when he is hearing the other actor's words. Think about Myrna Loy. Think about how her eyes swim with the words William Powell speaks to her. Even in *The Thin Man*, when they're bantering back and forth and swilling martinis and tossing off double entendre—"

"What's double entendre?"

"It's sexy talk disguised in humor," Miss James said.

While she said the word "sexy" she straightened up the papers on her desk and started to ready herself for the day.

"Even during that kind of talk, she is hearing all the words, and making them better, even the ones that seem to flutter by. Today, when you read with Joel, listen to him, look into his eyes, and let the words become bigger than the two of you and let it show in your eyes. If Joel is awake, he'll respond in kind."

Boys responded to me, this I knew!

. . .

At first it seemed really odd to me, taking in Romeo's words fully, instead of waiting till Joel stopped speaking so I could speak. I found out many things. What Romeo had to say was as compelling as what I—Juliet—had to say. And, when I listened intently to the words, so did Joel. It was infectious, evidently. When we finished our scene, the whole class applauded. Miss James seemed to be offering me a shy, secret smile. She was a very smart woman, I had to agree with Sue.

44

S U E

MYRA HAD STARTED attending our high school that fall. She was just out of leg braces, and still walked with a pronounced limp. There were a number of students in wheelchairs and on crutches or with braces in our school though, so her limp didn't stand out too terribly. Myra and I usually ate lunch together, and I tried to set her at ease a little. She was shy, but not somehow as shy as she'd been before her illness, which was a mystery to many but not to me. I had come out of my shell at the isolation hospital too, out of necessity.

Fanny and I had talked Myra into getting her hair cut from the waist-length-braid style she had worn to shoulder length, so she could curl it and fluff it out, as was the style. She did have beautiful clothes to wear, since Aunt Millie was such a wonderful seamstress: crisp cream blouses, long tweed skirts that deemphasized her limp.

It was a problem for Myra that so much of our social life revolved around dancing and roller-skating, neither of which Myra could do. She could only hope to meet a boy so crazy about movies that that's all he wanted to do.

As much as I thought about how to help Myra attract a boyfriend,

I didn't want one myself. I corresponded with Morrie all the time, two letters a week, and I still considered myself his girl. Chicago seemed as far away as China, but I had dreams that we could get together, in the end. Fanny was peeved that she couldn't double-date with me anymore, but I'd lived with Fanny's peevishness all my life, and I sometimes even thought I'd miss it were it to suddenly evaporate.

I worked at Kresge's twice a week after school and on Saturdays. Fanny and I were building up quite a nest egg for our trip to Hollywood, but I still wasn't sure it was where I wanted to go. My plan was to go to teacher's college right out of high school; Fanny hoped to work at the Muny those summers, and do more seamstress work for Famous Barr the rest of the time. In two years, Fanny would have more acting and costuming experience, and I would have a teaching certificate. But after that, did I want to go to California with Fanny or to Chicago to be with Morrie? It was so strange to conceive of living without Fanny that I usually didn't consider it. Anyway, if Morrie and I were meant to be together, couldn't he come to California?

My boss had me working Saturday evenings at Kresge's because I didn't go out on dates; I was the only living, breathing seventeen-year-old he knew who didn't go out on Saturday nights. On the Saturday before Halloween, some kid spilled candy corn down by his feet, after which he was whisked off by his angry mom, leaving me to clean up the mess. The corn was stuck to the rung of the counter footrest, and it was stuck to the floor, too, thanks to the Coca-Cola this same kid had spilled. I was down on my hands and knees unsticking the kernels, when Myra came into the shop with Aunt Millie. They had just seen the twilight show of *Topper*, and came in to have a milkshake before Uncle Donald picked them up.

"Sue, my heavens, your dress will be ruined," Aunt Millie said.

I stood up to show her I had on my Kresge's uniform; I would never have done this work in any dress of mine.

"Oh good!" Aunt Millie said, then she sat down at a small table nearby.

"Do you need some help?" Myra asked.

"Heavens no, no need for that. They're paying me the big dollars for this." I chuckled and rose with the cluster of sticky corn in one hand and my wet rag in another, while Myra sat down next to her mother.

"What can I get youz two?" I asked.

"We're both having vanilla milkshakes," Aunt Millie said, pulling off her coat. Uncle Donald had finally been able to afford to buy Aunt Millie a new coat. It was a lovely violet, exactly the color of lilacs. I admired it, then I helped Myra pull off her blue wool coat, which had been her mom's, but was expertly made down for her.

"I personally believe a milkshake is not a milkshake without chocolate, but . . . the customer is always right!" I exclaimed. "Especially when they're family."

"Oh, we saw Fanny going to the next show after ours. She was with that new boy, what's his name?"

"Horace Munroe!" I had to holler a bit because the milkshake machine was roaring. I left my hand on the cannisters because I loved the vibration, especially when the metal got slightly warm in spite of the freeziness inside them.

"Oh? He looked nice, but what was wrong with Bert?" Aunt Millie asked.

"Nothing was," Myra said softly. I only heard her because I'd released the cannisters from the machine. I turned to look at her, and I saw a blush coloring her cheeks like someone had blown cinnamon powder across them. I realized for the first time that Myra had had a crush on Bert. Now I remembered that he had been awfully sweet to her whenever he'd seen her over the summer.

"Fanny just likes to sort of try on different boys like we might like to try on dresses," I told Myra.

Myra's bad leg jerked a little bit under the table. It did this of its own accord sometimes. She put her hand on it to still it, and said, "You found the right one first thing, didn't you?"

"That's for sure." I got a little teary-eyed for a moment, thinking of Morrie. I wiped my eyes with a napkin, poured their milkshakes, and set the glasses down in front of them.

Then one of my regular customers, Mr. Loomis, walked in. He was a widower who worked in the neighborhood, so he often came here for his dinner.

"Grilled cheese, mashed till it hollers," he ordered. He smiled; he said this every time but always found it humorous. "And hot coffee, Sue."

"As opposed to the cold coffee I serve the others, Mr. Loomis?" I teased back.

"Fanny will love *Topper*!" Aunt Millie said.

"Is it good?" I asked. I put the frosty creamer by Mr. Loomis's coffee cup.

"Oh, so funny!" Aunt Millie exclaimed, her hands up in the air.

"Even though it's about ghosts?" Mr. Loomis asked. He turned in his seat and saluted Myra and Aunt Millie with his coffee cup.

"Oh the ghosts were hilarious. Weren't they Myra?"

"Cary Grant was a caution," Myra agreed.

I took the metal spatula and squashed Mr. Loomis's grilled cheese sandwich to within an inch of its life. Cheese spiraled out the sides, making it look like the aura that surrounded the sun, at least from the pictures we saw in science class.

After I had given Mr. Loomis his dinner, I reached up to a high

shelf above the milkshake machine to restock glasses. Just as I extended my right arm, a hot, sharp pain radiated from my fingertips
all the way down to my toes. "Yow!" I hollered out.

"What's wrong, Sue?" Aunt Millie cried.

I heard Mr. Loomis scramble behind the counter, and the last
thing I remember is that Mr. Loomis caught me in his arms as I fell
into a dead faint.

45

FANNY

CARY GRANT WAS my current favorite movie star, and I had been looking forward to *Topper* all week. The movie theater was full tonight, and there was a buzz of laughter building even as the movie began. Though this was only our second date, I liked Horace rather a lot, and we were already holding hands, our fingers slick with butter and scratchy with salt. I told Horace I liked Cary Grant because he was debonair but had no fear of being ridiculous as well. Who would have thought a ghost could be so appealing, I thought to myself.

Horace had a deep laugh that sounded like thunder when it is just fooling around before a storm, hearty enough to make the popcorn box shake. It was only this year that I finally had been able to eat popcorn again. I could see now that it wasn't the popcorn that had been at fault in my accident, but my own impatience, which had injured me in a variety of ways over the years.

As I reflected on popcorn, not to mention how well cut Cary Grant's suit was, I saw at the very edge of the movie screen a ribbon of fire. I blinked my eyes, sure it was some sort of trick, something in the movie itself, but no! There was a murmuring in the audience that got louder as it made its way up the aisles.

"Fire!" someone down front screamed, which meant that in one simultaneous motion, the whole audience got to their feet and turned to run from the theater, Horace and me included. We were in the middle of the ocean of people trying to move out, and right away we were all stuck. Everyone kept turning toward the exit door and then looking back to the screen hoping, like I had, that it was all a big mistake, but now a flame really was looping out of the screen, and it had lit up a stage curtain on the side and was licking onto the wooden floor.

"Horace!" I screamed. There was so much noise in the theater, screaming was the only way to communicate. His face was drained of color, but his arms were strong. He held me and tried to guide me in the slow, torturous movement of people down our row of seats. We heard the theater manager and ushers shouting for people to stay calm, but this seemed only to increase the hysteria. The flames had begun to close in on the front row of the theater, but mercifully no one was still down there. The movie was still running, and I gasped to see Cary Grant engulfed in flames, which ate away at his beautifully chiseled chin and features, up to his dark cushiony-looking crown of hair. We finally reached the end of our row and entered the aisle.

People were pushing with all their might, and I came close to losing my grip on Horace's hand, but I roped my hand around his waist and grabbed onto his belt loop. "We're going to make it," I heard him say in my ear. Then we were swept up the aisle by the tide of people. We didn't even have to move our feet. One man had a child clinging tightly to his torso. A pregnant woman cried out, "Please don't crush my baby." As we neared the exit door, I tripped over a very large man's boot. I was only down for what was probably a few seconds—long enough to feel a few shoe heels gouge at me— before Horace snatched me up and tossed me over his shoulder, carry-

ing me out to the lobby and then out of the theater into the fresh
night air.

Next thing I knew, I woke up in a hospital bed. Sue and Mom
and Pop and Bob were in the room looking down at me.

"There's our girl!" Mom said.

"How do you feel, honey?" Pop asked.

"What happened?" I asked. I didn't remember, but I felt that my
body was sore all over. It even hurt to use my mouth to talk.

"There was a fire at the movies!" Bob shouted.

"You got trampled a little bit coming out of the theater," Sue told
me. She took my hand very gently and held it.

"Trampled a little bit" seemed like a contradiction in terms. But
when I looked down at my body, I didn't see my legs or arms set in
any casts, though when I took a deep breath, there was a stabbing in
my chest. I saw I was wrapped around in bandages there.

"Did I break my lungs?" I asked. I guess I knew from science class
this wasn't exactly possible, but . . .

"You cracked a couple of ribs," Pop said, "so they taped you up,
but you'll be good as new."

"The rest of it is bruises, a lot of them. You're as purple as a
cluster of grapes," Mom said.

I looked at my arms and saw that they did look purple and blue.
I was glad my legs were covered by a blanket; I couldn't stand to see
them because they were one of my best features, or at least they had
been.

"Everything will heal up, honey, it will just take some time," Mom
said.

"Ooh!" Bob said, as he examined the colors of my arm. He was
in awe and I would guess even envied the kaleidoscope of colors on
my arm.

"Where's Horace?" I asked.

"He stayed with you till we got here, but then he thought he'd better get home and let his folks know he was okay. He'll see you tomorrow, honey."

"He didn't get hurt?" I asked.

"No, he's a little bruised up, but he's okay. You'll never guess who else got a little banged up tonight." Mom glanced over at Sue.

"What happened to you?" I asked.

"I was at Kresge's working, and I had a sharp pain in my arm and down my side and then I fainted on the floor. I woke up and Aunt Millie and Myra, who had come in for some milkshakes, were pressing cold cloths onto me. Mr. Loomis had carried me out from behind the counter and set me on Aunt Millie's and Myra's coats."

"Here's the strange thing, Fanny," Bob said. "It's like out of Buck Rogers or something!"

"What?" My arms and legs were throbbing.

"We think it happened at exactly the same moment you were being trampled at the movies," Mom said.

"It's another great twin story!" I felt nearly jubilant. "We should call the papers." I was always ready for a little publicity.

"Now, now," Pop said. "Do you want to be photographed looking all mottled and such?"

Pop sure knew how to appeal to my good sense. "No, I guess not."

I felt sleepy then; there was a medicine the nurse had given me to make me sleep. All my family kissed me on the only spot of me that didn't hurt—over my left eyebrow—and they left me to sleep in the hospital.

SUE

FOR OUR EIGHTEENTH birthday, we had a small backyard picnic with a few of our friends over. Mom and Aunt Millie had made us dozens of tea sandwiches—egg salad, minced ham, and chopped olive spread—and we had lemonade and coffee, too. A few of the boys tried to bring in bottles of beer, but Pop intercepted the bottles before they entered our yard; he told our friends he'd keep the beer someplace safe.

After we ate, we set up some card tables and the girls played bridge, and some of the fellows started games of poker. Randall taught Bob how to play; he had an extra soft spot for Bob since the eye injury (which left only a whisper of a scar on Bob's eyelid) and was determined to make it up to him at every turn.

Myra was excellent at bridge. She was my partner. We played against Fanny and a girl named Louise who was new at our high school last fall; she had acted in some school plays with Fanny. Myra and I won the first hand easily, and our victory made us thirsty.

I took a pitcher into the house to get some ice water, and Tommy Grayson followed me into the kitchen. We were the only ones in the room, though I could hear my parents and aunt and uncle in the living room talking and laughing.

"Need some help?" Tommy asked.

He lifted the ice pick and began chipping some pieces off the big cake of ice before I could say anything. I rinsed the stickiness of lemonade out of the big green glass pitcher. "Thanks!" I told him.

"Sue, could I take you to the prom?" Tommy asked suddenly. His icy palm touched my bare forearm, making me jump a bit.

I was stunned. Tommy was a good-looking, smart fellow. And with him so close by I was overcome by his pleasant, spicy scent. I had always liked him quite a bit, but I was still startled to hear myself say, "Let me think about it."

As it was turning to dusk and we had decided to give up on cards, Mom brought out a large square cake, a white one with pink frosting. In red frosting, it said, "To Fanny and Sue with love from us all." No wonder she had needed such a big cake, not just to feed us all, but for a nine-word message! Bob had decorated the cake with eighteen gumdrops on the edges, since there was no room for candles on top. He plunked the nineteenth, a red one (to grow on), into the *o* of "to."

We ate cake and then opened presents. We would open our family gifts later, but from our friends we got bottles of honeysuckle cologne, linen hankies, a few books (for me) and a few movie magazines (for Fanny). The last gift I opened was one that Morrie had mailed to me. My family had hidden it from me till this day. It was a beautiful chiffon scarf of palest green, with an enamel pin in the shape of a pansy, violet-colored with bright green leaves, attached to the knot of the scarf. I smiled and willed myself not to tear up. I avoided Tommy's eyes the rest of the evening.

· · ·

I had a lot of thinking to do in the days that followed. I still got weekly letters from Morrie, but now that our last year of high school was drawing to an end, I wasn't sure what I wanted to do about us. I had received several invitations to the prom, and I had been fending off invitations to dances and roller-skating parties all through the school year. But was a girl supposed to give up her very last school event, one this big? Fanny, of course, said no indeed. I had kept the candle burning for Morrie for a long time, but I hadn't seen him since last summer. He had told me he would try to take the train down for a visit over the holidays last year, but that hadn't worked out, and he couldn't come for the prom either. His father's new store needed constant attention. How was I supposed to know if I was even still in love with him? I knew I loved his letters and our memories, but if a real live breathing boy here in St. Louis wanted to escort me to the prom, did I have to say no?

I went to see Miss James, our English teacher, to talk to her about it. Fanny and I had walked to school early together; she was going in to run lines with another girl for a skit for the final school program. The weather was beautiful that May, my favorite time of the year. The mornings were cool, and our feet were magnets for dew if we cut across the grass anywhere, which Fanny always insisted we do. Our cotton sweaters were buttoned to our chins in the morning, but by lunchtime they would be tied loosely about our shoulders.

Miss James was sitting behind such a high stack of books that at first I didn't see her. But there she was, working on a text inventory sheet.

"Sue!" she exclaimed. She never got the two of us mixed up. "Walk me down to the teachers' lounge, and let's get some coffee."

We returned to her classroom a few minutes later with two cups of coffee and a couple of cake doughnuts Miss James had wrapped in a napkin for us as well.

"What do you want to talk about?" Miss James asked. She held her doughnut over her desk blotter and took a big bite.

"Well, it's about Morrie, my old boyfriend. He moved to Chicago last summer, and I have been trying to stay true to him."

"Ah, I see." Miss James took a big sip of coffee and sighed with pleasure. "I love coffee so much I fear someday there will be a Prohibition movement for coffee."

I sipped my own cup. "I don't think President Roosevelt would go for that! But anyway, several boys have asked me to the prom, and I wonder, do you think I should go? I hate to miss my prom, and Morrie can't come down for it. The last boy who asked me was Tommy Grayson, and, well, I told him maybe."

"Oh honey, yes, you have to go to your prom. You deserve that, no doubt about it. I think that even Morrie would understand, don't you?"

"He's a very understanding person. But, what if . . . well, what if I end up liking Tommy?"

"Eat your doughnut!" Miss James told me. "You *should* like the boy who takes you to the prom, Sue."

I swallowed a bite of doughnut and thought carefully about my next words. "I'm afraid I will like him too much. I'm afraid maybe I already do."

"You aren't engaged to Morrie, are you?"

"No, though he did ask me last summer. We were more . . . promised to each other."

"I think your feelings for Morrie were real and they were strong enough to carry you this far, to let you forgo some of the fun your sister Fanny has been having. You could have been double-dating with her; you could have been dancing with a dozen boys since last summer, as I imagine Fanny has."

"Yes, at least that many, in Fanny's case," I said, as I drained my coffee cup.

"But how can you know for sure you want to spend your life with Morrie when you're only seventeen?"

"Just turned eighteen."

"Congratulations! Go to the prom, have a good time. See how you feel when you're out with another boy."

"Maybe you're right. I know Morrie thinks I might move to Chicago. But if I go there and marry him, I'll never get to go to teacher's college. And I think that's what I really want to do."

"So that's the real question, isn't it, Sue? You would make a wonderful teacher, you know."

"Yes. And I could teach anywhere, couldn't I? Fanny wants me to go to Hollywood with her. She says she'll wait for me the two years while I go to teacher's college, and then we can go."

"You'd have to take a few courses in California to get your credentials for that state, but you could do it, no doubt about it. Do you want to leave St. Louis and go to California, or is Fanny pushing you into it?"

Then the early bell rang and some students came into the classroom. "We can talk about this more tomorrow if you like," Miss James whispered.

I stacked up our coffee cups, just like the waitress I was, bid her goodbye, and took the cups back to the teachers' lounge.

The lounge had a very familiar look to me. I could already see myself sitting on the gold-flecked green couch grading a big stack of compositions, drinking too much coffee, like Miss James did, bantering with my fellow teachers as they arrived with their own stacks of papers or their waxed-paper-wrapped sandwiches or their cigarettes to squeeze in between classes. I knew this was what I wanted. And I realized that Tommy had been an accessory to the real decision that I needed to make.

I spent many hours composing a letter to Morrie. I wrote that I cared for him and I always would, but that I had applied for admission to Harris Teacher's College here in St. Louis and that I wanted very much to get my certificate and then to teach. I also told him that I would be going to the prom with Tommy Grayson. Fanny, who had no problem at all dating two or three boys at a time, had advised me against this, but I had decided I wanted to be honest about everything.

I didn't hear from Morrie before the prom, and I felt funny going without his blessing, but I guess a blessing was a crazy thing to expect or even to desire, in this situation.

47

FANNY

WE COULDN'T WAIT for the prom. I was able to get beautiful, sweeping gowns for Sue and me at Famous Barr at a very deep discount, and since I could alter them myself, it was cheaper than if I'd sewn them from the start. My dress was a periwinkle organdy and Sue's was a cream-colored taffeta. With her Kresge's discount, Sue got us eye pencils, rouge, lipstick, and hair clips—all to match our gowns—and we were ready to go!

I went with Horace; he and I had dated off and on since the fire incident, though not exclusively. The fire memory drew us together in one way: I would always be grateful that he'd picked me up from the floor as fast as he had; another few seconds, and the stampede would have broken more than a couple of my ribs. Horace wanted to talk about the fire more than I did, however. He had been injured less than I had, though the psychological effects had stayed with him more. He and I and a few other kids from our high school who had been at the theater that night had gotten together to talk about it a few times. But for me, the minute the bruises faded away, I wanted to forget the whole thing.

I was back at the picture shows just a couple of weeks after the accident. Of course, nothing would have kept me away from movies, though that particular theater was still closed for repairs. When I went to movies in the few months after the fire, I had developed a habit of examining the edges of the screen. *Bringing Up Baby* was worth the slight anxiety I felt in the theater. The clothes were exquisite, including the sheer negligee wrap that Cary Grant wore when his regular clothes weren't available to him. I laughed so hard my earrings jumped off my ears. I only hoped that Cary wouldn't be too old for me when I was ready to act in the movies. Though, even with a twinge of gray at his temples, I felt sure he would still be the most handsome thing going.

That was the reason I had needed to date others besides Horace, though. He would not go to the movies with me after that time, not ever! A girl couldn't go to the movies by herself, could she?

But I was glad Horace was my date for the prom, and I was even happier that Sue would be going. She had been staying home way too much, in my opinion, because of Morrie. He was a swell fellow, but he was hundreds and hundreds of miles away, and her blood couldn't stop coursing through her veins because of that, could it? This Tommy she was going with was a sweet fellow, and he was book smart too, just like Sue. They would probably get all moony over poems, just as she and Morrie had.

Sue was nervous getting ready, I guess because it had been so long since she had been out with a boy. I buttoned the back of her dress for her, and then she got all nervous, feeling back there, insisting that I'd left part of it gaping open.

"Sue, you goose, don't you remember the keyhole design in the back? You act as if you'd never seen your dress!" I held a hand mirror to her back and then angled her up to the big dresser mirror.

"Well, it's kind of drafty!" was all she could say.

And after I'd labored buttoning those twenty covered buttons into tiny button holes! Sue was very modest; I guessed she had chosen her profession just right. Me, I had a halter neckline, which showed off my shoulders beautifully, but I couldn't wear a proper camisole beneath this one. It was just me and the friendly scratch of organdy there, plus the beautiful coral pendant my mom had loaned to me. I wore a shawl modestly draped over my shoulders as long as my pop was watching, then flung it off once we got in the car. I no longer cared to cover the scar on my arm. I had decided it was what made me distinctive, memorable. Like our baby-sitter Lorraine had said all those years ago: It was my beauty mark.

48

SUE

I T WAS A gorgeous night. The stars were strewn above us like powdered sugar, and the cool air tickled our hair, making the wavy ends float up toward the sky. I felt at ease with Tommy, who looked so handsome in his navy suit, punctuated by a burgundy tie. It didn't feel so strange to be out with another boy after all. We held hands as we walked into the high school auditorium, which was awash in glittery confetti. Horace and Tommy took our wraps and found a place for them, and then we all moved onto the dance floor to swing dance to "Jeepers, Creepers." It was a rousing start to our evening.

There were sandwiches cut into star shapes and the usual punch, but it was a pulsing sort of pink blend; some said it was mixed with Jell-O. We were fairly sure there was gin in it too, for the mellow feeling that soon came along with drinking the punch. Soon everyone sported strawberry lips, the boys and girls alike. There were sugar cookies, along with a big pan of ooey-gooey butter cake, which stayed untouched till late in the evening; no one wanted the mess of it on their good clothes.

There were chairs out in back of the school, so we could sit and watch the night sky and reminisce about our high school years. We were reminiscing already! A soft laughter ruffled up and radiated through the crowd. In the shadows, some girls sat on boy's laps. The chaperones didn't seem too intent on breaking things up; some said they were a little loose on the pink gin punch too, though most of them seemed to stick to coffee.

I loved dancing to "Where or When." It was a thrill being held close again, and I felt myself melt onto Tommy's right shoulder. I hated to admit this, but Tommy was a better dancer than Morrie had ever been. We moved as one, and we had never even danced before this evening.

Tommy asked me what my plans were, would I work at Kresge's full-time? I told him I was waiting to hear from Harris Teacher's College, and he told me there was no way I wouldn't get in. I told him I would go to school days if I got in and work nights at Kresge's, to pay for tuition and books.

"Well, I hope you'll have some evenings to spend with me. I've been told I'm more fun than wiping down counters and pouring up milkshakes."

"Oh, you are," I said. "What will you be doing?"

"I may go to the School of Mines in Rolla, but I've got to earn some money too; I probably won't go for another year. I'm going to be a soda jerk too, honey, over at Crown Candy Kitchen."

"Well, can competing soda fountain employees still go out, I wonder?"

"Oh, they can," Tommy said, "they can and will, if I have anything to say about it." Tommy danced me right off the dance floor and out the door.

We whirled past Fanny and Horace; I saw Horace salute Tommy. Fanny was smiling her Hollywood smile at me. I knew she was thrilled I was out again, finally.

Tommy and I kissed under a maple tree till our lips ached. Then the teachers in the auditorium were flashing the lights, and some were hollering, "Good night, graduates! Go home, graduates!"

We found Fanny and Horace behind an oak, straightening out their clothes a bit.

"Let's go get something to eat," Tommy suggested.

We got all settled at a table at Parkmoor and ordered burgers and fries and cherry Cokes. All that dancing—and perhaps the necking too—had made us ravenous. Tommy told Fanny and me that he and Horace had been in the physiography club together.

"What in heaven's name is that?" Fanny inquired.

"Well, it means we like rocks," Horace said.

Fanny's eyebrows did a little dance. "No, really?" she asked.

"Really!" Horace answered. He kissed Fanny on her neck, right in front of us!

It was a very lively night in Parkmoor. There were a lot of kids who'd come from the prom. It seemed odd to see people in such dressy outfits gobbling down fries and burgers. Fanny pulled her maraschino cherry out of her Coca-Cola and she nibbled on it in a way I felt came straight out of some movie, though I couldn't think which one. A hotsie-totsie actress, no doubt.

While the boys were paying the bill, Fanny and I went to the restroom to fix up our lipstick. Fanny took one look in the mirror and let out a bloodcurdling scream. Her neck was bare. She had borrowed Mom's good necklace, and now it was gone.

"Why didn't you notice?" Fanny demanded.

"I . . . I forgot you were wearing it," I answered. I hated when she could turn me into a six-year-old again, struggling for words.

"Well, I'm not!" Fanny retorted. She was running her hands over her throat as if she could have overlooked it somehow. She peeked down into her cleavage to see if it could have fallen there, though surely she would have felt it if it had. It was a rather large pendant, Mom's best piece. Pop had bought it for her for their fifteenth wedding anniversary.

"Mom will kill me!" Fanny began to cry.

"No, Mom will cry. Pop will kill you," I told her. "Okay, let's tell the boys we have to go back over to the school and look around, probably out back, right? Hopefully out back, the school itself is probably locked." I hugged Fanny. "We'll find it." We fixed our lipstick and went back out into the restaurant to the boys.

We all giggled a little because it took Fanny and Horace a while to remember which tree they'd been necking by. All the school dances we'd been to over the years? We'd known a few trees in our time. Finally, they determined the right tree; Horace and Tommy went to work, down on their knees, looking for the gem. We felt terrible that there might be grass stains on their good dress pants, but better on those than our beautiful gowns. Luckily, a full moon was our guardian; it was almost as bright outside as if there were electric lights turned on. Horace found it. In his palm we saw the bright patch of pinkish orange, glowing in the moonlight. The chain dangled, silvery and fluid-looking.

"My hero!" Fanny sang out. She ran and jumped into his arms, a true stage leap. She had copied the dancers at the Muny and practiced till she got it just right. Luckily Horace's fingers had closed around the pendant before her leap, otherwise we would have had to look for it all over again.

49

FANNY

RIGHT AFTER GRADUATION, I auditioned for a chorus girl job at the Muny. Sue held my hand right up till I went on stage, where I was asked to sing one song—I did "Where or When," and my voice stayed pretty steady and hit the high notes, as far as I could tell. For my dance steps, I did a short tap routine I had learned from watching the movies and trying to copy the steps at home. Some people sight-read music, I could do dance steps that way. Thank you, Ginger Rogers! I was glad of the flippy new circle skirt I had sewn for the audition; it flew up and about in a fetching manner, I thought. After my audition, I flew into Sue's arms, stage right. She whispered, "You've got it! I'm sure!"

The next day I got the news by telephone. Bob took the message and delivered the news to me when I got home from my job at Famous Barr. When I came through the front door, Bob beat out a little drum roll and said, "Please welcome Fanny Logan, chorus girl for the Municipal Opera of St. Louis! Future star of stage and screen!" I made a graceful curtsy for Mom and Sue, who sat on the sofa clapping wildly. Pop wasn't home from work yet.

Oh was I happy! The chorus job paid very little; I would keep my job as a seamstress at Famous Barr to save money for my move to Hollywood, but four times a week, I'd be dancing my heart out at the Muny. While I didn't have aspirations to be any sort of Ginger Rogers, I knew that many actresses had worked their way up from chorus girls. I did have pretty legs, and I could follow the choreographer's directions easily, which made me a natural.

Our first production of the summer was *Babes in Arms*, a musical about a bunch of teenagers who put on a big show in order to avoid being sent to a work farm for the summer. It was great fun getting to know the other kids in the chorus. At first we were all arms flying in different directions, feet kicking each other sometimes by accident. Occasionally the kicks were on purpose. I had always considered myself a very competitive girl, but now that I saw what some girls would do for positioning in the lineup, well, there were some things I *wouldn't* do.

We were measured for our costumes by a tall, blond older woman named Elka. "Darling, stand up straight!" she told us all. She measured us girls in our underclothes, and she joked around with us so we wouldn't feel so odd having our bubs wrapped in a tape measure and our behinds as well. Who knows what the boys were facing down the hall?

The costume designs looked wonderful. I told the costumer I worked at Famous Barr as a seamstress and would be happy to help out with the costumes if he needed it. He told me that he was a paid professional and had a staff working for him. "This isn't simple hems and tucks, girlie," he told me.

Of course, I knew my seamstress abilities were much more advanced than that, but I didn't make a big thing of it. Sewing wasn't what I was there for anyway.

The first few days of learning the dance steps were exhausting.

We had to repeat the same moves over and over again till we wanted to cry. The choreographer, James, was a slender middle-aged man who always wore a green beret. He had a good sense of humor and always cracked wise to make the time go faster. For our rehearsals, most of us wore dungarees and shirts tied at our waist and tap shoes. We girls tied our hair up tight on top of our heads; the last thing you wanted was a hank of hair clouding your vision during a high-stepping maneuver. When we did a shuffle step there was a thunderous sound, with sometimes a squeal from a loose nail on someone's tap. If you didn't check your shoes before each practice, the nails could be loose, and boy, if James caught you not taking care of your shoes, you were in hot water. The worst was when he lectured about how we could break our necks if we had a nail loose.

He also lectured us about warming up before practice. If we didn't stretch and bend and bounce our legs, we could have a leg cramp, which would be dangerous or humiliating or both. Worse yet, what if we tripped up one of the main stage actors if we took a fall? Finding the time to warm up was hard for me, since by the time I caught a streetcar over from Famous Barr on Thursdays and Fridays, I barely had time to put my practice clothes on, but I did follow his advice.

We had a voice coach who taught us how to sing the chorus lyrics. He was a squat man named Mr. Fring; none of us could figure out how old he was since he had a baby face, but with a nest of wrinkles at the corner of his eyes. He always wore a sort of wraparound kimono-type jacket over his pants. These theater people were so exotic! He liked my sweet soprano voice and said my notes were very true, but that I didn't project enough. He gave me a lot of vocal exercises to do at home to build up my diaphragm. I really hadn't known before how important the diaphragm was to singing. When I did my practice exercises in the living room, Bob teased me mercilessly, so I usually had to do them in the closet in Sue's and my bedroom to get some privacy.

The songs in *Babes in Arms* were a lot of fun. The prettiest was "Where or When," which is why I had chosen it for my audition piece; it had a gentle, haunting beauty to it. But I loved "The Lady Is a Tramp" the best, especially the line about diamonds and lace. I sang this while I took a bath, while I rolled biscuits, when Horace drove me around town. Horace was very proud to be going out with a chorus girl; he couldn't wait to come on opening night.

On the other hand, Pop wasn't too sure about this whole thing. We talked about it over dinner the Sunday after my first week of rehearsal. Pop loved music, and he had enjoyed going to shows at the Muny, though he didn't go as often as the rest of us did. He was very apprehensive about me "cavorting" around the stage in costumes he thought were too skimpy, worried they might "blow up and show too much of my baby girl to the world."

I argued that I was one of thirty girls in the chorus and would hardly be singled out for scandalous legs, and I assured him that the costumes were well sewn and fitted. We were just playing regular teenage girls, wearing swirly dresses and skirts and blouses. There were no low bodices to shame him.

"I don't know what a bodice is, missy, though the word sounds scanty even on its own. I just don't like these public spectacles."

"Jack, my love," Mom pleaded. "Fanny has a real talent, and this is how actresses get their start. You don't want to hold her back from getting started, do you now?"

Mom cut him a little extra slice of white cake (he'd already polished off a full one), and I knew she was hoping this would sweeten his disposition a little, make him not worry so much about my being onstage.

Pop ate the tender vanilla cake in two bites and pressed the tines of his fork all around the plate to gather the last crumbs. "This is just the start of things. She says she wants to go to Hollywood, and even to take Sue with her. Do you want to lose your girls to Hollywood? They make good pictures there, I know it, but I don't like the way those directors operate. They're wolves!"

At this, Bob made a spectacular, protracted howling sound.

"Son, quiet down!" Pop cuffed Bob gently on his jaw.

"I'll take care of her out there," Sue said. Her voice was respectful, but firm and full of assurance.

I reached my hand to touch hers beneath the table and squeezed it. I felt so glad of heart to have her as my twin. Over the years we had had our fights, but when it came right down to it, Sue was always on my side, and I on hers. There had been a number of family discussions recently about my show business goals, and she always stood up for me. She knew that deep inside I was already an actress, and I just had to let the world know it.

"We'll see about that." Pop set his coffee cup on its saucer and said he was going to read the newspaper out back, which we all knew really meant he was going to have a smoke.

After he left, Mom's eyebrows lifted, and she smiled faintly. "I don't want you to go either, because I'll miss you too much." Her eyes had misted over a bit.

Bob, wary of Mom's tears, asked to be excused and went off to listen to the radio.

"Oh Mom!" I cried. "You'll come and visit us! When I get my first part in the movies, I'll be able to afford a train ticket for you! First day you're in town, we'll take you to the Bel Air Hotel for crêpes suzette!"

"Whatever on earth is that?" Mom asked.

"French dessert pancakes!" Sue exclaimed. "With orange sauce."

"Well, I never," Mom said.

Sue took Mom's hands. "It's her destiny," Sue said. "I don't mean the crêpes, I mean Hollywood."

I watched Mom closely. She wiped her eyes a bit with the edge of her napkin. "Will you like teaching out there? Who knows what those

Californian children are like?" She said the word "Californian" like it was a foreign word.

"Mom, children are children, right? I just want to teach, and just think how nice it will be for me that the children can always go outside to recess? No snow to keep them inside climbing the walls, right?"

"You see the good side of everything," Mom told Sue.

I told Mom, "She learned that from you, I guess!"

Mom gave us both a squeeze and a kiss on our cheeks. Then we all carried the dishes out to the kitchen.

"Thank heavens you want to go with her," I heard her whisper to Sue. "You can feed her *regular* pancakes, till she makes it to the French ones."

After four weeks of practicing and working harder than I ever had in my life, it was opening night. Everything was smooth as silk onstage, but the chaos backstage! I loved it. The quick costume changes meant sometimes you'd see one of the important actors without his pants on, in only his underwear. That night, the lead actress, Jane Prue, had a mishap as well. One of her bosoms burst out the top of her camisole. She tucked it back in like it was just a hair out of place, and they popped her dress on her, and she was out into the bright lights once more.

After all of our jitters and our hundred hours of rehearsal, our dance numbers went nearly perfectly. Helen Ember tripped a mite bit over Jim Massey's knee in a quick spin, but the audience didn't even see it, and neither did we; she just showed us afterward the bruise that was blossoming on her ankle. In fact, we all had bruises purpling our own ankles and elbows, not to mention feet that were swollen and aching.

Everything was going along fine until the second week of the show, the Thursday night performance. I got to the theater with plenty of time to warm up, but there was a boy I liked a lot named Joe Finster (after all, I was not going steady with Horace), who wanted to talk to me about something before the show. Our talking quickly turned to necking. My, what a good kisser he was.

So, I didn't warm up my muscles, though my lips felt tingly and warm. I didn't think it would hurt this one time. Everything went along just fine till the next to the last number. My left calf suddenly cramped up while we were doing the "shuffle off to Buffalo" sidestepping exit, a very simple step I'd mastered weeks ago. I let out a groan that was muffled by the orchestra and fell slightly to the side, mashing into Jenny Pinker. "Oof!" I heard her say, and then a little chain of groans along the last five dancers as we moved off stage left.

"Cripes!" I hollered. I fell to the floor backstage. "Cramp!"

"A cripes cramp, eh?" One of choreographer James's assistants, a fellow named Louis, chortled. He sat on the floor cross-legged, grabbed my leg, and massaged it very hard.

When I cried out, he said, "Shhhh! If James finds out, you're out of the show. You didn't warm up, did you?"

"I . . ." The pain was lessening slightly but still my leg throbbed, and it was nearly time for the next number.

"You go back onstage for the next number, or you're out of the show. And not just this show, the whole summer!" Louis told me.

I rose from the floor and felt my leg, testing it on the floor. "I think I'm okay."

"Give her a belt!" someone hollered, and before I could decide if I wanted it, someone brought a sip of bourbon to my lips.

Then I was linking arms with two other girls and doing the aptly named cramp roll (toe, toe, heel, heel) back onstage. I promised myself I would never go without a warm-up again, not even for the sweetest, warmest kisses on earth.

Afterward, Louis told me I'd recovered like a champ, no need to tell James, who by great good fortune had been in a dressing room smoking during my faux pas and had missed the whole thing. Lucky for me!

50

SUE

I STARTED HARRIS Teacher's College in September, and even the first day of it, I knew I was in the right place. All of us loved studying and enjoyed the teacher's lectures. During breaks we shared ideas over big mugs of coffee in the teachers' lounge. Already, we were in the teachers' lounge!

I woke excited every morning in anticipation of the day and got up to wash my face and dress before Fanny rose. I had the task of waking Fanny for her job at Famous Barr. The summer shows at the Muny were all over, but she still had the sore muscles to show for them, and she was catching up on her lost hours of sleep. Once I managed to get her up and into the bathroom, I could go down and drink coffee and eat toast with Mom (Pop was already off to work), and then see Bob off to school. At thirteen, Bob was experiencing a wild growth spurt and he kept Mom, Aunt Millie, and Fanny busy with letting down his hems and sewing him new shirts. His voice was just starting to change the slightest bit, and it shot wildly around the scales without warning in any given conversation. Fanny sometimes teased him about it, but she risked a swift kick under the dinner table when she did.

One early October morning Fanny was particularly hard to wake. She had been out late with Horace, I guessed, since she hadn't been in bed when I went to sleep. We took different streetcars, she to Famous Barr, me to Harris Teacher's College, but we usually walked the first few blocks together before going off to our separate stops.

Once we began our walk, Fanny had an idea brewing; I could sense it. She kicked at the piles of leaves as we walked along.

"You know that Doublemint chewing gum? I saw an advertisement in *Modern Movies* that featured twin girls. Double girls, double mint, you see?"

"Sure."

"So I thought, why shouldn't we be a part of that campaign? We're as pretty as the girls in the ad, and they were blondes and we're dark, so don't you think they'd enjoy the variety?"

I realized I'd have to run to get to my streetcar stop on time. Fanny too. "Run! We'll talk later!"

"See you tonight!" she hollered.

"Oh, wait, I'm working tonight! Tell Mom to hold me some dinner!" I yelled, dashing off to catch my streetcar.

Us the Doublemint twins! Boy, I hoped that idea would disappear fast. Fanny had so many ideas, and this was just another one, albeit a little crazier than usual. I boarded my streetcar and opened my British literature book and settled into *The Canterbury Tales*.

I forgot all about Fanny's Doublemint plan till the subject re-emerged just after Thanksgiving. Fanny had been dating a fellow named Hap Henderson, a studio photographer at Famous Barr who was five years older than her, which made Pop extremely dubious about the courtship. He didn't exactly forbid Fanny to see him (after all, she was over eighteen), but he gave Hap more of the third degree than he did most of our dates. But Hap was a handsome and very friendly man; if he hadn't been, I would have recognized her ulterior motive much more quickly. She went out with him a few times, to the movies, to dinner, to a holiday party for Famous Barr employees, then she asked him to take some portraits of her to use as audition pictures for Hollywood, but she also asked him to take some photographs of the two of us, so that she could submit them to the Wrigley Chewing Gum Company. I found this out one evening, a couple weeks before Christmas.

"So, will you let him take some photos of the two of us?" Fanny asked me. She had made me a plate of fudge and brought it to me in our room after dinner. Boy, she wanted this bad!

I closed my *Theories of Learning* text and ate a piece of fudge before answering. It was delicious. "Are you just going out with this fellow because he's a photographer?" I asked Fanny.

"Well, I'll say this. I'm glad he's a photographer. That's what first drew me to him, you're right. I knew I needed some good head shots for auditions." She paused to eat a piece of fudge. "But he's actually a pretty swell fellow. It's nice going out with someone older. He's no Cary Grant, but he's not bad!"

"So you won't drop him flat once you get your photos?" I asked. I could hear Bob thundering up the stairs, in search of fudge no doubt.

"No, I promise I won't," Fanny said, holding the plate out to our hungry brother.

"Okay then," I said. "I still think the Doublemint idea is crazy, but it would be nice having some photos of the two of us, some good ones."

Fanny leaned to kiss my cheek, enveloping me in chocolate aroma. We looked at Bob, who had several pieces of fudge stuffed into his cheeks so he could quickly exit the room, and we laughed.

·   ·   ·

It was two days after Christmas when I went down to Famous Barr to pose with Fanny. Now that the rush of Santa photos was over, Hap had time for us. I had about an hour before I had to go to my job at Kresge's, and I was already tired from a full day of classes. There was a light snow falling, and as I got off the streetcar, my left foot slipped way to the side and my right foot straight forward and I fell into a soft snowbank. A teenage boy put his hand out to me and helped me get my footing.

"Thanks!" I cried out, grateful there was still some chivalry alive. But then the boy began to brush at the snow on the back of my coat and, very briefly, I thought he cupped his hand to my backside. So much for chivalry. I hurried off to Famous Barr.

The Christmas displays at Famous Barr were a big attraction in St. Louis. I was glad they hadn't been taken down yet; I could never get my fill of them. The display window was enormous. Inside, a mechanical Santa distributed presents to delighted girls and boys (painted wooden figures that looked surprisingly real); snow that looked as real as the snow that now dusted my eyelashes fell and elves scampered about. There was an enormous electrical train chugging all around too, with open boxcars piled with presents wrapped in silver and gold paper. I loved seeing the children with their faces plastered to the windows, leaving a trail of fog with their breath.

I met Fanny up in the sewing room, where she and her coworkers made magic with wedding gowns, formals, and, just recently, all manner of fancy Christmas dresses for little girls as well. They also sewed layettes; Fanny enjoyed sewing lace onto little crib blankets, though she sure didn't know what to make of actual babies.

Fanny and I changed into outfits she had handpicked for the photo session. We wore red sweaters with tiny white buttons and long navy blue skirts, identical ones, and she styled our hair identically too; smooth on top, brushed curls at the ends. We hadn't dressed and styled ourselves identically since we were small children (except for the roller-skating marathon), and it made me feel a bit silly. We took the elevator down to the photography studio. It was just closing up for official business, so several employees were leaving, but not before they gave us the classic double-take.

"Too much good looks to fit into one girl, so God made an extra!" one of the photographers said.

"Oh yeah," Hap agreed.

Fanny gave Hap a quick embrace and peck on the cheek, careful not to smear her lipstick. I knew that she was getting a higher than usual store discount on this session, and I watched her with him carefully, to see if she had real feelings for him. He gave her a little squeeze at her waist and she smiled with real delight.

He certainly seemed to know what he was doing, with the lights and angles and screens. He had Fanny and me first pose facing into each other, then sitting back to back, and even with our faces stacked up vertically, chin to crown of head. It was more fun than I'd thought it would be. Hap was very good at making us feel relaxed, or me anyway; Fanny was securely in her element when there was a camera around. She had already posed for her single shots with him several days before.

After the session, Fanny told Hap she would meet him later at the Fox to see *Holiday,* a new movie with Katharine Hepburn, who Fanny adored. Fanny and I bundled up and walked over to Kresge's, where she let me make her a grilled cheese sandwich and a cherry Coke.

"Oh, I can't wait to see those photos!" she exclaimed.

I sat down with her for a few minutes; the night crowd wasn't in yet. "Don't get your hopes up so high about the chewing gum ad, okay, hon?"

I don't think she even heard me. She was already visualizing our photo in a nice, slick magazine, as she parlayed that vision into a

Hollywood career. I stole a cherry out of her Coke and ran back behind the counter to pour up some coffee for Mr. Loomis.

I simply pictured our photos in glossy cherrywood frames, a nice present for Mom and Pop to display in the living room.

I wondered how it happened that we two twins could see the world so differently.

FANNY

I T TOOK A while for my dream to come true. I had nearly given up on hearing from Wrigley, when one day in May, soon after our nineteenth birthday, we got a telephone call. The Wrigley Company had been inundated with photo submissions from twin girls around the country. Who knew there were so many identical twins? They had selected a number of pairs from different regions of the country, and we were the girls selected for the Midwest! The money we'd make would really fatten up our savings account for Hollywood.

That night for our celebration dinner, Mom made Sue's and my favorite meal, salmon patties and mashed potatoes and creamed peas. We had telephoned in a message for Pop at the Public Service main office, and he came home with a bouquet of flowers for Sue and me; they sat in a vase in the middle of the dining table now, pink and purple and yellow, smelling beautiful. Pop's approval meant the world to me, since this would be a rather "public display," much bigger than when we were in the *Post-Dispatch* for the roller-skating marathon.

After dinner, Uncle Donald and Aunt Millie and Randall and Myra came over with an ooey-gooey cake that Myra had pulled right from the oven; they had driven over with it steaming hot on her lap, nearly burning her legs through the hot pads and her skirt! We ate it with coffee on the front porch, enjoying the evening breeze.

"We are so proud of you girls!" Aunt Millie squealed.

"You'll be running off to Hollywood right away then?" Uncle Donald asked.

"No sir, I'm waiting for Sue to finish teacher's college. That's the plan. We will just have more money to set ourselves up when we get there." I clasped Sue's hand.

It was great to see Randall; we hadn't seen him since he was a motorman in training for Public Service. He showed us his crisp uniform, much like Pop's. With Uncle Donald a rod man and Pop a veteran motorman, Randall a new one, our men would keep the whole city running. Bob already talked of the day when he would be a surveyor for Public Service. He was smart enough for the job.

"I wonder if they'll post the Doublemint sign featuring you girls on my streetcar," Randall said. "I can get extra money for giving out your phone number to the boys," he teased.

Pop frowned and put an end to that sort of talk.

Early in June, Wrigley sent a special photographer over from Chicago to take the photographs; Sue and I posed in a series of identical hats. That was the theme of the series of twin ads: twin girls peering out from under hat brims. We posed in a black saucer hat with pink wax flowers, a Tyrolean hat with feathers, several cloches, and a hat with a shovel front brim. Sue thought the last one was too silly for words, but she was a good sport about it. The stylist at the photo shoot said we had "good heads for hats."

In October, Sue and I showed up in a number of magazines in the black saucer hat. "Double your pleasure; double your fun!" the ads entreated gum chewers. It was very catchy; I heard it a few times a day, from young men I didn't even know! The photo was very becoming to us. Our faces tilted together, hat brims meeting, and the light illuminated our bright smiles. Even Pop overcame his unease with public displays and brought a copy of *Life* magazine down to the Public Service Company; he told us the boss had him hang it from the bulletin board in the employee coffee room. Mom showed a copy of it to all her friends, and some of their young daughters came around to meet us. They were giggly and awestruck; some had their own dreams of modeling or acting.

Sue handled it all fairly well, though she didn't crave attention as I did. She said she got extra wolf whistles over at Kresge's, and sometimes folks wanted her to pose holding up a pack of Doublemint for a photo. Her boss didn't mind the extra attention for his "favorite girl soda jerk" and the extra gum and soda sales were fine by him too. Down at Harris Teacher's College, it was business as usual for Sue. She didn't tell them about it, and few of her fellow students seemed to discover it; most of the time their noses were buried in textbooks, which had no chewing gum advertisements.

Bob wasn't terribly impressed until they started doing the Doublemint advertisements on the radio. They had double piano players playing, double violinists, and even double talking comedians; the latter was what funny Bob loved the most. Then we heard there was a billboard going up on Highway 66 that featured Sue and me in our hats. That weekend it was cold out but sunny at least, so Mom packed us up a picnic lunch, and we all drove out to see the sign. We had planned to drive to a park for lunch, but when we saw the massive sign, Pop pulled over, exiting the road by a few yards, and we ate lunch right under the sign. Bob was finally genuinely intrigued by our newfound fame. He kept looking up at the photo.

"Hot dog!" he managed after a few speechless moments. "Your heads must be ten feet tall."

Sue and I got the giggles. Sue said, "You can't blame us for having *big heads* now!"

We ate ham sandwiches and apples and jumbo ginger cookies that were "almost as big as your heads," Bob said. Often people would slow down and examine Fanny and me against the sign. We pointed up to it attractively, and if the motorists had their windows down, we shouted liltingly, "Double your pleasure, double your fun!" Soon car horns were tooting, and Pop said we better turn around and go home before we caused a traffic commotion.

Mom hugged Sue and me, one to each side like a set of parentheses around her smile, and we all got in the car and drove home.

Of course, one of the best parts of this whole business was the paychecks Sue and I received for the advertisement. Indeed the money would be more than enough to cover our train trip to Hollywood and even a few months rent of an apartment and our basic necessities. We put the money in the bank to gain a bit of interest till we left the next year. But first we took the whole family out to dinner: Mom and Pop and Bob and Uncle Donald and Aunt Millie and Randall and Myra. We went to an Italian restaurant on the Hill. We had never gone to a fancy restaurant, or hardly any restaurants besides Parkmoor. We gathered around a very long table in the restaurant, and we were all decked out in our best clothes.

Myra would be graduating from high school the following year, and by this time she had grown into a lovely girl, with gleaming brown sugar curls and a winning, if still a bit shy, smile. She was wearing a hand-me-down dress from Sue, a pale lavender cotton that made her eyes glisten like lilacs.

Randall had completed motorman training and had his own route now. He had moved into an apartment and was nearly engaged to a girl named Julie Crowner.

"How can you be nearly engaged?" Pop inquired. "She said yes or no?"

"Jack!" Mom murmured. "Don't be so blunt!"

"Means I haven't asked her yet," Randall said. "I've been saving up for the ring. I think I'll have enough by Christmas. I might need a twin or two to help me pick a ring out for Julie though. Or are you girls too famous now to help out your old cousin?"

Me, I never passed up an opportunity to look at jewelry, and naturally I had the best taste going. "I'll go with you!"

We shared a bottle of wine, all but Myra and Bob, who were too young, and Mom, who never touched a drop. We passed the wonderful garlic bread in its basket up and down the table. Bob was pulling at his necktie so much I was afraid it would soon glisten with butter.

The spaghetti and meatballs were wonderful. Mom and Aunt Millie speculated so much on what was in the meatballs, Uncle Donald said, "Ask the girl!" But the waitress told us the recipe was top secret.

What a fun time it was. I had been so set and determined to go out to Hollywood, and now that we had this great Doublemint credit, I had considered trying to talk Sue into leaving teacher's college and going out to Hollywood right away. But this dinner reminded me of what we would be leaving behind: our beautiful family.

Over the Christmas holiday, several stores asked us to make appearances as the Doublemint twins. Sue was busy with finals at school, and I had a hard time making her see the importance of doing them. We were St. Louis's twin celebrities now! The publicity could help me a lot. Finally, we did two appearances that were close to our hearts—one at Famous Barr of course, another at Kresge's. Our bosses both gave us very kind bonuses in our Christmas checks.

Naturally, in the store appearances, I was the one to talk to the young men who clustered around us; I would have no problem with this part of the Hollywood scene, I knew that. Sue enjoyed talking to the children, some of whom were extremely startled to see identical twins for the first time in their lives. One time she gently quieted a shrieking toddler who couldn't make any sense of what he was seeing and apparently considered us worthy of a full-scale fit. I could see what a terrific teacher she was going to make. Sue was so good with children, even the snotty ones who said rude things to us. I could never think of a single appropriate thing to say in response to their taunts, but Sue was warm and friendly even to them. All in all, Sue and I handled the crowd quite well. I knew it was a bit of a strain for Sue to put on a public face, but I had to give myself a little credit: She had learned a thing or two from me.

SUE

V ERY SOON I would have a teaching certificate good in the state of Missouri, even though I wouldn't get to teach here. I couldn't wait to teach, but I still could not quite imagine California, what it would be like. Its enormous shape was daunting, the way it closed off the whole western side of the United States in a big, encompassing arm. I had never been near the ocean; I simply could not conceive of it. I loved swimming, so perhaps I would love it, though they said the Pacific was saltier than Saltine crackers if you swallowed a bit of it.

I had made some very good friends at teacher's college, and I knew I would miss them. One of my best teacher friends was not from the college, however; I had stayed in close touch with Miss James. Now she was Mrs. Reynolds, married to a milkman, and she had had to quit teaching. The school officials believed children would be led astray knowing that their teachers would soon be in the family way. And Emma, as I now called her, was in fact expecting. Often when I had a free hour or so I would bring her around the salted nuts she was craving, and we sat and talked while she ate them. She said she already missed teaching very much, that she thought women should be able to teach and be wives and mothers all at the same time. However, of course she was very happy that by summer she would have a baby to hold in her arms. Personally, I hoped it would come before Fanny and I left for Hollywood, but in case it didn't, I had already finished knitting a blanket for the baby, all of pink, yellow, blue, and green yarns intermixed, since we didn't know yet if it would be a girl or a boy.

"This is so dear of you!" Emma said, when I gave her the package in a white box I'd tied with green satin ribbon. The blanket had turned out well; the colors blended together like what you could see if you looked into a kaleidoscope. I had thought this to myself, and then Emma said it aloud.

"You know, Sue, I think that Hollywood will be like a kaleidoscope too. It will be so full of good colors. Think of Scarlett O'Hara's green dress made out of the drapes from Tara; oh, and think of Mammy's red petticoat that Rhett gave her! Now, I know that's the magic of movies, but I can't help but think that the town itself must be pretty magic, to stir up all those good colors on film."

"Do you think I'll be teaching the children of the stars?"

"You never know! But Hollywood has to have some 'real people' too, the people who run the markets and the buses and the people who deliver the milk, like my sweet Joe."

"I guess that's true." I offered then to get Emma's clothes off her clothesline; I knew it was hard for her to get around these last weeks before the baby came.

Out back, I smiled to see the baby clothes she had already purchased dangling in the May breeze. There were so many T-shirts lined up it looked like she could outfit a whole baseball team. I unpinned them from the line and let them drift into the straw laundry basket like so many leaves falling to earth.

FANNY

Mom and pop threw us a going-away party the weekend before our departure. It was a surprise party, and Sue and I were truly surprised! Mom said it had been a cinch to pull off, since we'd been so preoccupied with our final preparations.

Mom had invited about a dozen or so of our high school pals, as well as our new friends from the Muny and the teacher's college. Emma and her husband and new baby, a girl named Ruthie, came to the party. Also on hand were our aunt and uncle, cousin Myra, who brought a boy named Stewart, who was sweet as pie, and Randall, who brought his fiancée, Julie, who was actually worthy of the rose gold engagement ring Randall and I had picked out for her. Randall was embarrassed about the tiny diamond, but Julie loved it: She flashed it around like it was the size of a grape.

Mom said it had been hard to know which of our old beaus to ask, but she'd invited the ones who had turned into true pals: Bert Singman, now a bus driver in south St. Louis, and Horace Munroe, who was dating a new girl but still threatening to follow me out to Hollywood later; he was a home builder and thought he could build great sets for the directors out there. Tommy Grayson came for Sue. They had dated till he went to Rolla School of Mines, which was well outside of St. Louis. But she had not had the intense feelings for Tommy she'd had for Morrie, so they had been able to part well. Morrie had sent flowers for the party, but a couple weeks before, Sue had gotten word that he was marrying a Chicago girl. She cried when she got his letter, but later said she was happy for him, too. "I knew we weren't meant to be together forever," she confided to me. "And I'm not sorry he was my first love." She was a brave one, my twin.

Oh, our party was a fun time. Pop cranked the radio up higher than he'd ever allowed us to, and he even rolled back the rugs and let us dance till the wee hours. We listened to the entire "Your Hit Parade" program on the radio. Pop and Mom even danced; they were as graceful as Fred and Ginger! And I saw that suddenly Bob, who we'd feared would always have two left feet, was sweeping a neighbor girl, Lucy, about the room like a real smoothie.

Pop allowed a few bottles of beer into this party, but he kept a close eye on things. Sue and I split a beer; that's all we needed to have a good time, half a beer! Our party would have been the best, even without it. We received a few farewell gifts, some practical things to set us up in our apartment in Hollywood, tablecloths and tea towels, and a few more sentimental items. Myra gave me a pair of black, rhinestone-decorated "movie star sunglasses." Tommy gave Sue a copy of *You Can't Go Home Again*, by Thomas Wolfe, though in it he inscribed, *However, you and Fanny most certainly can come home again! See you two soon! On the silver screen, or down at Parkmoor!*

Our trunks were packed and so were our carry-on satchels. We had decided against paying a higher price for tickets in the train's sleeping compartment; we wanted to keep as much money as possible to start out in Hollywood. Mom was worried we would get no proper sleep on the long journey, but Pop pointed out that we could take turns sleeping with our heads on each other's laps. Mom and Aunt Millie had sewn us some lovely lap cushions, of soft polished pink cotton, for just this.

Mom packed us some food to eat, probably too much, but she had thought it out very carefully. Fresh food, ham sandwiches and fruit, for the first day, and then things like crackers and nuts and raisins and pillows of shredded wheat for the days that followed. There were club cars of course, but she had heard those were very overpriced. We thought we might want a hot egg or a bowl of soup now and again anyhow though.

Sue's bags were heavy with books. I knew she would read most of the way out, but the treat was that sometimes I could still get her to read aloud to me. Wouldn't her students adore her sweet voice running over them each afternoon in the yellow California slice of sun? I guessed I would finally get an earful of *Winesburg, Ohio*, still her most treasured book because it had been her first grown-up one, and perhaps she'd read me some of the new Wolfe book as well. I asked her to read me the fiery parts of *Gone With the Wind*, too. I had seen the film six times over and was still trying to forgive Selznick for making the movie before I had a chance to hit Hollywood. I would have made a perfect Scarlett!

We had tickets on a very early train on the last day of June. The night before, we had a quiet evening, listening to the radio after dinner, then driving down to Ted Drewes's custard stand for a concrete milkshake, our last one for a while. Bob flirted with the girl server behind the counter. Our Baby Bob, now fifteen years old! He had shot up to our shoulders, and by the time we saw him again, he would be taller than us, most likely. Sue and I made him sit between us in the back of the car when we drove home, and we both lay our heads on his shoulders at the same time, with no plan of it beforehand. He smelled like Brylcreem, which had managed to wrestle his wild patch of hair down into a nice pattern.

When we returned to the house, Mom worried over our clothes, counting undergarments and stockings and blouses and sweaters and skirts and shoes. She checked all the garments' buttons to see if they were knotted on tightly and inspected all the hems for any loose stitches.

"Ah Mom, we can sew and knit, you know? We won't run out of clothes," Sue told her. She pulled Mom back from her hunched position over our trunks and kissed her on both cheeks.

"You can't sew shoes!" Mom said.

"Oh Mom, don't worry. Shoes must last twice as long in California, with no snow to wear them down!" Sue smiled, and she clicked the lids of the trunks down, decisively.

"Not to mention, I will be famous before our shoes wear out!" I told Mom, and kissed her too. "Then I will buy Sue and me the best shoes in town."

Pop stomped up the steps and came to stand in our bedroom doorway. "I hate to see you girls go," he said. We ran to him and hung on him, in spite of his pungent cigar aroma. I guessed we would miss that smell, before long.

I saw a tear glinting in Pop's eyes. And you didn't have to look too hard to see more than one in Mom's.

The brilliant morning sun shone a swath of lemon yellow on us where we sat on the train as it chugged out of Union Station. We had finished drying our tears and were glad of the many handkerchiefs Mom had slipped in our purses. We had a very long trip ahead of us. Sue and I held hands like we were little girls. We didn't care what anyone thought.

"Sue, honey, thank you for coming to Hollywood with me. You're a peach," I told her. I knew that she would have enjoyed teaching in St. Louis; I knew that she was scared of what Hollywood might be. And I knew, more than anything, that she was the one who would be at my side in the adventures that lay ahead of us.

IN THE DARK of night as the train chugged through Colorado, Fanny and Sue curled up in their seats with their feet criss-crossing. They both wore flowered slippers lined with rabbit fur, one of their farewell gifts. Fanny dozed off first, her head pillowed on Sue's warm, fuzzy-sweatered chest and the soft pink lap cushion. Sue glanced out at the purple mountains rising around the train before her eyes fluttered shut. The twins smiled in their sleep. Oh, the days ahead of them.